SONGS *of*
Deliverance

Books by Marilynn Griffith

Rhythms of Grace

Songs of Deliverance

SHADES OF STYLE

Pink

Jade

Tangerine

Turquoise

SONGS *of* Deliverance

Marilynn Griffith

Revell
a division of Baker Publishing Group
Grand Rapids, Michigan

Published by Revell
a division of Baker Publishing Group
P.O. Box 6287, Grand Rapids, MI 49516-6287
www.revellbooks.com

Printed in the United States of America

Library of Congress Cataloging-in-Publication Data
Griffith, Marilynn.
    Songs of deliverance / Marilynn Griffith.
        p.   cm.
    ISBN 978-0-8007-3279-0 (pbk.)
    I. Title.
    PS3607.R54885S66 2009
    813'.6—dc22   2009032712

Scripture is taken from the King James Version of the Bible.

Published in association with the Books & Such Literary Agency, Janet Kobobel Grant, 52 Mission Circle, Suite 122, PMB170, Santa Rosa, CA 95409-7953.

This book is a work of fiction. Names, characters, places, and incidents are the product of the author's imagination or are used fictitiously. Any resemblance to actual events, locales, or persons, living or dead, is coincidental.

09   10   11   12   13   14   15 | 7   6   5   4   3   2   1

For my grandmother, Goldie Freeman,
whose humming was the soundtrack of my childhood.
Thanks for letting me daydream.
I'll love you always.

Thou art my hiding place; thou shalt preserve me
from trouble;
thou shalt compass me about with songs of deliverance. Selah.

Psalm 32:7

1

Zeely

Then

My roommate, the bishop's daughter, noticed first. Her timing was terrible. Both of us were exhausted from pulling an all-nighter to get our papers done and class was in one hour.

"Has it kicked yet?" she asked from the desk behind me, her voice no different than when she said goodbye before going to class.

I didn't turn around, didn't want to see in her eyes what I'd been hiding, even from myself. "Huh?"

She didn't play along with me. "The baby. Has it kicked yet? That costs more."

The room started to spin. I felt myself falling. The bed seemed to rise up to meet me. I rolled over onto my back as a cold wave of fear washed over me.

Pity passed over my roommate's face, but it was replaced quickly by a resolve I had only seen in my mother. She stopped writing. Her paper was due today and she was an honor student. Mine was typed neatly on the desk next to my bed. Somehow I knew that mine wouldn't get turned in either. Not today, anyway.

On her feet now, she came toward me, still talking in that horrible, even tone. "It's not so bad. I've done it twice. Lots of girls here have done it more than that. You'll do fine, but you're going to have to listen to me. Do you think you can do that?"

I shook my head no. She wasn't making any sense. None of this was. I couldn't be pregnant, could I? I'd just been busy, that's all. Stressed. Mama said that happened sometimes . . . And then I thought about it, counted the days, the weeks, went all the way back to what I started that night after graduation.

"Don't fool yourself. Your mother told me everything about you. Twenty-eight days like clockwork. Well, I've been waiting and your clock ain't ticked yet. Now it's my mess too. Do you know how hard it was for us to get away from home? From the church? They'll have us all home by the weekend. For good. Face it, girl. You're pregnant. Now, I know it's hard the first time. Are you going to do what I say?"

I shook my head again, then nodded.

Lord, forgive me.

My hands trembled when she reached out to pull me up. I had to get to Cincinnati to see Ron. He'd know what to do, what to say. "Drive me to UC, to see my boyfriend. I have to tell him," I said.

The girl, Sara was her name, shook her head. "That's the last thing you want to do. The men are overly sentimental about babies. Not that they want to take care of them, you understand, but they want you to have them."

My mouth hung open. Sara really was crazy, and so was my mother for thinking this girl could keep an eye on me.

"Look, I've got to tell him. Here." I shoved my last twenty dollars at her, knowing that was more than enough for gas to get us from Central State to the University of Cincinnati and back again.

"Well, I ain't turning down no money, but I still think it's a bad idea. This is going to take all week, I see. You're taking the hard way. Freshmen always do. Come on."

We had to stop three times on the ride, once for me to pee and twice for me to throw up. It was as if admitting I was pregnant gave my body permission to have all the symptoms at once. By the time we pulled up on Ron's campus, Sara was really regretting the trip.

"Let's just find him and get it over with, huh? No long talks and all that. Just tell him and let him know what you have to do. It won't take much convincing. He doesn't want to drop out of school."

I was starting to think that it was Sara and not the baby that had made me throw up. How could she say things like this? Was this the same girl who had sung in the state youth choir with me and served on the national missionary board? She was a bishop's daughter, for goodness' sake. What scared me more was that there was a ring of truth to her words, like somebody reporting news ahead of time. My news.

A friend of Ron's who knew me somehow, probably from my pictures, let us into his room. I lay down on his bed and sighed with relief, glad for just the smell of him. When I heard a key turn in the door, I sat straight up and gave Sara a hard he'll-be-different-just-watch look, willing Ron to come in, but he didn't, not right away. He was talking to someone.

"Look, I want to rush the fraternity and all, but I can't get with those girls you were talking about. I've got a girlfriend and it's pretty serious."

"Long-distance love, huh? Everyone here has a girl at home. This is college, man. Lighten up."

"She's not that far. Right over at Central State. We see each other every weekend."

The other guy got quiet, then he got loud. "Central? Are you kidding me? Isn't that a black school?"

Sara's eyes got big. I hadn't told her anything about what Ron looked like. I hadn't thought it mattered anymore. Until now.

"Yeah. She's black. So what?"

"Look, I'm just trying to help you out, okay? I can see you're real smart but you haven't had anybody to tell you how things work. You're going to be a lawyer. You can't marry a black girl. You can keep her, sure, but you can't marry her. I'm telling the truth and you know it. C'mon, you don't want to be broke all your life, do you?"

When Ron didn't answer, I didn't stay. I nodded to Sara and we opened the door and pushed between them. For the first time, Ron looked like what he really was, what my mother had seen when she saw him—a white boy. The blond bum Ron was talking to almost fell inside the door when we came out, but I didn't apologize or explain. I just kept moving.

Ron didn't stop to help the guy up. Instead, he came after me.

"Zee? What are you doing here?" He was running, but not as fast as I knew he could. He seemed scared to catch up to us.

I was scared too.

"Baby, what are you doing here? Did you hear all that?"

I was going down the stairs now, two at a time. I'd vowed not to say anything else, but I couldn't help myself. "Yes. I heard," I shouted as we banged out of the front door of the dorm and into the parking lot. Ron came through the door right after us.

Sara took out her keys.

"Wait, Zee! None of that meant anything. None of it. Please."

He said more, but by then I was zoned out, focused on getting in the car, getting away from the one person in the world I thought would never hurt me.

If he'd had a car, Ron would have chased us, I'm sure of it. He ran half a mile behind us as it was. By the time I stopped crying, we were on the highway.

Sara took out a cigarette and took a long drag. "You left a lot out of that story, girl. A whole lot. It's a shame too. That's the finest white boy I have ever seen. Woulda been one pretty baby." She blew a smoke ring out the window and handed back the twenty I'd given her. "This ride's on me, girl. You're gonna need that money later."

I shoved it into my bra and curled up and went to sleep. When I woke up, we were in Dayton at an abortion clinic. I'd come here for a prayer vigil years before. I felt sick again remembering the looks on the faces of the girls who'd broken our line to go inside. Many of them had worn crosses around their necks. A few were girls whose churches I'd sung at. How, I wondered then, had girls like that ended up in a place like this?

Now I knew. Church girls ended up here the same way everyone else did, by letting our behinds rule our minds, as my mother so wisely said. She'd been right . . . about everything.

Sara broke things down for me on the way inside. She was loaning me the money because I was one of those soft types, and if she took me back to campus now, I'd never go through with it. I shrugged as she pushed me along the sidewalk. She told me how I was angry and confused and sometimes anger was good because it could make you strong enough to do what you have to do and blah blah blah. She was pushing me and talking, but everything was blue-grey, like some sort of mist. I heard Sara but couldn't really see her. Nothing made sense.

"It would kill your mother for you to come back to the church pregnant. It happened to a friend of mine. She told her parents and her mother dropped dead, right there."

That made sense. I started walking on my own.

The clinic waiting room was full. More men than I had expected:

fathers with their daughters, husbands with their wives, a few brothers and boyfriends. I stared at the married couples the most, thinking of all my brothers at home and the nine or ten kids at Jeremiah's house. (I never could get the numbers right on the younger ones in their family. I was the baby girl at my house.) He'd be the one for me, my mother had said, my beloved. Only Jeremiah thought differently. He'd chosen the cheerleader with the shortest skirt and made his apologies.

Though my dream husband had a different face than the one Mama had for me, I still wanted a house full of children. Okay, so maybe not as many as the Terrigans. But still, when I thought about it, which one of my brothers would I do without? Which one of Jeremiah's little sisters would I pick to scratch out? None of them. I loved them all. Even if their brother didn't love me. And that was just as well, because I loved someone else too.

Or at least I had.

Sweat broke out on my forehead. I told Sara to get her money back. I couldn't do this. It would hurt my parents either way, but this was their grandchild too. Mama would come around, somehow . . .

"Ann Terrigan?"

Sara pulled me up by the arm when I didn't respond to my middle name and Jeremiah's last name. He'd failed to marry me, but I was going to get something out of him. I didn't use my own name or even Ron's. You never used your real name in these places, Sara said. She picked the last name to remind me that if I didn't do this, Jerry or any other good church boy would never marry me.

"That's you, remember?" she said, pulling me out of the chair. "That's the name we used." She said you just never knew who was in these places. People were quick with names, especially with our fathers being in ministry.

"Hang on," she said as I disappeared behind the door. "I'll be here waiting for you. It won't take long."

She was right. They were quick, too quick, with everything. We were back on campus by dinner. Sara smiled and laughed, flirting with every guy who passed us by.

"You can pay me back a little at a time. One day you'll thank me," she leaned over and whispered when one of the football players smiled my way.

I knew then, as I know now, that it cost my soul.

With interest.

2

Ron

Now

She slid through my hands, falling away from me. Again. I caught her, pressing my hands too tight around her shoulders. I couldn't help it. I yelled for a nurse as Zeely's head flopped between her knees. Blood stained her jeans, pooled between her shoes. Her eyelids fluttered.

"Help me. Please." It was me talking for her, saying what she would have said if she could. I screamed for somebody, anybody to come. Finally, I had her in my arms, but like always, she was slipping away from me. Only this time I felt like if I let her go, I'd never get her back.

"Sir? You can let her go now. Sir?"

The nurses came from everywhere. They pushed me aside and slid Zeely on a gurney. They waved for me to follow. "Come on. Are you the husband?"

Something broke inside me. I could have been. I should have been. I wasn't. "No. Not exactly—"

"Call the family. What's her name?"

"Zeely. Zeely Wilkins. We were just released. There was an incident. A gun . . ."

"The Okoye woman?"

"Yes. Grace. She is Zeely's friend. Her neighbor. There was a man, Malachi—"

Someone pushed a chart into my hands. I filled out what I knew and shoved the papers back. There was too much to tell and not enough time to tell it. The night rushed past me: Brian running toward Grace's screams, me running to Zeely's condo. In that moment, I thought I knew how much I loved Zeely, how much I'd loved her since the first day I stepped foot in a church and thought her father was Jesus himself. I'd vowed to Brian that day to marry her. Now, it seemed that the night, the past, had taken her from me after all.

The cart rounded the corner, leaving me where it felt like I belonged. Alone. I tried to run after them, but my body refused to move. Instead, I stood there, staring at the smear of blood left on the floor. After all these years, all the waiting, all the secrets, surely God wouldn't let it come to this.

A hand touched my shoulder, a hand that I knew—Brian's hand. He was my brother by blood, though not the kind that runs through a mother's veins. We were related by the blood he'd wiped from my wounds. We were bonded by the only thing that united my white life and his brown one—our losses and loves, things no one else knew or cared about. He was my closest relative and a stranger to me all at once. It had only been through the madness of the past few months, the panic of tonight, that we'd come back together.

I reached for him now, knowing that after the bullets and blood we'd seen last night, we were again brothers. One look in his eyes told me he was hurting too.

He beat my back with his fist, not hard enough to hurt, but just enough to make me feel better. Him too. When he touched me, I saw it all again.

Brian feels things sometimes. I do too, but not the same way. He had a hunch, so we went back, like the fools we are, to check on the women we love, the women who don't love us back. We were just going to cruise down the street, in neutral or something. They were both at Zeely's, he said. That's where he'd left Grace. Her condo was dark. That feeling Brian had, it was probably nothing.

Then, a light clicked on in Zeely's upstairs. I'd sat outside her place on enough nights to know that she didn't get up at that time of night. Another light clicked on downstairs. Zeely didn't move that fast unless she was dancing . . . or running.

I grabbed the door handle even though the car was still moving. Brian looked at me like I was crazy, and then we heard the sound that changed everything.

Grace's scream.

The car jerked to a stop. I was out before Brian opened his door. The snow crunched under my feet as I glanced back and yelled, "I'm going for Zeely. I'll call the cops. I'll find you . . ."

Brian was out of sight already, cutting behind a building like somebody on fire.

I felt him on that. I'd jumped all Zeely's steps and banged on the door. "Zee-ly! Open up. It's Ron."

She didn't open the door at first. I could hear things opening and shutting, turning over, like she was looking for something. Then, I got a glimpse of Brian down around the back, a few condos down. And he wasn't alone.

"I've got to go. I see them—"

Zeely came flying out the door as I went down the steps. She had on a leather trench coat way too big for her, but she kept up. When we had almost reached them; when we could see Grace on the ground, bleeding and not moving; when we could hear the unbelievable words the man with the ski mask was saying, Zeely pulled out a gun.

"I did love her, you know. Always. Even the first time. I just didn't know it yet."

I knew that voice. I'd heard it from the pulpit of a church I liked to visit. Malachi Gooden, the bad boy turned preacher. We'd known him growing up, though Brian knew him better. He'd been the founder of the gang that now terrorized Testimony. He'd once been known all over Ohio for his exploits. It seems there was one more to add to his rap sheet—the rape of Diana Dixon, now known as Grace Okoye, the woman Brian had come for, the one who lay breathless and bloody in the snow.

And Zeely had a gun.

Whatever had gone blank inside of me roared back to life. "Birdie . . . put that gun down. You don't know what you're doing."

She cocked the hammer in response. "It was him. He messed up everything. Took her away from me. Then he tries to marry her? Comes into my house and takes her away? My house. Nobody is taking anything else from me."

Her hands were shaking, but I knew the shot would ring true if she took it. I didn't know where she'd gotten that gun, or when, but this wasn't my sweet baby from the church choir. No, this was another woman, one I'd had a part in creating. We were all paying for our past sins tonight, only I wasn't sure I could afford the atonement.

The truth hit Brian hard too. He tried to get up but fell back on one knee. Malachi started running. Right toward us. Brian was up then, behind him like a hungry bear. Malachi kept coming, kept running, right into—

"Zeely, no!" I pushed her arm but the bullet crashed through the pistol anyway.

Mal kept coming, then fell, grabbing his shoulder.

The gun hung from Zeely's fingers. She stared at it like it was going to explode. I took it from her fingers. Kissed her hair.

Eyes wide, throat raw, she jabbed a finger at Malachi. "You come into my house and do this? You never loved her, but I did. She was finally going to be okay. We all were."

Now, looking into Brian's eyes, I wondered if we would be okay. Any of us. Mal Gooden had fooled everybody, even me. Only Brian had seen through the man's clergy collar and big words.

And now, standing in the hall where they'd wheeled Zeely away, Brian saw right through me too.

"Is Zeely okay? I still can't believe she shot him. Did you know she had a gun?"

I stared at him for a second as the numb of the night wore off and the reality of it broke in. We could all have been killed. And maybe, in a way, we had been.

"They took her away. She passed out. She was bleeding . . . and I couldn't stop it. I couldn't get anybody. It's like she was dying, B. Right in my hands—"

"But she didn't. You said they took her, right? They're going to take care of her. Grace too. We've just got to believe, like you always tell me. Just believe."

"Is Mal dead?" I asked.

"I don't think so," Brian said. He spoke through clenched teeth like the words hurt to say. They definitely hurt to hear. It was too much, all this, and both of us knew it. We also knew better than to say it out loud. How can you tell God that you need a timeout? Life didn't work like that. We were tapped out, both of us. Neither of us had slept in over a day now. It seemed like a lifetime.

Brian's eyes opened from what sounded like a pitiful prayer. I agreed inwardly, thankful that God answered those too. Brian wasn't hugging me now, but his hand was on my shoulder. He was gripping me hard, hard enough to hurt, but I knew he didn't realize it. I didn't mind either. The pain let me know that I was still alive.

"Was Zeely bleeding? Was it from the shooting? Did he—Mal— did he hurt her somehow? They checked her out at the scene, right?" Brian was looking at the blood now, the smear on the ground. Someone had just arrived to clean it up. We stared at each other, thinking of the other blood we'd seen tonight, scarlet against fresh snow.

I pushed away from Brian, whose muscle-bound touch was suddenly far from comforting. It magnified who we were—two men alone in a hospital. I started walking. He knew to follow.

"I don't know what's going on with her, but it didn't look good," I said. It hadn't felt good either. "She'd been smiling the most beautiful smile, telling me she was sorry, that she needed to tell me something and then she passed out in my arms, you know? Just like that."

Brian shoved his hands into his pockets. His almost waist-length dreadlocks hung in front of his eyes. I knew what he was thinking— that everyone we loved died—but I was thankful he didn't say it. Even Joyce Rogers, the teacher who had seen something in each of us that no one else did, the principal who had called Brian and Grace back home, brought all of us together. Her cancer had marked her as someone else we would lose, but not yet. Not today.

For a moment, I was tempted to go to Joyce's hospital room and tell her everything that had happened. The truth might have killed her. Malachi had been her student too. She'd believed in him as much as the rest of us. And Grace? Grace had been the best dancer Joyce had ever taught, the one who would be her legacy until her virtue was stolen and her parents took her away.

Zeely would make it. Grace too. I had to believe that things could be different.

Maybe Brian believed it too. "We've been through worse. She's going to be okay. I feel it."

I stared at Brian, trying to believe his words. His "feelings" usually turned out to be true. He'd always known when my mother would come home walking, drunk and barefoot, ready to do to me what my father had spent so many years doing to her. Back then, Brian had said that I'd be okay. And he was right. Sort of.

As we reached the nurses station, Brian took my hand again. He squeezed. I didn't squeeze back.

He held on anyway. "Lord, you've brought us this far. Now we need you to take us the rest of the way. Let Zeely be all right. Grace too. All of us . . ."

For once, Dr. Brian Mayfield fell silent. Speechless.

"Amen," I whispered as I pulled away. "Amen."

They wouldn't let me see her. Not for a while. They weren't supposed to tell me anything since I wasn't family, but a nurse who knew me from church whispered to me that Zeely was in stable condition. That sounded good. At least she wasn't critical.

I tried to get Brian to go home, but he wouldn't, even after he slid off a chair in the waiting room—while we were talking.

"Just go, man," I said. "You're too tired to drive. Get a visitor's room in the annex next door. Go there and wait for me."

"I'm good," Brian lied, wiping the corners of his mouth and looking around. Having shared a room with him growing up, I knew that for a few seconds he'd had no idea where he was.

"You're not good. They have rooms here, kind of like a hotel.

20

It's right next door. Get one and go to sleep. I'll come over when I know something."

Brian caught himself before he slumped over again. "You're sure?"

I wasn't. I wasn't sure about anything. "Positive."

My brother folded his arms, stretched his legs out in front of him. "I need to check on Grace in a few hours anyway. I'll stay . . ." His eyes closed, swallowing his promises.

They gave me a blanket for him, but it wasn't long enough. His hair hung almost to the floor, so I piled it underneath his head for a pillow and called Zeely's father. I should have called Jeremiah, my friend and Zeely's fiancé. I should have, but I didn't. I couldn't.

Obviously Zeely's father, Reverend Wilkins, hadn't had the same problem. He bounded into the hospital corridor with a determination that defied his age. Jeremiah stumbled along behind him. He headed straight for me.

"What happened? They said something about a shooting? Mal Gooden, they said? The preacher?"

He *was* a preacher—however, as soon as he healed up from the bullet Zeely'd put in him, Reverend Dr. Malachi Gooden would be an inmate. "Long story." I just didn't have the energy to explain it all. The hurt was too fresh, especially with the man Zeely was going to marry by my side. Brian had told me that first day, so many years ago, that Jerry would win, that I didn't have a chance. I'd been stupid enough to think my love was stronger than destiny. As usual, I'd been wrong.

Jerry was on his feet now, following Reverend Wilkins to Zeely's room. I grabbed him.

"Wait. It's only family. You can't—"

Jerry shrugged me off. "I am family. She's my wife."

21

I marched into the dark room behind him, trying not to scream what I was thinking: *She isn't your wife. Not yet.*

Zeely was definitely delirious when she opened her eyes. She said we looked like the angels hanging over her mantel, me and Jerry. If she'd been herself, she'd have known that we were anything but. We both wanted a piece of her, the piece that we'd lost ourselves in, the part of us that only she could unlock.

Her father watched in silence as his daughter pressed the button to incline the bed. She groaned as the bed brought her forward. Jerry and I both lunged for the button. As usual, he got there first. The Reverend cleared his throat.

Zeely rubbed her nose. She was funny about scents. "What's that smell?"

"Antiseptic, I guess." Jerry lifted her hand.

She frowned, then stared at me. We both knew better. We'd smelled the odor before. Blood. Zeely's blood.

Jerry leaned closer. She turned away, saying she couldn't imagine how rough she must look after last night. She tried not to look at me and touched his arm instead, saying it was nice that at least one of them looked good.

I squinted at Jerry. I'd been too mad to notice before really, but he did look good. Since his divorce he'd been looking like a truck had hit him. But now he was clean-shaven and wearing a fresh suit. He looked like he had the first time I'd seen him, towering over the church choir, especially tiny Zeely. Things would have been easier if I'd have just accepted that day how things would go. I didn't though, and I wasn't so sure I could accept it now. I didn't do easy very well.

Reverend Wilkins moved forward from where he'd been standing. "Would you two gentlemen move aside so that I can talk to Birdie, please?"

"Yes sir," I said, embarrassed that he'd had to ask.

Birdie. Just thinking Zeely's nickname made me remember how she'd sung to me that first night, that first time . . .

I swallowed down the memory. It'd only hurt worse to think of it now.

Reverend Wilkins reached out his hand and touched Zeely's face. He kissed her cheek, then did something curious. He put his hand on her stomach. She grimaced, but he didn't move his hand. When he closed his eyes, I knew that he was praying.

When Zeely spoke again, I wished that somebody had been praying for me.

She looked at Jerry first and then at her father. "I lost the baby, didn't I?"

My eyes went out of focus for a second, so when Jerry went to comfort her, all I saw was a blur of the grey of his suit against the darkness of Zeely's skin. All I saw was my life passing by. We'd had a baby too, Zeely and me. I'd followed her that day she'd come to my dorm. I'd lost her on a back road, and when I found her friend's car again, it was too late. Just like it was too late now. When I stepped back from the bed, no one seemed to notice.

Then she stopped crying and shook her head at whatever Jerry was saying. Her lips were moving, but no sound came out. It took me a second, but I made out the words.

I'm so sorry.

The beep of machines in the room drowned out the sound of my heart breaking . . . again. For a moment, I was rooted to the floor, until I saw Reverend Wilkins's face shift with concern, his eyes narrow with worry.

Zeely looked like something had been drained from her. Though Jerry was bigger than me, I somehow shoved him aside and punched the call button for a nurse.

"We need some help in here. Now!"

My call was answered as yet another victim of this conflict—this war of love—entered the room, Jerry's ex-wife Carmel. At that moment though, she wasn't Jerry's ex-wife, she was Zeely's nurse, and thank God, she acted like it.

I leaned in to touch Zeely's forehead as Carmel rolled Zeely onto her side to check the bleeding.

"You all need to go, even you, Reverend. She needs to rest through the night. We'll keep you posted."

Zeely eased onto her back, looking more afraid than earlier tonight when she held that gun. I wondered if I'd had the gun whether the outcome would have been any different.

Probably, I thought. I would have aimed for the heart.

"I'm sorry. About everything," Zeely said, barely above a whisper and to no one in particular.

As Carmel fluffed her pillow, we all tried to explain that it wasn't Zeely's fault, that none of it had anything to do with her. I stopped, as a wave of anguish crashed back over me, reminding me of why we were here. It wasn't because she'd been shot in the altercation with Malachi. It was because she had lost a baby. Jerry's baby. And here we all were: Carmel, Jerry, Zeely, and me, tangled up as always in each other's business, in each other's love.

Then Carmel did something she hadn't done since she entered the room. She looked into Zeely's eyes—and I realized that Zeely's apology hadn't been for any of us men, but for Carmel alone.

"I'm sorry too, Zeely. I'm a woman too and losing babies hurts worse than having them sometimes. I don't know how, but we're all going to have to get through this."

Zeely nodded, but Jerry raised a hand. And his voice. "Hey, hold up. It's not—it wasn't—my baby—" He paused to glare at me. "I

24

haven't been with Zeely or any other woman like that since the day we got married, Carmel. Can you say the same?"

What a night.

"Last time I checked, that was none of your concern, Jeremiah. And furthermore, I don't think that your fiancée's hospital bed is the right place for us to have this discussion." Carmel noted Zeely's vitals and positioned the sheet as though this was a routine check on a stranger. I made a note to pay more attention to Carmel in church. Whatever kind of Holy Ghost was moving in her section of the pews was powerful and much needed on my end.

Reverend Wilkins agreed that the conversation wasn't one that needed to take place here—or now. Jerry cut me a sharp look before agreeing. I tried not to laugh. Did he have the nerve to think that I was the father? What a joke. No, it wasn't me. Not this time. Maybe he was just bluffing to cover for himself. I sent him back a glare of my own. Malachi had fooled me and Zeely had broken my heart, but I wasn't going to be anybody's fool today. All were guilty until proven innocent.

Even you, Ron?

Especially me, Lord. Especially me.

Carmel filled the water jug and put Zeely's chart back in the slot on the door. She turned back to her patient. "I'll be back to check on you in ten minutes and clean you up. I expect all visitors to be gone by then. Is that clear, gentlemen?"

Crystal. I couldn't get out of there fast enough. If I'd known what was coming, that Zeely'd had a miscarriage instead of catching a bullet, I'd have headed over to the room with Brian to catch some sleep, but I hadn't known. I hadn't gone. I was here and it hurt.

Jerry reached for Carmel's elbow as she passed by. "Thanks," he whispered.

She shook his hand away like dust. "Don't mention it."

As she followed her former husband out the door, Carmel turned back to Zeely with a sad smile. "I don't know what's really going on, but you didn't need a baby to get him, sweetheart. You already had him. You've always had him."

She didn't stick around to see if the Reverend and I were behind her. For that I was thankful. I didn't want her to see what I must have looked like after absorbing the impact of her words.

Zeely closed her eyes and I felt Reverend Wilkins's hand against my back. The room blurred as I slipped into the hall, back into the shadows of Zeely's life. Unable to go farther, I crouched down in the first chair I saw and buried my face in my hands. Jerry was somewhere nearby. I could smell his smothering cologne. It didn't matter though—my heart unfurled right there, before the Lord, before the world.

Zeely had found the happiness she'd waited so long for and it wasn't with me. Instead, an old pain had found me again—the empty ache of a baby, Zeely's and mine, the one we would never know.

My guilt was back, like a cancer, daring me to live.

3

Zeely

They told me Grace was coming, but I didn't think she'd make it. I'd been strong for her when we first got here, told them not to hurt her. And then . . . all my secrets had died, bled out on the floor for everyone to see. I had no strong words, no sisterhood left for Grace now. The bullet I'd put in Mal had been my best gift for her, and even in the state I was in, I knew that was no gift at all.

When they wheeled her in, she tried to dismiss the orderly, but he shook his head and said he'd be just outside the door. She pushed herself up to my bed and smiled.

"Some things are meant to be private, you know?"

I knew all too well.

"Thanks for coming," I said, surprised by the raw sound of my own voice. It'd been almost a day since I talked to anyone, though Ron came and stood in the hall this morning. I could see his reflection in the window. I'd almost gathered the nerve to tell him to come in.

Almost.

Grace rested her hand on mine. I could feel the cut on her palm.

They'd tried to stitch it, but it's a hard place to keep closed. I knew it hurt her to touch me like that. It meant more than any words that she did it anyway.

"It's awfully dark in here, Zee," she said quietly, finally pulling her hand away. "Not that I'm one to talk. I just started keeping the lights on myself. It seems like I've been asleep for a week. I had no idea that you were even here until Brian told me."

Great. So he knew too.

"I turn the lights up when Dad comes, but I'm not ready yet. I can't explain it, but I just need to be like this."

Grace understood. That much I could see on her face. She knew the dark, had known it for a long time, but I had always soared above it. It scared her to see me here, in her darkness. Me, her fearless friend, who'd shot the bad guy, hiding in the dark. Hiding from God. Hiding from myself. It scared me too.

She tried to smile, but the cut on her cheek pulled when she did it. I reached out and touched her face. She recoiled at my touch.

"Anyway. Thanks. For everything. I didn't have time to say anything, you know, that night. Everything happened so fast. I'm sorry if trying to save me made this happen to you."

That made me smile, the way she said "this" instead of what had happened—that I'd lost a baby no one knew I was carrying. We didn't just dance in front of people, Grace and I danced around each other too. I didn't have the strength for dancing now though. Acting either. Brian got on my nerves most of the time, but I had to give it to him for saying things like they were. He'd probably told her as carelessly as mentioning the selections for lunch: "There's roast beef, jello, and, oh, Zeely had a miscarriage. She's right here in the hospital too." He was a trip like that.

As far as Grace knew, I was a virgin, so she had to be plenty confused, but considering the circumstances, it all seemed to make sense somehow. Still, I didn't want to be here right now, didn't want to have the conversation that would eventually come, the truth that we'd have to finally get to. I closed my eyes.

Grace's wheelchair began to back away.

"I'm not sleeping," I said finally, reaching up to click on the light over my bed. "Don't go." I was going to have to face my life sometime. Grace was the best place to start. Daddy still hadn't asked me what happened. I wasn't sure he ever would.

Grace eased back to the bed. "You were so quiet. Looks like they're keeping you comfortable. Are you okay?"

I shook my head, which probably looked bare without my weave. I raked my hand through my own curls and patted my pillow.

"I'm not okay," I said. "I don't know if I ever will be. I'm a murderer." The last part came out in a whisper. It surprised me as much as Grace. I shouldn't be taking guests yet. I wasn't ready . . .

Grace's stitches scratched the top of my hand as she clamped her hand on mine. If it hurt, I couldn't tell. She tried to stand up, but before I could call for the nurse outside, she eased herself back down. She'd had a rough run through the snow, one that it was going to take a while to recover from. Still, she seemed to be doing a lot better than me.

"Murderer? Are you talking about Mal, honey? He didn't die, Zee. He's still breathing, right here in this hospital, no less. He's on his way to jail, but still breathing. The officer came and told me that they'll be taking him to County soon."

I stared at my friend. Bless her heart, she still didn't get it. Perhaps she never would. And how could she? The child had almost married the man who once raped her. Ski mask or not, I'd have known that fool a mile away. I never had liked him anyway. I didn't blame Grace, though. She was just an innocent soul, someone who always saw the best in people. I'd lost my innocence long ago.

"Isn't that something. We're all here in this hospital together: Joyce, me, you . . . and Malachi. If that isn't a mess, I don't know what is."

She chuckled, finding humor in it all despite everything that had happened.

"Listen at you, still calling him Malachi. You're so regal that way. Even now, you look like a queen. Murderer mutterings aside, you're still Zeely, never thinking in contractions or contradictions like me. My life feels like a nickname, a stand-in for something that should have been. Mal turned me from Diana Dixon, dancer, to Grace Okoye, someone who I realized this morning I don't know very well at all. Please tell me that my best friend hasn't become a stranger too."

I didn't know what to say to that. It was usually me seeing through Grace. Me setting her straight. For once, I felt like water, like she could see through me.

"I never planned to use that gun. I was just being practical. A woman living alone, they said. I never thought . . ."

She put down the rail and laid her head on my chest. "I know. And I teased you, called you a Girl Scout and all that. He had me, Zee. He really thought he loved me somehow even though he was hurting me. I feel sort of sorry for him in a way. Isn't that crazy?"

I sat up in the bed, ignoring the pain shooting up my legs. All those women on TV lost babies once, but not me. I was just losing and losing and losing. "It's not so crazy. The man definitely needs some help though. Seriously."

"Well, you helped him all right." Grace eased up from her wheelchair, over the side of the bed, and hugged me. I almost lost it then, at the feel of her unassuming, open hands. All my other touches—from Carmel, Jerry, Daddy, and even Ron—had been unsure and full of questions. Grace hugged me liked she saw me, like she knew who I was.

"Girl . . . I always thought it'd be a burglar, not a preacher. You're asking me how I am. How are you? I mean, all that time, not knowing that he was the one who . . ."

My voice trailed off. Grace and I had never really talked about what happened to her that cold night in 1984 when the bus never came. We never mentioned how I'd felt when she never showed up to the recital and I had to dance the lead part, the part I'd been playing ever since.

We'd probably never talk about my babies either—the one I'd just lost and the one I let them take. The secret had grown for so long, gotten so big inside of me, I wondered if I'd ever be able to get it past my lips. And if I did, would Grace ever forgive me for not telling her? She'd been right there at UC too. How different could things have been if I'd gone to her room instead of Ron's? There was no use playing the what-if game now. Nobody ever won.

Grace lifted her head. "So are we going to discuss your Immaculate Conception or are we cutting straight to Brian because I don't know what to do with him. He says he'll wait for me. He says he loves me."

For the first time since they'd put me in this stinking, ugly room, I laughed.

"Let's skip to Brian. That seems pretty cut and dry. He loves you? So love him back. It'll take some time, but if the brother says he'll wait, I'd take him at his word. He's good for it."

At least somebody is.

"And you think that's simple? I don't know when I'll be ready to accept his love, let alone return it. I can hardly look in the mirror at myself. Now, I'm starting to get dizzy, so let's cut to the chase. What's with this baby business and why didn't you tell me?"

I turned away from her.

"There's nowhere to run for once, now spill. How does this work exactly?"

"With an abandoned egg and a whole lot of money." Wow. I'd actually said it.

Grace let go of me. "So it was a virgin birth after all. I thought I'd really missed something. Which I guess I did. Quite a lot, in fact. If I wasn't so tired and hurt, I'd be mad. Maybe when we get out of here . . . I thought for sure it was Ron's. Or maybe Jerry's, but I hoped it was Ron's."

Me too. Every day.

"Well, you didn't have to worry. It was neither of them." My voice was muffled in the pillow that I held to my face for a second to keep from screaming. Why hadn't I left that stupid light off? "I rescued a fertilized egg. I checked the couple out thoroughly. Don't judge me, okay? I've been praying about this for a long time. I'd just made it through the first trimester. I thought I was going to make it."

"I'm so sorry. I didn't know."

"I didn't tell you."

"True."

My heart beat loud against my robe, against my brain.

"You act like you never need anybody, like you never want any-thing, but under it all, you wanted a baby. And you lost it trying to save me."

"No."

"Yes."

We sat there, breathing, thinking. She didn't reach for me again and though I desperately needed to reach out for Grace and let her know that none of this was her fault, I didn't move except to reach up and turn out the light.

Grace pulled up the bed rail. "I didn't know. I told you to stay upstairs. I never wanted you to get hurt . . . The only reason I went with him was because he threatened to hurt you. I didn't want to bring danger to your door, but somehow I did it anyway."

This was getting too sappy, too close. I was always the one who pointed the fingers and bound up the wounds. The strong one. The only thing about that was it meant that someone else had to be the wounded one.

What I said next stopped us both cold.

"What about you and your baby, Grace? The one you gave up. Now that you know who raped you, are you going to go after your kid?"

It was Grace's turn to shift in her seat. Even in the shadows, I could feel her unease. We'd made it to the rape, but not the baby.

"I don't know," she said. "I wanted to talk to you about that too, but I wasn't sure how much you knew."

Somehow I managed to reach out for her. This time she didn't pull away. "You tried to tell me. I didn't want to hear it. I didn't want to have to tell my own secrets."

"About the baby? The one you lost?"

If only that's all there was to tell.

"About a lot of things."

Grace looked at me in that dark room and narrowed her eyes. She held my heart in her hands in those seconds, weighed my soul and found it wanting. With a sigh, she left my line in place and didn't cross it. Door number one would be opened on another day. For that, I was thankful.

She went back to her own door and flung it wide. "I always thought that if I ever found out who did that to me, I would make him pay. I'd prayed about it, been through counseling, but there was still a part of me that wanted payback, you know? What Mal did changed my family forever. Especially Daddy. He was never the same after."

"Mine either." I nodded. All the men had changed after what happened to "Trey Dixon's girl."

That caught Grace off guard, I could tell. I guess she didn't want to think about Daddy knowing what had happened to her, but not much happened in Testimony that he didn't know about. I could attest to that truth personally.

"As I lay there in the snow and heard Mal tell Brian that he did it, something lifted off me. He is sincerely mentally ill."

I snorted. "Umm hmmm. Pray for me. After what he's put us through, I'd like to say I wouldn't shoot him again if I had to do it over, but I don't know."

"Please don't say that. I know you didn't mean to shoot Mal, just like I never meant for you to lose your baby. Wait. Are you and Jerry still getting married—"

"Probably. I got pregnant before we got engaged. It's why I said yes, I think, to be honest. Not that it matters. I'll never have a baby now. It's hopeless."

"Hopeless? I've never heard that word from you, Zeely. I don't like the sound of it. That's my kind of talk."

I pulled the blanket up around my chin. The door opened behind us and the orderly came in. He didn't say anything, but his presence said it all—time was up. And I was glad of it.

Not that it shut Grace up or anything.

"On what do we fix our hope, Zee? That Jesus will come on time? I left this town when I was fifteen years old. And in a few months, my whole life had been turned upside down, but God is still with me. With us. Everything hasn't gone according to my plan, but I know that he's coming right on time. Just like your bullet, Lord forgive me." She reached for my hand as the orderly turned her wheelchair toward the door.

"I'm not fixing my hope on anything. You shouldn't either. Jesus ain't coming. Not for the likes of us."

She rolled away from me.

I turned away from her.

"Zee . . ."

"It's been longer than three days, Grace, or even three years. It's too late. Maybe there's still a chance for you, but my hope is gone."

4

Brian

Eleven minutes until my next class. Just enough time for a phone call, one I'd considered making ever since we'd found those gum wrappers in Grace's apartment that implicated Sean McKnight in the break-ins at her place. I'd always hated that Jerry passed out candy to the kids who got the most right answers in math and thought Bazooka to be an especially childish choice. How could I have known that that would be the evidence that might keep Sean from the chance to become a man outside of prison?

I had every right to make the call, but after all that had happened, I didn't have my usual zeal for tying up loose ends.

I called Ron instead. He picked up on the first ring.

"Ron Jenkins."

"It's me."

"Hey. I was just going to call you. You still need me to cover some classes at the school? I can do it, starting next week."

Why he'd suddenly be free from the law firm I didn't know. I wasn't sure if I wanted to know. When Ron was ready, he'd tell me.

Right now, I just needed him over here any way that I could get him. "Next week would be great. But that's not what I'm calling for."

I felt bad asking Ron to come work at the school at all, especially since I'd probably have to put him in Jerry Terrigan's math class for part of the time. I hoped they were both man enough not to start any new drama. There was already enough to go around. Ron had his meek and mild Jesus side, but I knew there was still a part of him that would fight for the people he loved. I was one of them, I should know.

"Okay, what's up?"

I cleared my throat. "Okay, so you remember that somebody broke into Grace's apartment, right? Before all that stuff with Mal went down."

"I remember. The night you two were supposed to have dinner and Joyce took a turn for the worse. What about it?"

"Well, they found some gum wrappers there. The same gum wrappers that a kid from the school is always dropping around. The boy I had the problems with last year and was involved in that violence in the cafeteria on Labor Day. Sean McKnight. The detective told me to call him if I remembered anything and I'm thinking of giving him a call. Grace is home from the hospital and she's not really talking to me so . . ."

"So you want to put some kid in jail over a gum wrapper to keep her safe. I feel where you're coming from, B, but this seems kind of drastic. Don't you think you've had enough of trying to be the hero? I know I have. Let the police do their jobs—"

"I've got a beep. I'll see you next week."

"You're going to do it, aren't you? I'm coming over. Wait for me."

"Don't bother. Gotta go." I clicked over. "Hello?"

"Dr. Mayfield?"

"Yes."

"This is Detective Stein. I gave you my card some time back? At your girlfriend's house?"

I took a deep breath. Girlfriend? Not even. "How can I help you, Detective? I have class in a few minutes. I may need to call you back."

"I understand. Sorry to impose. I know this has been hard on all of you. There's just one last piece of the investigation and I think you can help. You seemed like you were holding back that night, like you had an idea of who might have broken in? Am I right on that?"

"I don't know. I was probably jumping to conclusions."

"Maybe not. We're considering a student at your school, the boy from the school shooting. Sean McKnight. Do you think he could be capable of something like that?"

My beard started to itch like crazy. Must be starting to heal. At least something was. "I'd like to say no, Officer, but Sean and I have had some run-ins. He keyed my car last year—"

"So he has a history of violence against teachers? That's the kind of thing I needed to know. Thanks, Doc. I know just where to find him too."

"Wait, I'm not sure—"

The line was dead. The class bell filled the silence. Ron would be here soon and I had no idea what to tell him. I'd go over to the station once school let out and make sure Detective Stein understood that I wasn't sure. Ron was right—playing the hero wasn't working for me. I'd been on the wrong side of everything since the night I saw Grace again. And yet, I couldn't let her go.

From behind the glass enclosure that served as my office, I watched the students fill the room. This had once been the kiln room when the building was the Charles Chesnutt Recreational Center.

Ron and I had waited in line here many summers for our crooked pots and mugs to be glazed. The building still held the hopes of so many, including the principal and my former teacher, Joyce Rogers, the one who'd brought us all back together: Grace, Zeely, Ron, Jerry, and me. Next week, Ron would make the team complete, all of us trying to save the dream of the woman who saved us.

If only we could save ourselves.

That's My job.

I swallowed hard at the voice of God in my heart, so new but so old too. I'd forgotten how God could do that, just sort of plug into you. I'd tried so many things since leaving the church, but none left me feeling like I felt now—needy.

And now wasn't the time to be in need. I faced another class of frightened, red-eyed students who hadn't recovered from their dying principal, wounded teachers, and the overall mood of distress.

Only one boy, a senior who was knocking on the glass now, seemed to be above the fray. Quinn Rankin was helping out in my class in Zeely's absence, and though I'd never admit it—and he'd never tell—he was also providing the spiritual support I needed until Ron could get here. Quinn was Imani's best student and, to be honest, the closest thing I'd had to a friend on a lot of occasions. His newfound faith had been a problem for me over the past year until lately, when I'd given up my shrine to myself and accepted Christ too.

Only now I didn't know quite what to do with Jesus or with Quinn, who assured me that God was hard at work whether I could understand it or not. Almost losing Grace and watching Zeely shoot Mal wasn't exactly the spiritual awakening I'd hoped for, but hey, God was God and I wasn't. As the old folks used to say, I'd understand it better by and by.

Or not.

"Coming." I shoved my cell into my pocket. This class had been the rowdiest period a few months ago, but now the kids had a somber quietness they couldn't seem to shake. Under other circumstances, I would have been glad to have their attention, but these days I wanted someone to pass a note or try to text a friend under the table. I wanted someone to smile.

"Have you heard anything from Miss Okoye?" a student called out as I stepped out of my office.

I paused, unwilling to admit to myself or my students that Grace hadn't answered one of my calls. I'd told her I loved her that night in the hospital, thinking the feeling was mutual. Now I was too far gone for even that to matter.

Another student waved her hand. "What about Miss Wilkins? Somebody told me she died. She didn't, did she? Please tell me she didn't."

A burly boy who'd never said more than "here" all year turned on the other student in a fury. "She didn't die. She popped the guy who kidnapped Miss O. Get your story straight, girl."

"She shot him? Dang, that's cold. I could see that. You know Miss Wilkins ain't having it. I didn't know she was packing though."

"I know, right?" Another student laughed.

A scream was building in me, pushing up from my toes. A scream that took me back to that night in the bright snow, when I realized that the man who'd once tried to send me to prison because I wanted out of his little gang had also been the one who'd raped Grace and then . . . tried to marry her. The hard thing was, Mal really believed that it had somehow been love. It pained me to think about it.

"Enough already! As I've said before, Ms. Okoye and Miss Wilkins are recovering and will be back to school as soon as they can. I know you all have been through a lot this year, but listen, adversity breeds character. We're still going to pass that proficiency test and with even higher scores than before. Now let's get started. Mr. Rankin, pass out the books, please?"

That little speech had almost depleted my store of words, which was strange considering I'd once spoke half a day at a conference without so much as a sip of water. Those were the old days, when I was a visiting professor with a bestselling book. Now I was a nobody, teaching a bunch of kids nobody cared about.

And I was glad of it.

The class gave me their full attention for the next fifty minutes, including the impromptu quiz I threw in at the end. Quinn shook his head as the students' faces strained with concentration. He was probably having flashbacks to his own days in my class, days when he and Sean McKnight once battled for the highest grade point average in the school. These days they were in different battles as Sean, now a grade behind his old friend, seemed to have disappeared all together. Sean's father, who'd always communicated with me before, hadn't returned any of my calls.

I know just where to find him, the officer had said. I wished now that I'd asked the detective what he meant by that. Something told me it might work out better if I got to Sean first. Ron would probably think that was a bad idea too, but he'd come with me. That would probably be our errand after school, looking for Sean. Try as I might to get out of this mess, I kept sinking deeper into it.

As the bell rang for lunch, my shoulders sagged. Returning to work immediately had been my decision, although my doctor and the police had advised against it. With Joyce battling cancer and Grace and Zeely out, I didn't have a choice. Closing Imani Academy was just what the city commission wanted. Our site was valuable real estate in their plan to push the poor out of town and turn this side of Testimony into a historical district that no modern person could afford to live in.

Ron's former boss, John Bent, had said as much in one of the meetings. "Why don't you all just give up that school, Mayfield?" he'd asked. "Those kids aren't going to do anything, no matter how many tests they pass. Just pack it up and be done with it. You're standing in the way of progress."

It wasn't the first time that I'd been told that the low-income and minority students in Testimony didn't matter. A principal had once spoken similar words over the first class of Imani students. Ron, Zeely, Jerry, and I had sat with our mouths open as Joyce was told to offer us crayons to pass the time. Instead, she'd called each of us to her desk and spoken destiny over us. We'd all lived up to her words in some way, but underneath all our achievements was a brokenness, a wounding, that we'd brought to the school, infecting it with sorrow.

Lord, help me. I know I try to fix things myself. I feel like I've got to do something. Like somebody has to do something. But only you can do it. Please. In Christ's name. Amen.

Though I hadn't said the words out loud, Quinn had somehow known that I was praying. His hand lighted on my shoulder as he added his own amen. I smiled at him, this boy who looked like a man, who sometimes knew me better than I knew myself.

"Go and eat, son." I said, tensing at my own words. Quinn wasn't my son, but sometimes I slipped and called him that. I meant it in a general way and said it to other boys in the school too, but it meant more with him.

"I just want to make sure that you're okay, Doc. You want to read some? The psalms always make me feel better in hard times." He flashed a goofy smile that made me laugh in spite of myself.

"I've been feeling the psalms myself lately, but believe it or not, I'm studying the book of Job. Ironic, isn't it?"

Quinn chuckled. "Not really. That sounds just like you. Don't you ever lighten up?"

I sighed. "Maybe I will, if life ever does."

He squeezed my hand. "You did all you could. She's safe."

"But he could have—"

The boy nodded. "He could have, but he didn't, Doc. You've got to remember that. It's wondering that'll drive you crazy. Life has tests too, but I'm finding that they're all open book." Quinn pulled a pocket New Testament out of his jeans and forced it into my hands.

I accepted it. I might have been Quinn's teacher for the past three years, but I had a lot to learn about being a Christian. "Thanks, man. You've really got this all figured out, huh?"

Quinn laughed. "Nope. I don't have a clue most times. That's what keeps it interesting."

Another sigh escaped me as Quinn waved a goodbye. He'd never get any food with all the students eating lunch at once now. Some cute girl would offer him some fries or something though. Quinn had it like that.

The phone rang just as I was heading toward the small refrigerator in my office to excavate for something edible.

"Hello?"

"Dr. Mayfield? This is Detective Stein again."

"Right. I'm glad you called. About Sean McKnight—"

"We've got him."

"What?"

"Apparently he was already picked up. Violation of probation from the gang-related incident at your school in August, maybe? I'm not sure, but we have him."

I looked toward my coat. "He's in juvenile detention?"

The detective cleared his throat. "Actually, no. I don't know all the details, but he's in County, sir, being tried as an adult."

My chin hit my chest. I'd wanted Sean off the streets, but not like this. "I'm coming for him. How much is bail?" I fumbled in my desk for my keys, wondering who could cover my class. I could ask Lottie, but I didn't have too much to say to her either. She hadn't been a part of what had happened to Grace, but she sure wasn't sad about it.

"I'm at the jail now, Doc. There's no need for you to come down. They're releasing McKnight since Gooden is in custody. I guess he got picked up the night everything went down, but he had a hearing today. There's already someone here waiting for him. Wilkins. That pastor from the church down by your school?"

That figured. "Yes, Reverend Wilkins. His daughter teaches here. All right, well, thanks again for calling."

"No, thank you. I had no idea that was the same kid from September. I'll be keeping an eye on him now. We're starting a gang activity task force and he's first on my list."

I closed my eyes. "Look, Sean has had some problems, but so have we, right? If Joyce hadn't looked out for us, there's no telling where any of us would have ended up—"

"Everybody just isn't going to make it, man. You know that by now."

I knew it all too well. "I hear you, but please, don't make him a target because of anything I've said. Before all this happened, he was really starting to do better in school again. Try to give him another chance."

There was silence on the line for a moment.

"I'll do what I can, but I can't promise anything. I think your young friend may have used up all his second chances. Can I call on you if I need you? To talk to him and our other little gang initiates?"

"Anytime," I said before hanging up.

Everything Joyce had ever tried to build in Sean had probably just been torn down. By my hands. I'd wanted so badly to have some good news for Grace when I talked to her again, something to pull her out of the dark funk she'd been in, so far from me that I couldn't reach her. And now I'd gone and done this.

True enough, the kid was no saint, but I hadn't been one either growing up. Somehow Joyce had managed to cover me until I could make it, until I could become a man. Still, when I thought about all Sean had done . . . What had he been doing in Grace's apartment anyway?

You don't know he was there.

The thought, like all the others that had invaded my mind since I'd sat in my cold car outside the church and given my heart to God, caught me unaware.

I wiped my forehead. I wouldn't have felt this ambivalent about Sean getting in trouble if that detective had called last year when the boy ran a key down the side of my Jaguar . . .

Grace ran into that same car. You're not holding that against her.

God was playing a game with me and I didn't like it. Sure, Grace had hit the Jag on her first night in town, but it was much easier to forgive people that I loved.

Why did you hold a grudge against Ron for so long then?

That was too much to ask, even for God. I started ransacking the fridge in my office, even though I knew I wouldn't find anything to eat. I'd just tossed an out-of-date carton of yogurt into the trash when I smelled burritos—Miss Thelma's burritos. I must have been dreaming with my eyes open.

"Here, Doc. I brought this up for you. Figured you might have forgotten your lunch. Again." It was Quinn, whose handsome charm had evidently worked out well for the both of us.

45

Grateful, I took the burrito, wrapped in a grease-stained napkin, and the iced tea, probably sweetened just how I liked it. Six months ago, I'd never have held this, let alone eaten it. Now I was simply thankful. "Thanks. You done for the day, son? I know you have a job now and not many more classes to take."

Quinn nodded. "I can stick around if you need me, but if not, I probably will head on out. I'm doing some classes at the community college too."

I nodded, remembering the dual enrollment recommendation I'd filled out for him last year. That seemed like a lifetime ago. BG. Before Grace. She'd turned my world upside down.

"All right then. You go on. I can handle things from here. Thanks for helping out. I couldn't have done it without you this morning."

Instead of leaving, Quinn dropped into Grace's seat and threw his head back, staring at the ceiling.

Oh, come on. Somebody had to keep it together around here. "Boy, get up and go on. Like I told the kids, it's all going to work out. Really. Open book tests, remember?"

He lowered his head, his eyes meeting mine. "Yeah, about that. It seems I had a pop quiz of my own on the way downstairs. I need to confess something to you before I lose my nerve."

I swallowed my food and waited, praying again.

"Go ahead, Quinn. You know you can tell me anything."

Quinn looked my way, but avoided my eyes. "Remember when your car got scratched up last year?"

This could be bad. "Of course. Sean and I got in that big fight that got me sent to anger management, remember?"

"Yeah, I remember." Quinn shifted in his chair. "It wasn't him though, Doc. It was me. You tore up my test that day because Sean was talking to me. I went nuts after school. I should have told you then, but I was too embarrassed to have lost it like that. The next day, when you two blew up, I tried to say something but nobody would listen. Anyway, downstairs in the line, God sort of pushed me to come up here and tell you the truth. I know Sean's done some bad stuff, but he didn't do that. I'm so sorry and I'll take whatever punishment you want to give me. I deserve it."

For once, no words came to me. Silence passed between us like water being poured carelessly from one glass to another, sloshing over the sides. Maybe God was working on me after all. I just wished he could find less painful ways to do it.

"Doc?"

I forced myself to look at Quinn but knew better than to speak. I'd say something I'd regret. The silence seemed to be hurting Quinn more than any words could have, but he had no idea what I was capable of.

"Look, Doc, I know that you're disappointed and everything but say something—"

"We'll talk later. You go on and study and I'll figure out what you owe me and I'll get back to you. You know I can't let this go."

Quinn nodded. "How much do you think it's worth? The damage, I mean."

My fist slammed the desk. So much for calm silences. "I'm not sure yet. Maybe a couple hundred bucks . . . maybe Sean's life."

5

Ron

I didn't recognize her at first. Brian did though. But then he always had.

"That's your mom."

I'd snickered and walked on. "Don't start the 'your mama' jokes with me just because you almost sent that kid upstate for a gum wrapper."

Brian didn't laugh. He didn't move. He walked over to a tired, leathery-looking woman and extended his hand. "Miss Marie? It's Brian, Eva's son?"

My heart stopped beating for a second, I think. Some people trying to get into the restaurant gave me a gentle nudge. I stepped back from the middle of the sidewalk. Could this small, invisible woman be the same person who I'd been so afraid of?

"I remember you, Brian Michael," she said softly. "Hello, Ronald."

The sound of her voice dismantled me, though I'd long ago learned how to keep from showing it. She had started this—my problems with women. I'd never understood a one of them after her, not really. Only Eva had ever made sense. And Zeely, for a time.

"Hello, Marie." I didn't say she looked well. That would have been a lie. I couldn't call her "mother" either because, well, she'd never been one. Still, she was my mother and I wanted to gather her up and take her home. I wouldn't though. She knew it too.

"I don't want nothing from ya. Neither of you boys. Just watching to make sure you're all right. Heard about that shooting and all."

Well, wasn't that something. I could count on my hands the number of times I'd seen my mother since she'd cursed me so scathingly in family court when Eva had taken custody of me. They'd asked me what happened. Tell the truth, they said. And so I'd told them. Just a little though, not all. Not enough to get her into any trouble, I didn't think.

It was more than enough. She'd gone to jail, and except for a few unhappy run-ins like this, I'd never seen her again. Last time I'd gone looking, one of her street friends had told me she was dead. *Gone*, he'd said. *She's gone*. It never occurred to me that she'd simply moved or something, that she might be watching the news or reading the paper looking for me.

"We're okay, Miss Marie. Thanks for asking. Why don't you come inside with us, let us get you something to eat." Brian talked gently with her, like he was talking to someone special. Precious.

She looked around, fumbled in her pockets. "No. That's okay. I'm not supposed to get close to him. I hurt him bad. I'm bad for him. Just want to see him, make sure he's all right."

I bit my lip and determined not to cry out here on this sidewalk. Not for anything.

Brian made no such decree. He didn't even try to wipe the tear going down his face. Even with Grace and the shooting, he hadn't cried.

"Miss Marie, that was a long time ago. We're grown now. We know you wouldn't hurt Ron. Will you please just come and eat with us?"

She stared at me then, like she'd done when I was little, when things were good between us. She saw all the nastiness I hid from people, the fear that I'd never belong anywhere, hurt that made me unable to do for my own mother what I'd done for Joyce so many times—reach out and hold her. Help her. I just didn't know how.

"He don't want me, Brian Michael," she said finally.

I shook my head then. She couldn't have been more wrong. With all that had happened between us, I'd always wanted her, dreamed that one day she'd come back and get me. That one day she'd love me. In that moment, I knew what had caused my hesitance to answer that boy back at UC the day Zeely came to my room to tell me what I now knew—that she was pregnant. I was thinking about my mother and how she would treat Zeely, how she would treat our children. I was so sure then that there would be children, lots of them.

Brian stepped closer to my mother, his hands extending instead of mine. I silently thanked him and hated him for it too. "Come on," he said, his arm grazing against her shoulder as though she might break. "Just a little food. No need to stand out here in the cold."

Her face went blank. "No. Just tell him that I love him and that I'm sorry. I was wrong about you all, you coloreds. I know that now. Ronald's father was just so crazy against them. He told me to hate and I hated. Or at least I tried. It was on account of Sadie, you know—his grandmother. It wasn't right though. Not at all. Now I ain't got nobody."

I couldn't take any more, even though I knew it'd end badly for me. It always did with her. But it was so cold. Colder than I'd ever felt. "Mama, please. Don't go. Come go home with me. I'll get

50

somebody to take care of you. You have somebody. You always will. Let me take care of you."

Now Brian was looking at me like I was the nutcase. He'd wanted to get her dinner, but this taking her home plan wasn't okay. I could see the subtle "no" as his head turned ever so slightly back and forth. Though the lashes on my back had never scarred his skin, Brian had always been there, waiting outside the window to take me to his house, the place that eventually became my home.

My mother smiled like she remembered too. She was missing a few teeth but seemed more lucid now than ever. "I'm not alone, laddie. I got Jesus with me now. It's too late for us to play house, but I appreciate your offer. You just be careful and don't let that pretty colored girl get away. I go listen to her sing sometimes. Thought you would have married her by now. Don't wait. Tomorrow comes too fast. Too fast . . ."

She turned and disappeared into a hole in the fence that I'd never noticed in all our years of coming to this restaurant. I tried to follow, but she was gone. I couldn't breathe. I'd seen my mother and she knew about Zeely. More than that, she'd given me the key to understanding everything my father had tried to hide, the big secret that had driven him crazy—Sadie.

6

Grace

"Don't go there."

That's what Zeely had said when I told her about the notebook. *The* notebook, the one I'd written in at St. Andrew's Infant and Maternity home. In the early passages, the words were blurred with tears, but now I had read to the end, to the painful delivery that made me shiver now when I thought of it.

Zeely went home before I did. She'd insisted that I stay with her when they discharged me. I did, for three days. I'd told her about the notebook, even gone home for it—she went with me—and showed it to her.

"Don't go there," she'd said. I hadn't wanted to, but with Mal out of the way, there was just my baby now, and I had to go back, it seemed, to get her.

> *I'm at the hospital. Toxemia they said. Mom and*
> *Dad are on their way. I hope they get here soon. I wish*
> *Zeely was here too. It hurts so bad.*
> *Diana Dixon*

It hurt to read that. Secrets make great walls, but people usually forget what—or who—the walls were hiding. My parents came to the birth, but they couldn't look at me, didn't see me. I couldn't see them either, just the white-hot pain.

Somehow, Joyce had seen, had known, that one day I would be ready to read these words, to feel these feelings. I hadn't believed her really, but I'd continued writing in the journal that had been required to stay in the Ngozi dance troupe. Joyce said that writing in our journals would keep words in our hands.

Write it down. You'll want it one day. I promise. God will turn this pain into something precious.

I remember laughing at that, thinking that nothing about any of it would ever be precious, but that was before I saw the baby. Writing had made me feel better. I'm glad now that I listened to Joyce and wrote some of my feelings down. In my heart, I wrote hoping one day the baby would read it. I'd given up on that thought now. This time, the baby that must be born was me.

> *They gave me something in my back for the pain. It hurt real bad. Gave me a headache. Something went pop when the needle went in, but now it doesn't hurt so much. I heard them whispering, saying it's another girl from St. Andrew's , so young and isn't it a shame. If I could get my words out, I'd tell them how much of a shame it really is.*

My breath quickened as I read those words, remembered the coldness of the room. The doctor had a kind smile and eyes that I wanted to believe in. The nurse at the home had noticed my blood pressure at my check at the home and sent me over. It wasn't time. I wasn't ready . . .

Zeely was wise to recommend that I leave all this alone. If there was another way, I would have gladly taken it, but it was time to let God get down to the bone, to the marrow.

If you ever loved me, you'll come, Joyce had written, asking me to come and teach at Imani Academy. Along with the letter had been the notebook. I still couldn't figure out how Joyce had managed to find it. I'd meant to complete it and give it to her, but once the baby was born . . . I don't know where it ended up.

I swallowed hard and got up to change into a pair of my favorite jeans and sling a belt made of daisies crusted with turquoise across my waist. By the time I'd slipped on my toe rings and frizzed out my hair, I knew I had to call Zeely. A bad low was swooping in and I wasn't going to outrun it.

"Hey."

I didn't have to explain. She knew from my voice. "You've been reading it, haven't you?"

"I'm sorry. I know you said not to."

"I knew you would. I would have too."

Tears were coming now. I ground the heels of my hands into my eyes even though it hurt to do it. The weight of all that had happened and what might never happen—finding my child—crashed down on me.

"I'd pushed it away, you know? Just accepted it. She's not mine. I gave her away. I have no right. They raised her. I mean, every day I think of her. Every night I pray for her, and that was enough. And now . . ."

"And now it isn't."

"No."

"And it isn't going to be. Go find your baby, sweetie. Nothing will be right until you do. Trust me."

I hugged my knees closer to my chest and rocked back a little. This couch I'd loved a few months ago now seemed huge and stiff.

Perhaps it was because my friend, the fortysomething-year-old virgin who'd miscarried some strangers' eggs, sounded like more of a mother than I'd ever been.

"That miscarriage must have really hit you hard, sis. You're sounding like a mama for real."

I shouldn't have said that, but she let it go. "Do you want me to come over?"

"No. You've got your own stuff to deal with. Tell Jerry I'm sorry for interrupting. I saw his car down there. I just needed—"

"It's okay. And you didn't interrupt anything, trust me. He's asleep on the couch, snoring like a lumberjack. And you can call me anytime. Whether you know it or not, I think about that baby of yours every day too. She's mine too in a way. Many times, I've looked into the eyes of girls at Imani wondering if one of them could be the one."

Me too.

"You go on and find your baby. Then we'll work on me."

"I'll try. Pray for me."

Fourteen minutes later, I pulled up in front of the place I'd been dreading coming to since I got to town: Testimony Social Services. The heat of the lobby steamed my breath as I stepped inside.

"May I help you?" The silver-haired woman at the information desk didn't turn around.

I walked around the counter, moving into the woman's view. This was too important to risk on someone's back. "I need to update my file."

The woman looked up over her glasses at me, prepared to scold me. Instead, she covered her mouth with her hands. I knew I looked a mess, but was it that bad?

"Oh my goodness! Your hand. And what happened to your cheek? Do you need an abuse counselor?"

I forgot how I must look to people. To me, it was so much better than what it had been. That's all I could see. "No, I'm fine. There was an . . . incident. The offender has been caught and arrested. I'm here about *my* case." I'd spent enough time talking about Mal. It was time to talk about me.

"Be more specific. We have lots of cases. What's your name?"

Now for the hard part. "Diana. Diana Dixon. That was my name then."

"Changed your name, huh? We get that a lot here." The lady tapped at her keyboard, while I fumed inwardly and filled out the update file. She stopped typing as a file filled her screen. "Ah, yes. Here we are. Actually, your file is flagged as under investigation and in process. Once I update your information, who knows?"

I was still stuck a few sentences back, on the "under investigation" part. "Can I speak to the caseworker assigned to my case?"

The woman made a face as though I'd requested court with the King of England. "I'm afraid not. Our investigator is only here part-time. He works at that new school, you know, the one for bad children?" She extended an all-too-familiar business card, the same one I'd been given my first night in town when I crashed into a purple-black Jaguar. "His name is—"

"Mayfield. Doctor Brian Mayfield."

The secretary's eyes lit up. "You know him? He's wonderful, isn't he?"

"Yes . . . he is," I said, forcing a smile and heading for the door. A little too wonderful.

I didn't call. I didn't email. I went straight to his house.

That was my first mistake.

He was talking on the cell phone when he answered the door, but when he saw me, he shut the phone and pulled me inside.

And I let him.

I was supposed to be angry, hot-mad with him. I was supposed to yell and roll my neck and wave my finger in the air. I was supposed to say the speech I'd rehearsed about respect and boundaries and something else I couldn't remember. I was supposed to, but I didn't do any of that.

Instead, I let him hug me for what seemed like eternity. It wasn't a roaming-hands, booty-grabbing kind of hug either. It was an embrace, the way you held something broken, something hurt. It was like his touch brought everything back—the knife slicing my hand, the fist crashing into my face. I'd thought I was strong, but maybe I wasn't because when he held me like that, all my heart slid sideways. And somehow Brian managed to catch it.

Light flooded into his front room. I'd only been here once before, but I had every corner memorized. It all melted together as he took my good hand and led me down the hall.

He stopped in front of a room that I prayed wasn't his. I didn't think it was. He wasn't that crazy. When he opened the door, and I smelled rose and vanilla and saw the obviously feminine décor, I was both relieved and disappointed. It must have been the guest-room.

When he turned on the light, my breath caught in my throat. On the west wall was a mural of a dancer with twists in her hair and flowers springing from her thighs. She had a crown of thorns on her head and stars beneath her feet. Beneath her was one word— GRACE.

I was tired of crying, truly I was, but somehow I summoned up a few more tears. I turned into his chest and let out the real cry, the one I'd been scared to release, scared that if I did, I'd never make it back.

He held me close; firm, not easy like before. "I come in here and work on it when I can't sleep. When you're on my mind and I'm praying for you. I think it's my best."

I'd never seen anything else Brian had painted, but I couldn't imagine that anything could be better than this. It reminded me of that first billboard I'd seen about Ngozi, with the girl flying in the sky, big behind and all. I didn't bother trying to give him any promises, any words that weren't really there. Coming, but not there.

"I could tell when I opened the door that you weren't happy with me. Maybe you never will be. But can you just hold your anger for a few hours and let me take care of you? Just for the day. Please."

No, I thought. No man will ever take care of me. Hadn't I learned that the hard way already? My daddy took care of me the best he could and even he couldn't protect me. No. I had to get out of here . . .

My hands balled into fists. My palm felt like it was on fire. Brian plucked my fingers open, one by one, like petals. He raised my palm to his lips and kissed it, gently and on the edge so it wouldn't hurt.

I sat down on the bed and covered my face with my hands.

"Please. An hour. Nothing more."

All I could do was nod.

He tugged off my coat and then my boots. When he started peeling off my socks, all of me pulled away.

Brian stopped. "I won't hurt you," he said. "I promise. I'll be right back." He picked up a remote I hadn't noticed and clicked a button. At his command, a fire roared in the fireplace at the foot of the bed. I'd missed that totally.

When the door closed behind him, I crumpled onto the bed.

How could I be here, barefoot in Brian's spare room? I fumbled in my pockets for my cell while trying to get my socks back on. Zeely didn't pick up.

Brian returned and caught me twisted up like a pretzel, but he just smiled and pulled a huge bowl covered with roses from under the bed. My feet dangled over it.

He took off my toe rings one at a time. He kissed my big toe and then apologized under his breath. I thanked him under mine. My feet had danced on many floors, but they had never been kissed.

Something that sounded like a teapot on steroids whistled from the kitchen. Brian left again but came back quickly with a huge tureen that I'd seen in old movies. It had flowers on it too. He unfolded a piece of wax paper from his pocket and dropped rose petals, lavender buds, and chunks of some kind of salt into the bowl under my feet. He poured the steaming water on top of it.

Into another smaller bowl he poured the rest of the water and mixed it with something green. I could smell comfrey to be sure.

"Don't worry. It won't be that hot when you put your feet in. That's just to dissolve the Dead Sea salt. I'll put the room temp water in next."

I just stared at him.

"I took care of my mother, my wife. Trust me. You can even ask Ron—" His lips clamped down, as if he'd said something he hadn't meant to.

He didn't have to worry. I had no appetite for Ron's secrets. I had enough of my own. He went into the bathroom and filled the kettle and poured into both bowls. No more steam.

"See?"

I saw all right. I saw that I'd had a temporary loss of sanity but I was slowly coming around. "I don't think—"

Brian's locks brushed my face as he whispered into the curve of my neck. "If you ever loved me, even back then, when we were kids, or if you think you can ever love me in the future, please. Let me take care of you. You don't have to stay."

Of course I wasn't staying. As he placed my feet into a sea of warm rose water and put a warm compress on the horrible gash on my face, I heard music inside me. New music.

Brian's song.

7

Zeely

I should have taken my own advice and left well enough alone, but well enough wasn't good enough and I was tired of being alone. Not that Jerry wasn't around. He was around all the time. I saw him at school, work, after work . . . The time I didn't see him now was church. After Daddy had told me that he couldn't bless our engagement, Jerry said he couldn't set foot in Mount Olive anymore. He was going to Tender Mercies now. Everybody was going there now, it seemed. Ron certainly seemed to love it there.

He was even planning to get married there next spring. A mercy wedding to keep Mindy Bent, a girl he'd been engaged to until he found out she was pregnant by someone else, from getting an abortion. His penance, I suppose. I couldn't judge him. I had drama of my own. Wasn't I about to marry someone I didn't love too? Pretty much.

Still, people thought Ron had been paid off by Mindy's father, John Bent, who practically ran Testimony. Ron worked for Bent's law firm. From the outside, it seemed like the perfect setup, but I'd learned long ago that what looks perfect rarely is.

And for that reason, I couldn't step foot in there. That and the fact that since that day at the hospital, I'd been avoiding Ron. He'd sent food over a couple times, a date plate from the rib place we used to go to, three cards by mail, emails every few days. If I was honest with myself, I was ashamed to face him.

But tonight I wanted to see him.

"Hello?"

"Who is this?"

"Um, Zeely. Is this . . . Mindy?"

"Yes. Ron's in the shower. Can I take a message."

I swallowed, thinking how horrible Ron and I were with timing. "No message."

"Zeely?"

"Yes?"

"Thanks."

"For what?"

"For not . . . leaving a message."

I hung up without saying goodbye.

Though it was the last place I wanted to go, I got dressed and went to the hospital to visit Joyce. She was in and out now, some days she didn't even recognize us. Other days, she was Dr. Rogers on the move and we had to almost restrain her in the bed. We'd all agreed not to tell her about Mal and what he'd done—or tried to do—to Grace, but somehow, she'd found out anyway. That didn't surprise me.

What did surprise me was who was already in her room when I got there.

Ron.

No wonder Mindy had been so grateful I hadn't left a message. She was trying to hold on to him too. Good luck to her on that one.

"Look who's here, Ronald. It's Birdie, I believe. Still wearing that loud perfume. I'd know it anywhere."

He jerked around and looked at me, then back at Joyce. "Yes, it's her. She's come to see you."

"Oh now she's going to come and see me? After she's been shooting up the town? Well, better late than never, I suppose. Have a seat."

Dread filled my stomach. Being here with Ron and Joyce could be more than I'd bargained for. Best to get out quickly.

"I just stopped by to say I love you. You were on my mind and so here I am."

Ron was looking at me now, taking in every bit of me with that concern of his. By now, he knew that I'd lost seven pounds and hadn't had my hair done for nine days. He'd know that I loved him too, if I were free to tell him.

Just tell Jerry to call it off.

And then what? Mindy wasn't going to just give Ron up. She needed a daddy for her baby too, and Ron was more than suitable. Until I'd seen that look on his face when he found out I'd lost a baby, I hadn't let myself think too much about how what I'd done had affected him. He'd never let on like he'd known.

"Please. I've been in this hospital for weeks and you've barely come up here. Grace probably wasn't answering and you know that Ron is usually here—"

"No, Doc. That wasn't it at all."

"And stop calling me, Doc, girl. I'm not Brian. I'm Miss Joyce to you when we're out of school. I'm old enough to be your mother, and I love you like a daughter, so just stop all that. Both of you. Haven't you wasted enough time?"

And with that scathing accusation, Dr. Joyce Rogers fell asleep, leaving Ron and I to face each other.

"You look good," he said, which made me mad. If we were going to lie all night, I might as well go home now.

"I do not look good. Stop being stupid."

"Okay, you look like hell, but I'd love to pick you up and carry you out of here and wake up next to you tomorrow. I'd love to have you be my wife and make you breakfast and whip you at assorted board games any time I wanted. Is that true enough for you?"

A smile spread across my lips. "Almost."

"Almost? Woman, you are insufferable."

"Isn't she? Now marry her already, I'm dying here, if you haven't noticed. Give an old woman some small pleasures."

We both turned and squinted at Joyce, who looked as fast asleep as she had a few minutes ago except for the small opening in her left eyelid. These days, I guess that was wide awake for her.

"She's marrying Jeremiah, Joyce. I told you that. Do you remember?" Ron said loud enough for the world to hear.

"I'm sick, not deaf, and that means nothing. Jerry will go back to Carmel in the end. They always do. And where will that leave both of you? Stop trying to make love into some social project. It isn't. It's just love. Ron, you can't save John Bent's pregnant daughter, and Zeely, no matter how many eggs you save from the freezer, it won't bring your baby back."

I froze then. Only one person could have told Joyce about that, and he was standing in front of me.

"I didn't have to tell her, Zee. She knew. Somehow she knew."

This wasn't fair. They couldn't have this little understanding while I'd gone on thinking I was alone. How many years had Joyce sat behind her desk at Imani knowing my secrets. "You couldn't even give me that, could you? You couldn't even let me have my pain to myself."

He grabbed me and kissed me quiet. I let him. That Cinnamon Binaca Blast gets me every time. Ron's kiss made me hungry. Ravenous.

"Listen to me. She knew. I don't know how, but she did. And I won't lie, I'm glad she did. You were never going to discuss it with me."

I poked my nail into his chest. "And I'm not going to start now."

He kissed me again. "Talking is overrated."

"What about Mindy?" I asked.

"What about Jerry?" he countered.

Neither of us had an answer.

Ron put on his coat. I'd never taken off mine. He kissed Joyce's forehead. Her eyelids, both closed now, fluttered, but that was all. He took my hand as though I belonged to him and we left the hospital together. When we got to his car—Brian's old one—he held open the door and I got in, giving no thought to what would come next. I was tired of thinking and planning and plotting. God was bigger than all of that.

We drove to Ron's house to the tune of an old praise CD that he must have copied from a cassette tape. It was me singing "His Eye Is On the Sparrow" and my voice sounded like a shadow of my sound now, but yet there was something free in it that I'd lost, something beautiful. I hit a high note on the tape and Ron reached over and took my hand. I took his too.

I didn't get out right away though. Mindy had answered the last time I called. Who was to say that she wasn't on her way right now?

"You're engaged. Mindy answered the phone before. I don't feel comfortable—"

"About that. Mindy overstepped her bounds. We'd just had a long conversation about us—about you. We'd just agreed to take some time and space to really think about this. She still loves her baby's father. It's complicated, but you don't have to worry about her coming over. Now come on."

When we got to his house, he went upstairs and got me one of his T-shirts and some pajamas. Then he went into the closet and brought out blankets. The same blankets he'd had in his first apartment. The blankets from our first time together. Before I could say anything, he was gone into the kitchen. By the time I'd changed and wrapped a blanket around my shoulders, he had every burner on the stove humming.

"I could chop some onions, get some beans going . . ."

He shook his head. "I've got this."

Truth was, he did have things in hand, not exactly the way I would have done it, but there was love in it. I could smell it. Once everything was going good, he did something I definitely wouldn't have done—left the food. He went back into the living room and pulled out the couch into a somewhat comfortable-looking queen-size bed.

"Thanks," I said softly.

Ron lifted an eyebrow. "This isn't for you. It's for me. You're sleeping in my bed. After I feed you, anyway."

"I can't."

"You will. Jerry has been all up in your face, but he isn't feeding you and you're not sleeping. You get crazy eyebrows when you don't sleep. I'll call Tisha about coming over here to do your hair in the morning."

Now that would be a front-page scandal. Right next to the national headlines. "Now you know good and well that girl can't come over here and do my hair!"

"She can and she will. Don't make me have to call the nail salon about a house call. You get cranky when you look bad and then you don't eat and then you don't sleep and I'm tired of worrying about you. Now sit down here so I can whip you in Bible Trivia real quick before you eat and go to sleep."

"Whip me?"

"You heard me."

"Man, please," I said before I draped my hand around his neck and kissed his eyebrows. He gave me a look that broke my heart . . . the same way I'd broken his.

"Maybe we should do Monopoly," he said, pulling my hands from behind his neck. I hadn't meant to tease him or even touch him really. Just like we hadn't meant to hurt each other.

I picked up a deck of cards from a side table. "Let's go old school. Let's play War."

He smiled at me. "I think we're already playing that. Any other ideas?"

8

Grace

"So he had rose petals for you to soak in?"

"Yes. It was glorious. I'm still salty with him and he knows it."

"Seriously, he could probably lose his job for that. It's probably illegal." Zeely was always quick to point out what was illegal, unless it referred to her.

"Probably. He took good care of me."

"You look better. I was worried that scar was going to stay like that on your face. What did he put on it?"

"What didn't he put on it? Arnica, comfrey, organic cocoa butter, some tea tree oil concoction. He has a whole health food store going over there."

"Now that's funny coming from you. You've got the same thing and that's in your bathroom alone. You two are both crazy with all your organic granola mess. Just put some peroxide and a Band-Aid on the thing. Goodness."

I hugged Zeely. I'm not sure why. Maybe because she could say that while peeling organic carrots for my juicer. "Let's talk about what happened with you and Ron because you, my sistah, are looking like new money."

Zeely ran a hand through her freshly permed hair. "I can't lie, girl. I feel so much better. Looking bad just makes me feel bad. I don't know why."

"Well, you look slim but healthy. Your face had begun to sink in. Then you disappear for a few days and come back looking like the old you. Only better."

"Ron and Brian must have planned that or something because neither of us knew what hit us."

Brian hadn't planned for me to come, I knew, but he was hopeful. And prepared. If Zeely was a Girl Scout, then Brian was an Eagle Scout den leader. Every time I'd turned around, he was pulling out something else. If we ever had kids, he'd pull a first-aid kit out of his hair or something.

Zeely waved a hand in front of my face. "What are you thinking about? I mean I know who you're thinking about, but what about him?"

"Nothing, silly. Listen to us. We sound like two high school girls, like we've gone all the way back in time."

Zeely looked distant then. "Maybe we are."

I didn't know whether to laugh or agree, so I handed Zeely an envelope that had come in the mail the day before.

Zeely held it out from her face a ways so she could focus. "Equal Employment Opportunity Commission? Is this about that mess with Lottie and Brian?"

I nodded. That mess, as Zeely called it, was as bad as I thought things could get two months ago. Boy was I wrong. Lottie Wells, a local artist and Imani Academy's art teacher, and Brian, my recent healer, had put me down as a witness to what Lottie said was harassment. It was a mess, if you asked me.

Just before Thanksgiving, Lottie had cornered me in the market and vowed to tell everyone about the baby I'd given up for

69

adoption if I didn't testify in her favor. It turned out that Lottie had been at St. Andrew's too. I'd known her then as Charlotte Ann. Zeely read the letter out loud:

Mrs. Okoye,
The case for which you were a witness has been
dropped. Your testimony is no longer needed. Thank
you for your assistance in this matter.

"Dropped?" she said. "Just like that? Now you know . . ."

I lifted my hands in the air. "I asked everyone at my old church to pray and I know Brian was praying himself. That could have jeopardized his teaching certificate. No matter what I think about him, I do know that he loves those students."

"And they love him too. They don't like to admit that either. I don't know about you, but I can't wait to get to school. Girl, why do you have all these messages on your machine? This is pitiful. No wonder I can never leave a message."

Before I could say a word, Zeely had already pressed the button for the first message to be replayed.

"Miss you. Love you. Praying for you. I'll come rub your scalp anytime, just call me." That was Onya, my bald Amazon of a hair-specialist-turned-therapist. Our friendship had started over my hair (or lack of it in places). It'd turned out to be about much more than that. Her quiet strength might be just what I needed tonight, but I knew I wouldn't call her. Not yet. From the tone in her voice, she knew it too.

The next message startled me, especially after having been at Brian's house. "Grace? This is Brian. I'm just checking on you. I hope you liked that spinach and mushroom pizza I sent last night. Tell Zeely I said hi. I lo—" *Beep.* The machine cut him off before he could finish.

Zeely took up where he left off. "Tell me you didn't eat a whole pizza."

"Of course not."

"Good, give me some."

"Go for it. Just don't take it all. I have to have some for my midnight snack."

"You're pitiful."

"I know."

Like everything else associated with Brian, the pizza was good— best I'd ever had.

"I just wish he hadn't done the whole investigation thing. Sometimes I think he just feels bad about what happened and he's locking on to me, thinking he loves me, like some kind of post-traumatic stress syndrome or something."

Zeely hit me in the forehead with a carrot peeling. "Why can't you believe that somebody might truly care for you?"

That hurt, and I didn't mean the carrot either. But two could play at that game.

"You know what—"

Zeely held up a finger. "Hold that thought. Let's hear another message!"

She had better be glad she was holding a carrot peeler.

"Grace, pick up the phone . . . It's Zeely. I know you're there." A sigh. "You left your toothbrush over here. Now if you want to go around with stank breath, that's your business, but I can have Jerry run it down—" *Beep.*

I shook my head. "See? See what I have to put up with? You know I wasn't thinking about a toothbrush when I left your house. I keep spares here anyway in case Mother ever shows up. You know that."

"Girl, I was just trying to get Jerry out of my house that day. He'd been up under me for hours. Next!"

71

Beep. "Ms. Okoye? This is the counselor from the police department. I came by your room at the hospital? I just wanted to see how you were doing and if you needed to talk. We have a small victims' group that meets at the hospital every Thursday, from six until—" *Beep.*

"Enough said there. You need to put this thing on a timer. Folks are leaving their memoirs on this machine. I don't even give them that long. You have to get your words together or . . . BEEP!"

I laughed. "Don't I know it. I've given up trying to leave a message on that thing."

"It's me again." Brian's voice sounded mellow. "I'm checking to see if you made it home safe. I really wish you'd have let me drive you. I would have gotten your car home. Anyway, I love—" *Beep.*

Zeely cracked up laughing. "Poor Brian. Everyone else can leave their life story, but let him start talking about how he loves somebody and he is so cut off it isn't even funny."

As she pushed the button again, I vowed to start answering the phone more, knowing that it probably wouldn't happen.

"Diana?" A woman sobbed on the line. "Baby, are you there? Some man called me from your school. He told me . . . Oh baby, please pick up. I'm so sorry. Please call me. I love you."

I reached over Zeely and smacked replay. It sounded like my mother. The voice at least. The words . . . sounded foreign. What did she say at the end? More love? I replayed the message, leaning forward at the end of the message. No mistake. Somebody else loved me.

Zeely put down the carrot in her hand and headed up my stairs. "Call your mama," she said. "Right now."

For once, I was eager to do exactly what she recommended. I picked up the phone and dialed my mother's number, pausing after each digit. As scary as this call was, I wanted to make it. "Mom?"

"Are you all right? Your friend called me. I heard about Joyce too. They told me everything. Oh honey . . . why didn't you say anything?"

They told her *everything*? I cringed at the implications. "I didn't want to worry you, and you haven't been very happy with me lately so—"

"Nonsense. We had words. Everybody has words. I'm sorry, baby."

I stared at the receiver. Who was this woman? "I'm sorry too."

"They told me they got him. That it was Malachi who . . ." She blew her nose. "I can't believe it. He ate in my house. I tried so hard to make you marry him—"

"It's okay. You didn't know. You couldn't have known." I shook my head. If anyone should have known, it was me.

"But I should have known. I'm a mother. Mothers know these things—mothers protect their daughters . . ."

The young girl in me, the Diana, had waited so long to hear those words. The woman in me didn't know what to do with them. I'd always thought my mother blamed me, not herself.

Lord, heal us all.

"It's not your fault, Mom. Or mine."

"I should have driven you that day. Your father told me to!"

"You had a meeting, Mom. You had to work."

More crying. "Work? I always had to go to work, and what did it get me? Nothing. You're father's gone. Your Aunt Ina's gone. I lost you a long time ago."

I sighed. Zeely had tried so hard in the last couple months to get me to call my mother. She'd threatened to make the call herself. I'd told her that I didn't want to trouble my mother, no use in upsetting her over something that was history. Maybe I just couldn't risk her rejecting me like she had the first time, telling me I should have known. Maybe the Dixon women didn't have to know everything after all.

"No, you didn't lose me. I'm still here. We'll just have to work on it a little at a time, okay?"

"Okay, a little at a time. Like in that letter you gave me last Christmas."

"You read it?" I wiped the tears off the phone.

"I did. I didn't like it, but I read it. And then I read it again. I'm reading it the third time now. I think I'm getting it. When you got raped, I got raped too. I just didn't want to accept it. I guess I'm just starting what you've been going through all this time."

Jesus. Sweet Jesus.

Tears blurred my vision. My mother was right. And wrong. I'd been dealing with the rape for years. Healing. Praying. Standing on God's Word. That part of the war was over. But my child . . . that war still waged. "I'm going to go now, Mom. Don't worry. I'm okay."

"All right, sweetheart. Go and rest. We'll talk soon. I'm going to come visit too. One question before you go."

"Yes, Mom?"

"Did you find the baby?"

9

Brian

Without the buzz of people, Testimony Social Services was like a shell. Without Grace, so was I. I walked on weary legs to the desk that bore my name. I shouldn't be here, of course. A reasonable man would have been at home resting, eating, praying even. But I'd learned long ago that I wasn't often reasonable. Most times it worked to my benefit. Like now. I knew from experience if I slowed down, if I stopped long enough to think . . . I might fall apart.

I hold all things together.

That voice, that whisper of God, was comforting, but not as reassuring as it should have been. There were other whispers now, the old questions, the ones that had driven me from the cross in the first place. I didn't try to answer them this time, but they muddled my mind just the same. There was only one thing I knew to do in times like this . . .

I emptied the pockets of my wool winter coat, now ill-fitting and hanging on my frame. My keys landed heavy on the desk. A worn CD came next, Fred Hammond's *Spirit of David*. I'd only started back to attending church recently, but I'd never been able to bring myself to get rid of that CD. For years I'd kept it, playing it over and over on nights when I'd wake up, reaching for my wife Karyn and pulling back air or talking to the mother who I'd never known. On those days, I'd closed the blinds and locked the doors and danced . . . in spite of myself.

Now here was Grace, a woman I loved but couldn't have—not yet anyway. Maybe not ever. She needed to heal. I needed to grow. When the Lord said it was time, I'd make a move. Until then, it was just me and Fred.

Thirsty for worship, I slipped the disc into a CD player on the corner of my desk. The Psalms said God inhabited the praises of his people, and right now I needed Jesus to occupy me, to take residence. I wouldn't make it otherwise.

The music flooded back to me like the scent of Eva's greens. I could almost taste it in my mouth. "When the Spirit of the Lord comes upon my soul, I will dance like David danced . . ."

I turned it up a little louder letting the worship strip away the walls, drawing me to a deep, crazy place for God's eyes only. I needed him to fill every crevice of my being, to wipe away my frustration, my hurt.

My anger.

I liked to think that I never could have killed Mal, but I knew better. Every time I considered that Mal had actually tried to marry Grace, knowing that he'd raped her . . . It was still a process. Reverend Wilkins asked me to visit Mal when things settled down, but I didn't know if I could.

With Me, nothing is impossible.

I let out a breath, my lips vibrating with the song. Weren't my own sins just as bad in God's sight as what Mal had done? Probably. Still, I struggled to feel for the man, to feel for myself. I danced through most of the CD until sweat ran into my eyes and peace lit my soul. For a long time, I sat quiet, not thinking, not praying, just there at God's feet. Just there.

Then my thoughts refused to quiet anymore. They ran toward Sean. He stayed on my mind a lot lately. Quinn too. The keying of my car had been a turning point in both boys' lives. Though guilty, Quinn had been driven to the cross. While innocent, Sean had been driven away from it. And I was the one in the middle.

Maybe I could talk to the judge . . .

No. My tampering hurt more than helped. I hadn't planned it that way. I'd believed in Sean once. Maybe even now. Okay, maybe not, but I wanted to. I needed to. Not for the first time, I did something I probably had no business doing and checked the social services database for the status on Sean's family. He and Quinn had both been given up for adoption. They'd had their days in foster care, but both had landed in permanent homes. I'd even thought that Sean's father was his birth father, as hard as the man had worked to keep the boy in line. When I checked Sean's status, a red check was next to his name.

I held my breath, knowing what that meant—birth mother update. I'd been looking for that check next to my own name ever since I started working here.

I probably could have gotten in to see who his mother was, but Sean faded from my mind and Grace invaded my thoughts as I gripped the keyboard. Sean's case reminded me of a truth that I hadn't wanted to face since Mal was arrested—he hadn't just raped Grace. He'd gotten her pregnant.

That was why she moved away, why she'd stopped dancing.

Why she was afraid to love me.

Sure, I'd known that about Grace's case and had searched for her baby. But now the reality hit me: the child wasn't only hers. It was Mal's too.

And mine, Brian. That child is mine. Just as you are.

I shoved back the office chair. It slammed into the wall as I turned up the music to full blast and unbuttoned my shirt. I pulled it over my head and threw it on the desk. If I wanted to forgive like David, I'd have to worship like him too.

10

Ron

My first day of school was easier than I thought. Zeely came back to work early, so I was paired with Brian instead of Jerry. The kids found my whack jokes a good balance to Brian's seriousness, and I had to admit, I enjoyed being with him. And them. I enjoyed being with Zeely too.

"So, are you coming over tonight?" I asked her in the hall, realizing that I was getting too comfortable too quickly with our secret evenings together. We were both promised to someone else, but the unspoken promise we once made to each other was becoming harder and harder to forget. I wasn't sure Zeely really took me seriously yet. I was serious though. I was prepared to talk to Mindy. Tell her everything. I'd always support her and her baby, but if there was even a chance—

She looked me with eyes that I hadn't really seen since high school. Eyes that trusted me, eyes that loved me, eyes that knew just who I was. She didn't pull away when I held her hand even though we were right next to Jerry's classroom. He was teaching radicals today and she said that always swept him away.

I knew the feeling.

"I'll be there. You'd better bring your A-game though. I'm bringing Scrabble tonight."

She smelled so good. I wanted to gather her up and take her home right then. We really, really had to make some decisions. I didn't want to push her, but my first word on the board would be MARRIAGE. Well, maybe not. It's a loaded word for both of us at the moment. This too shall pass.

Instead of kissing her like I wanted to, I squeezed her hand and took a step back. Brian wasn't too thrilled about all this "drama," as he called it. He'd try to do something crazy like fire me and then the two of us would be fighting in the hall. Can't have that.

"Scrabble on a week night? You're getting a little crazy, aren't you? That game could take us on into the wee hours of the morning."

"I sure hope so," she said, skimming a taupe nail down the curve of my arm.

I shivered and hoped she didn't notice. "I'd better go."

"Me too."

After school, Brian looked over his glasses at me, but he didn't say much.

"Be safe, man. Guard your heart. I'm pulling for you though. God knows I am. We've been going through this mess since middle school."

I wanted to correct him, to tell him that I'd been loving Zeely since the day I was born, but he had it about right. I wished I could do what he said and guard my heart, but it was too late for that. Way too late. All I could do now was pray that God wouldn't let me be crushed again, that if this wasn't going to work out, that he would finally take this love away from me. It cut me to the heart seeing Jerry's ring on Zeely's finger every time we were together. She swore it didn't really mean anything and that theirs was a relationship of conveniences, yet she never kissed me while wearing that ring. That said more than I wanted to think about. As much as I loved Zeely, the time was drawing near for me to draw a line, to establish who we were going to be to each other.

Three hours later, when Zeely showed up at my house smelling of orchids and onions (she'd brought dinner too), I got my chance.

"So you know, I think it's time we talk about the wedding," I said as she forked ox tails and rice into my mouth.

She sat back in her chair. "Which wedding?"

"Ours."

There it was, the elephant in the room, parading for all to see. I felt my lungs expand and then release.

"Ron . . ." Her voice was playful, but strained. I could see her shutting down before my eyes. She wanted to come here almost every night and be my girlfriend, but she still hadn't given up on being Jerry's wife. My chest felt tight again.

"What? Ron what? I'm serious."

She kissed my temple. "I know you're serious. I know. I just don't know what to say. Jerry is picking out houses. You and Mindy have stood up before your whole church and said you're getting married. I feel stuck. Caught. The only time I feel right is when I'm here with you."

Zeely rested her head against my chest. I wanted to run my hands through her hair—which was actually hers this week—but I forced myself away from her.

"So that's what this is? A safe place for you to feel better about making the biggest mistake of your life? I'm glad you clarified things, because that's not what it's been for me. Not at all. As much as I love having you here, I won't have pieces of you. We've been through too much for that. It's all or nothing. You decide."

"Wait. Don't—"

"You guys having a party without me?"

We both turned slowly toward the familiar voice, Jerry's voice. It was the worst time possible for him to drive over and use his key. A month ago, I would have been thrilled to see him. Tonight, all I could do was wonder how much he'd heard.

"Looks like you two are finishing up a game of Twister," he said, smiling a fake smile and laughing a fake laugh. He picked up Zeely's ring from the end table and forced himself between us and slipped it on her finger. "And look, darling, you dropped your ring."

He turned to me. "We can't have you losing that. We're going to need it for the wedding. Speaking of weddings, when is yours, old friend?"

I mumbled something, but in truth I'd forgotten the date, just like I'd tried to forget about Jerry and Zeely getting married. In my mind, it was just a matter of time until she let him go for good and came back to me where she belonged. What I hadn't counted on was that Jerry had finally fallen in love with his beloved and was now ready for the arranged marriage his mother and Zeely's mother had planned a century ago.

A black marriage creating a black family. There was no way for me to compete with that. I never thought I'd have to if Zeely could get over our past. Just when it seemed that she had, here was Jerry, closing the door on our future.

Zeely was silent, staring down at the ring Jerry had slipped on her finger. Then she stared at me. There was longing in her eyes, but there were questions too. Some of the same ones in my heart. We could both marry two people who loved us and live safe, reasonable lives . . . or we could close our eyes and freefall.

She took Jerry's hand. "Good to see you, babe. I brought Scrabble . . ."

Zeely never was much of an adventurer. So, safe it is. I hoped we could all live with ourselves when it was all said and done.

"You know what, guys? I'm going to call it a night. I'll see you both at work tomorrow. Let me know who won."

Both of them looked stunned as I got up and opened the front door. I was surprised myself, but glad. Zeely might be willing to throw our love away, but I wasn't going to sit around and watch her give it to someone else. As Brian had so wisely recommended, I had to guard my heart. Zeely certainly wasn't going to.

11

Zeely

Besides weddings I'd attended and churches where I'd led the choir on Sunday afternoons, I hadn't been to many churches besides my father's. After Dad refused to give us his blessing on getting married, Jerry suggested that I join him at Tender Mercies. I'd agreed weeks ago, but now that I was actually here, I wasn't so sure. For one thing, this was Ron's church. He shouldn't have to worry about running into us here. It was hard enough seeing him every day at school.

He didn't hug me anymore or laugh at my jokes. Though he gave me lingering looks in the hall, whatever hold I'd had on him was broken. I was proud of him for getting over me or whatever he'd done. I was still stuck between the Rock of Ages and the hard places in my heart. Sometimes I wondered if I shouldn't be by myself and leave Jerry alone too. Not that he'd make that easy. Like us being together at church today, we were together all the time lately. I didn't have time to think. Maybe that was the plan.

I squirmed in the padded movie seat just thinking about it. The seat beside me moved too. Connected. I guess that's how everything worked around here. That could be good . . . or bad. I looked around the sanctuary, sparsely decorated except for the lighted dove above the podium and the plants lining the stage. It was no four-foot-high cross, but it seemed peaceful.

Jerry cleared his throat beside me. "Don't worry. You'll like it. Trust me. Well, maybe not the music."

My eyes widened. "What do you mean, not the music? That's the best part." It was hard enough sitting in these seats instead of in the choir stand.

"I love the worship, but it's slower than you might like. And there's no choir."

No choir? I reached for my purse. "What kind of church did you bring me to? The pastor seemed nice enough on the phone but—"

A smiling couple squeezed by us into the next two seats. "Good morning. I'm Barbara. This is my husband Paul. Are you new?"

Jerry smiled. "It's her first time. I've visited before. With Ron Jenkins."

The man leaned forward. "The redhead? Nice guy. Came and visited Barb in the hospital twice last year."

His wife nodded. "Sweet as pie! He's a keeper."

He sure is. Only I didn't have sense enough to keep him.

Mindy hadn't made the same mistake though. She sat a few rows ahead of me, but had made time to approach us and extend her congratulations on our engagement. She looked relieved to see me with Jerry. I'd wondered as I stood there watching the two of them—Jerry and Mindy—if they shouldn't hook up. It would make about as much sense as what was going on.

Sometimes I dreamed that I'd waited to hear what Ron had to tell me instead of accepting Jerry's proposal. In my dreams, when Jerry arrived, I didn't say yes to his proposal, but "Thank you, but can I take some time to think about it?" Moments later, Ron arrives with his ring and his proposal. Being the smart woman that I am, I accept and give Jerry my regrets.

The bad part about dreams is waking up and realizing you'd done the dumb thing instead.

Perhaps I'd sealed all our fates the day I'd gone to the clinic and had one of their abandoned eggs implanted inside me. A baby. I thought that was all I wanted. All I could have. Now I knew better. I wanted love. And whether I'd ever have that with Jerry, I wasn't sure.

We were a sorry pair, the two of us. I'd accepted his proposal so that my baby could have a father. I think he proposed to me for the same reason—so that when his girls were with him, they could have two parents. I'd lost the baby and Jerry seemed to be just sort of going along. So was I. I didn't know what else to do at this point. I should have just told him about the baby. Ron too. But I'd tried that once. Sometimes you have to bear your own burdens.

I turned to the woman with a smile of my own. "I'm sorry to hear that you were in the hospital. Ron is always good about visitations. We attended the same church growing up. Are you all right now?"

"Yes. Two miscarriages. We're getting a bit old to keep trying, but we haven't given up yet."

I stared straight ahead, deflated as though someone had pricked me with a pin. Jerry started to say something, probably that I had just lost a baby too, but I glared at him and he pressed his words into a smile. I did too. "Yes, well, we'll have to tell Ron we met you."

A synthesizer crackled through the speaker. I recoiled. The lady, Barbara, touched my shoulder. "You'll get used to it. I grew up Catholic. I had a headache for the first few weeks."

I laughed as a plain-clothed worship team took the stage. One of them, a brown reed of a boy with a pair of maracas, looked familiar. Was that . . .

"Quinn Rankin," Jerry whispered in my ear.

I stood with the crowd as a familiar chorus poured through the microphones a few feet away. "Our God is an awesome God . . ." I closed my eyes and lifted my hands. The surroundings might be different, but the Lord was the same. My voice poured forward, sweetening the harmony. With each word, a tendril of despair snapped its grip around my heart. By the end of the song, the front of my dress was wet with my tears, and the root of bitterness that had buried itself in me when I pulled the trigger on Mal was gone.

Jerry leaned down, clapping as the next song began. "So what do you think?"

I took a deep breath and lifted the tear-soaked fabric from my chest. "I like it."

12

Carmel

If Monique hadn't insisted on stopping to get Sean a tie, we could have made it on time. But she had insisted and late we were. I lifted Justice, my granddaughter, from her mother's shoulder and walked faster. That baby had been waiting for this service all week.

A tanned man met us at the door of the shopping center unit. "Welcome to Tender Mercies Church."

I waited for him to give their motto, like, "Where Jesus makes the difference" or something, but he didn't. I guess they kept it cut and dried around here. That would be an interesting change. Still, I wasn't sure quite what to make of this movie star–looking man or this strip mall church. Who was tanned like that in the middle of winter? No God-fearing people I knew.

We'll see.

He passed us a bulletin with the week's events and a space for notes. "The nursery is just down the hall." He pointed to a room marked "Overflow." "Go in there until worship ends. Then you can go in."

Nodding my thanks, I stalked down the hall to the toddler room.

Monique ran beside me. "I'm sorry about the tie and everything. I just wanted it to be perfect, you know? You have to get right before you go to church."

A round face with cheery eyes appeared in the door. The grandmother who'd invited me to church when her own daughter had come through labor and delivery. She looked at Monique. "You have to get right first, do you? I'm glad nobody told me that. I'd still be sitting at home." The woman held out both hands. "Carmel, it's so good to see you. I'm glad you could make it."

I lifted Justice over the gate. Sean, the baby's father and, despite my mixed feelings, Monique's husband, reached in and sat the backpack on the ground.

"I'm glad we made it too, though I don't know how long she'll let us stay in there. Last night was a doozy. She cut another tooth." I hoped I wouldn't yawn during the service.

"Aw . . . Is that right, little sis? You just stay here with Grandma Betty. We'll be okay."

Monique stepped forward. "Mom, I'll stay with Justice, you go—"

The woman shook her head. "No. All of you go in. Justice and I will be fine."

The baby wailed in contradiction.

I frowned. "I don't know . . . I hate to do this to you. Little Miss can scream, now."

"It's nothing. Now go. Sit in the back. If there's an emergency, which I doubt, I'll flash your number. Seventy-seven." She handed me a red tag.

I nodded, feeling better and wondering when church nurseries had become so sophisticated. "Got it."

The door in front of us opened and teenagers streamed out, followed by their parents.

Betty shooed them toward the door. "It's the break. Go find a seat. I'll see you soon."

The three of us inched into the sanctuary, Sean leading the pack. He pulled up short after a few steps. I ran into him, but my new son-in-law didn't say a word. Not even his usual "excuse me." He gaped across the room. I sighed. Next time, I'd come alone.

Monique reached across me and tugged on Sean's jacket. "Is that—?"

He nodded. "Yup. That's Doc." The boy got a look on his face that he wore more often than not these days, the look of someone caught in a trap. I was surprised he'd agreed to even come to church, as strange as he'd been acting. Stranger still was the sight of Brian Mayfield in a house of worship. Wasn't he into all that African mess? I remembered Jerry always praying about that. At least one of his prayers had been answered. Maybe he should have prayed harder for our marriage.

Maybe I should have too.

Brian leaned over into the aisle as we passed by. "Sean, don't leave here without talking to me. It's urgent."

My son-in-law's eyes darted around, looking for the nearest exit. "Yeah. Okay."

Whatever this was about, I didn't know whether to be worried or relieved. Brian had never cared for me much in college, but he was always cordial. Today, though, he seemed genuinely concerned about Sean. Monique simply stared at the man as if he weren't real. I guess seeing your teacher at church was sort of weird.

I shrugged it off. There was only so much I could handle. Playing grandma was job enough. I tried to lighten things up some. "Where's the rest of your crew? I'm sure Ron's here somewhere."

"Visiting elsewhere," Brian said, as the pastor, a handsome Hispanic man, filed down the center of the room.

I grabbed the new Bible I'd brought and some paper and a pen.

Brian motioned to the right. "Your crew's all here though."

Against my better judgment, I let my eyes follow the carpet, up and around to the first bunch of seats. There was Jerry, holding Zeely's hand in his, and smiling up at the pastor like the happiest man in the world.

He shouldn't have her out this soon.

I crossed my legs and turned a new page in my notebook. Brian was right. The gang was all here.

13

Ron

I hadn't been to Mount Olive in years. Fifteen years to be exact. I mounted the steps one at a time, each one chiseled with memories. Vacation Bible School. Me and Zeely in a mock wedding, her as the Bride of Christ and me as the Bridegroom. I walked faster. Funny how things worked out the opposite.

"Is that you, Brother Jenkins?"

I turned at the voice, still familiar even after so long. "Mother Riley?" The sight of her face, creased with many years, brought me to a halt on the stair. How old must she be now? Ninety?

She smiled. "Ninety-two next Sunday. And I've still never heard a better preacher than you. Not in all my years."

"You're just trying to flatter me." I reached out and helped her up the steps, pausing on each one. "You don't have to give me compliments. You know I'm a pushover for you."

She nodded, bringing her left foot in line with her right. A knotted knee-high stocking peeked out from under her hem. "Stop lying. I've been asking about you forever. Are you preaching today?"

I pulled the door open with one hand and helped her inside. "No, ma'am."

The old lady frowned. "Young folks. You want God to bless you, but you're never ready. Never expecting. You're supposed to be ready all the time. In season and out." She shuffled to the Mother's bench, next to the organ. Her hand tapped the musician's shoulder on the way to her seat.

"This man can tell you. When he came here, he tried to sit in the back and stay quiet with all that voice. My Lord. I can't see very well anymore, but my hearing is fine. I went back there one morning and listened down the row until I found him. Isn't that right?"

The handsome organist laughed. When I saw his eyes, I dropped Mother Riley's hand. I knew that face. That shirt even. Where had I seen it? Pictures. This was my fiancée's lover, the father of the baby Mindy was carrying. The man whose place I was trying to take because Zeely had accepted Jerry's proposal.

The guy reached for my hand. "Yes, she got me with that, reaching down the pew to see who was singing. I see she's working on you now. Good morning. I'm Daniel Lazarus."

I shook his hand as a smile formed on my lips and a plan formed in my mind. "I think we've met already through a mutual friend."

The organist frowned. "I doubt it. I've only been going to this church a short while. I used to go to—"

"Tender Mercies. I know. I'm Ron, Mindy's fiancé. You, I believe, are her boyfriend."

We exchanged guarded glances before I found a seat on a back pew and sat down. An unsteady strain from the organ signaled the opening of the service. I hummed along with the opening song and stared out the window during the welcome, trying not to draw attention to myself. I looked up and met eyes with Zeely's father. It was too late to try to hide. He'd seen me.

"Would all the visitors please stand?" Reverend Wilkins smiled down from the pulpit in my direction.

I was too busy recovering from meeting Daniel to give much of a response, but I couldn't help but smile as I reluctantly stood. The first time I'd come here as a visitor, I'd thought that Reverend Wilkins was Jesus himself. Brian had tugged at my suit—well, actually it was his suit, I'd borrowed it—and told me to sit down.

There was no one here to quiet me this time, but I stood slower now, clasping my hands in front of me. I looked around the sanctuary, waiting, hoping for someone else to stand, but no one did. Of all the Sundays to visit, I would have to choose a day when I'd be the only visitor. The crowd had mixed reactions to my presence.

"What is that white guy doing here? Did you invite him?"

"He looks familiar . . . Is that the boy Eva raised?"

If they only knew.

I lifted my program to cover my face, but not before Reverend Wilkins pulled the microphone from its stand and stepped down from the pulpit. Though they'd updated the church, they still had that microphone with a thousand feet of cord. The Rev. would walk all over the church with that thing. Somehow, he'd never tripped on it. Now though, he wasn't looking like he planned to walk the aisle—his eyes were fixed on me. My stomach tied into a knot Brian and I learned at one of three Boy Scout meetings we had attended. I didn't remember the name of it, but I could see it in my head—like some kind of pretzel.

I closed in a simple, desperate prayer.

He wouldn't, Lord. Tell me he wouldn't.

Even as I prayed, I knew that Reverend Wilkins would do just what I feared—call me out. I must have been crazy to come back here. The swish of the Reverend's robe vibrated into the microphone, bringing back a flood of memories. It was here that I'd heard Zeely sing for the first time. When I heard someone call her Birdie, I didn't have to ask why. Nor did I have to wonder where my childhood preacher was heading as he stepped out of the pulpit and down the middle of the church. He was coming straight for me, just like he did in my dreams.

He stopped at the end of my pew and motioned for me to join him in the aisle. His voice filled the room as it had in the years before the new sound system and recording equipment. I could recount many of this man's sermons word for word. Even worse, I could still remember my own.

"Any of you all remember this 'visitor'? Coming up in here all quiet and such, acting like we don't know him. He done hurt my feelings. I had to come down here and tell y'all who this is, both to me and to the Lord. Y'all remember this boy, don't you?"

Many nodded. "Yes sir. We know him. Rodney Jenkins."

I almost lost it then. Rodney wasn't my name, but Miss Eva, who'd raised me and Brian, had always called me that. Her son Rodney had gotten too close with a white girl before people were ready for that sort of thing. Someone killed him for it. My name Ronald sounded like Rodney to her, so I let her call me that. If she were here now, I'd answer to it in a second.

Though Brian seemed to have forgotten the good times Eva gave us once he found out she wasn't his real mother, I would never forget. I couldn't. Before I moved into that yellow house with the roses, my life had been very different, and not in a good way.

Reverend Wilkins squeezed my shoulder and walked back to the pulpit, giving me an almost imperceptible nod that meant for me to follow. This was the part of my dream where I woke up sweating and ready to scream. Only this time it was real. Under the veil of many eyes, I followed him to the front of the church.

95

As we walked, he continued talking. "His real name isn't Rodney. I've been telling y'all that for years. For those of you who don't know him, this here is Ronald Jenkins. He grew up around here, and many Sundays he preached us old folk long into the night. Only we weren't so old then, right, church?"

While the congregation answered with hearty amens, Daniel plunked the wrong note in the background music. I stifled a laugh. This had to be awkward for him too. He didn't need to worry about me though. I was only marrying Mindy so she'd keep her baby instead of killing it. It wasn't the best foundation for a marriage, but we'd been engaged for real not so long ago, and well, I figured I owed in the baby department after what had happened with Zeely. The way things were going down today, I must owe in some other departments too.

Reverend Wilkins nodded to the organist. "Don't lose time, brother. Stay with me, hear? I'm telling the truth now. I see some of you all looking funny at this man because he looks different than most folk who come through our doors. That tells me I'm not doing my job quite right. Surely you all know better than to judge by the flesh. Don't make me have to give this fellow the pulpit. You'll all be shamed."

"Go ahead! We've got time." Mother Riley's voice sounded from the front row.

I looked around the room for help. My eyes searched the choir stand. After how things had gone down at the hospital, I knew Zeely wouldn't be there. It was part of the reason I was here, to keep from running into the happy couple at Tender Mercies. Right now, it'd be nice to look up at her and share a look. Only she could understand how it felt to be put on the spot by her father. She'd been enduring it all of her life. I'd advised Jerry to leave Zee home today, to let her recover some more, but I knew he'd do the opposite. The way things were going here, I might end up in the hospital . . . with an ulcer.

Charlene waved at me from the soprano section. She was the coat checker from the country club where Mindy and I had lunch sometimes. I hated that stuck-up place, but seeing Charlene always made it easier. "I say let him preach, Pastor," she said, beaming a smile at me. "These folks need to be stirred up."

I shook my head preacher style, just enough for Reverend Wilkins to notice, but not the crowd.

That was a mistake.

The old man nodded his head, a laugh on his tongue. "Brother Jenkins will teach this morning! Move over, Mother Riley. I want to have a front row seat for this."

My mouth went dry as the Reverend led me up to the pulpit and slipped the microphone back into the stand. "And don't hold back, either. If you do, I'll call you out. You home now, not 'cross town," he whispered into my ear on his way down the stairs.

For a second, my heart went wild. My lips pressed together so tight that I knew they could never open, let alone transmit sound. And then I realized it—I was finally tall enough for my arms to rest on the podium. That made me smile. This podium had seemed so big back then. So strong. Just like Reverend Wilkins. Now it seemed average. Ordinary. Old. But some things, like the feeling that went through me when I gripped it, hadn't changed. Not at all.

I stared down at the Bible on the podium before glancing back at my own Bible, still at my seat in one of the back pews. The Reverend tapped a deacon and pointed to a weathered Bible several rows back. "Take that up to him, please? The big brown one. Thanks."

No way out now. I accepted the book from the deacon and looked heavenward and then down at Daniel, sitting still at the keyboard with a skeptical look. Reverend Wilkins was right about one thing.

If I was going to do this, I had to do it the old way—step aside and let God do his thing. I pulled the mike from the stand in one hand and let my Bible flop open in the other. "I know what you're thinking. What on earth is this white boy going to say?"

The crowd laughed. It was an uneasy chuckle for some, a full-blown guffaw for others. Taut shoulders eased to normal position.

"Well, don't worry. I'm not going to talk long." I draped the microphone cord around my neck and stepped down the stairs and into the center aisle. The text was an easy choice—David, a victorious king whose biggest loss was his family. "I just stopped by to tell you a story."

14

Grace

I stumbled into Mount Olive twenty minutes late. I'd planned to make this my first Sunday back at Tender Mercies, but today's pain was an old pain, one I wasn't ready to yield to strangers. I'd made the mistake of reading another entry in my old notebook, this one from my sixteenth birthday, three days after the baby was born. When I finished crying, I hadn't wanted to come to church at all. Even now, the words lingered on my mind.

> *Tomorrow is my birthday. The nurse says they're going*
> *to send up a cake so I can celebrate. People are so*
> *stupid sometimes.*
> *Diana Dixon*

I could almost taste it now, the sweet bitterness of that cake. I'd eaten it for my mother, for the nurses, the nuns, and maybe even for myself. It didn't stay down long. There was nothing to celebrate and they knew it. They just didn't think I knew. I'd known then and I knew now.

The quiet surprised me as I slid into a pew past the middle but not quite in the back. I wasn't quite back-pew late, but pushing it. Usually there was a rocking laughter, a back-and-forth between Reverend Wilkins and the Amen Corner, the faithful who still called me "Trey Dixon's girl." Instead of laughter and call and response, there was the movement of shoulders and the nodding of heads. A low hum erupted from the first row as I sat down.

Even more shocking was who was doing the talking: Ron. Zeely's Ron. He walked toward my row with the microphone cord tangled in his collar, but passed me like he'd never seen me before. I'd seen that look on many preachers' faces before. Ron was in the zone.

"The story I just read was from First Chronicles, chapter twelve. David wanted to do something big for God. His friend the prophet said 'Go for it.' Only thing, they forgot to consult God himself."

Ron's wit and humor had impressed me before, during the few times I'd hung out with him and Zeely, but nothing had prepared me for this Ron—a man overflowing with the Spirit of God. My purse strap slid down my shoulder as I fumbled to find the correct passage in my Bible.

"David had a good plan, a divine motive, and even godly counsel, but he lacked God's blessing. When David did his do, Nathan the prophet couldn't sleep. How many of you know that people who hear from the Lord lose some sleep?"

Reverend Wilkins waved a piece of cloth at the front. "Preach, preacher."

"Nathan had to go back to his friend's house and tell David that God said no. He had to tell his boy that even though he'd killed the giant, even though he'd won the wars, even though he'd built a nation, he wasn't the one to build God's house. Too much blood was on his hands. David's son would do the building. And God planned to do some building too—a house for David."

I leaned over so far that I was hanging off my seat. This was why the Lord led me to Mount Olive today. This was a right-now word, my word, the one I'd needed.

"The Lord said no." Ron lifted his chin. "Don't look at me like that. I know that nobody preaches that. I know y'all came out to hear how you are going to get everything you say, everything you pray, but you're not. I'm not. God says no sometimes, and you know what? Sometimes that no is a blessing. It's all in how you respond."

No could be a blessing? There was more truth in Ron's words than I wanted to admit. I'd heard God's no many times in my life: Dancer? No! Mother? No! Wife? Yes—no! I shivered when I thought of where I might be if God hadn't said no to my marriage to Malachi, the man who'd raped me all those years before. I shook so hard that the woman next to me reached out and touched my shoulder, speaking softly in tongues.

I leaned into her touch and set my Bible on the pew next to me. This was going to be a laid-out-on-the-floor-before-it's-all-over sort of teaching, I could tell already. I wiped the sweat off my forehead and waited for Ron to speak again. He paused like few young preachers do nowadays, giving me time to get myself together.

"After hearing his friend the prophet's news, David didn't cuss Nathan out. He didn't rebuke any demons or have Nathan taken away. He didn't even pray. He just sat before the Lord, questions and all. Remember when you were little and God was big and you used to do that? Just sit before the Lord?"

I bowed my head, allowing all my questions to pour out of my mind and into my hands. They were heavy. Big things. Crazy things. One cut into my fingers, refusing to be silenced: why had God brought Brian into my life and let him love me—knowing that I didn't know how to love anymore?

Ron didn't give me too much time to dwell on it. He headed back to the podium. "David realized the real questions hiding behind his fear, his anger. Can God be trusted? Does he know what's best? In the silence, the king found an answer. When he speaks again, David doesn't mention the denial, only the blessing. He doesn't focus on what the Lord said that he couldn't do, but what the Lord promised to do for him. God had promised to build *him* a house!"

I blinked away tears. During my midnight dances, hadn't God promised me the same—a house, a family? I swallowed a lump in my throat, almost afraid to say the rest. A husband? But I had ignored those words then. I'd had men enough, drama enough, pain enough. Even now, I wanted to give myself to Christ totally, something that only a single woman could do.

"And here's the good part. Though David knows that he won't be the man to build God's house, he makes sure that his son won't lack for anything when the time comes. Instead of sitting around waiting for God's promise to emerge, he rolls up his sleeves and gets down to work. He draws up the plans, hires the builders, finds the best wood, cuts the best stones . . ." Ron took a few more steps and turned around. "Are we willing to do that, church? To release what we can't do and do what we can? Are we willing to gather the wood and cut the stones, trusting that God will bring the builder?"

I bit my lip until it bled. Only when the lady next to me offered a tissue did I realize I was sobbing like a baby. Joyce had asked me to come back to Testimony to teach. I thought she'd just meant to teach school. That had only been part of it. I'd come here to dance. I'd come here to finish what had begun in Ngozi, to take Joyce's wood and her tears and build a house of worship in the hearts of Testimony's children. The words of Joyce's letter to me earlier this year, when she must have known she was dying, came back to me:

If you've ever loved me, please come.

Who could turn away from a plea like that? But when she'd asked me to resurrect the Ngozi Dance Troupe, I'd stuttered like Moses, telling Joyce why Zeely was the best candidate for the job. She hadn't asked me about it again. And now, it was understood that I couldn't, that I wouldn't, be doing any more than trying to get my mind right so I could get back to teaching school.

These were my wood, my stones: the Ngozi Dance Troupe and Imani Academy. My heart pounded as Ron spoke on, urging me to accept the love, any love, God sent my way, whether it was from the baby I'd always be searching for or the man I seemed to always be running from. My pencil broke as I scribbled in the margin of my Bible, still on the seat next to me.

Do what you can. Love who you can. Accept the wood. Build the house.

"If we think we can hold our obedience hostage until God ransoms it with explanations, we can forget it." Ron closed his Bible and tucked it under one arm. "The Father didn't explain himself to Jesus. And we want an update from the heavenlies every few days before we'll do anything."

A middle-aged man at the far end of the pew shook his head back and forth. "You right. God knows you right . . . Umph. Have mercy, Jesus."

Ron pointed toward the voice, nodding. His eyes looked brighter than I remembered against his reddish-brown hair. From where I sat, he looked like a man on fire.

"He's got it exactly. Mercy. Isn't that what we all want? But we hold that back too. Nobody gets anything until we get our answers." Ron gave up trying to stand behind the podium he'd returned to and descended the stairs. "Well, you can forget that, friend. God never promised to answer all our questions, but know this: He is *the* answer."

SONGS of Deliverance

Despite the heated room, goose bumps prickled up my arms. Hadn't I offered the Lord my share of ultimatums?

Give me my baby and I'll do whatever you want.

I rubbed my biceps, then my elbows, but the chill wouldn't leave me. My baby was anything but a baby. She would be as old as the kids I taught now. Nothing could put that child back into my arms or go back through time and steer me away from that bus stop. There was just now, just Jesus, and it was time to tear up my ransom notes. Either I'd obey God or I wouldn't. Lots of people had been through bad things. Some a lot worse than me.

"I'm about to close. I thank y'all for listening to me. I know it wasn't a feel-good message. Nobody likes to think about God saying no to them, especially not church people. Blessings. Favor. Prosperity. I like to hear that stuff too. But today wasn't a dessert kind of day. This was vitamins and minerals, and it was for me more than any of you. It would have been nice to serve you some spiritual ice cream though. Maybe next time we'll talk about when God says wait. Sometimes it's not a denial, but a delay, amen?"

"Um hum." One person answered, barely above a whisper. Everyone else held a collective breath.

"Just remember. God is not as concerned with your doing as He is your being. He wants your heart." Ron walked to the stand where the collection plates were stacked. With that, he approached the first row and handed the microphone to Reverend Wilkins. He started walking toward the back, but Reverend Wilkins pointed out a spot on the front row.

The Reverend waved his hand as he took the microphone from the stand where Ron had replaced it. "Are y'all getting this?"

An old woman on the front pew clapped her hands. "I got it. I don't know about the rest of you, but I got it! I'm going home to gather some wood."

I stepped out of my shoes and into the aisle, stretching out on the floor in the best dress I owned, in front of half the town. It didn't matter though. This wasn't cute time. This was healing time. Other people were heading to the front to pray and be prayed for, but this wasn't a day for me to stand in any line and receive from the hands of man. My broken pieces had to be put back together by God himself.

Reverend Wilkins sang a song I didn't know, but his voice sounded distant, as if it were somewhere on the other side of a river. There was moisture here, a shiny fog I hadn't felt in a long time, the reality of an ever-present, all-powerful God instead of the one I'd substituted for Him in my mind. The sanctuary filled with something precious and rare—the glory of the living God.

"Thank ya! Lord, I just thank ya!" shouted the woman who'd been sitting beside me. She stepped over me on her way to the altar. I couldn't have moved out of the way if I wanted to. There was a surgery going on in my spirit and this carpet was the operating table.

After what seemed like hours, but must have been minutes because the music was still playing, I got up slowly, barely able to stand. I sat back on my heels, watching as a woman came out of the choir stand to embrace a pregnant girl with the same eyes and smile as her own. I clutched my sides as people filled the aisle around me.

Reverend Wilkins mopped his brow. "Whosoever will . . . let him come. Just come. He's seen it all—ha—he knows it all and he loves ya anyway—ha—Won't you come?"

Ex-husbands and ex-wives, current lovers and former enemies, all came together, pushing through the crowd. Finally, even the music went silent as the organist stretched out on the floor too.

"That's right, son, give it all to him. God knows how to make his own music anyhow. He's playing his best songs right now—the songs of deliverance. Don't you year it—ha—way down deep-uh-on your insides. Oh-oh-uhn. Y'all ain't hearing me. It's a good song. It'll set you free." His voice went up into a high hum.

"There it is, the first verse is redemption. And the sec-ond verse is adoption. The third verse is deliverance. That what he's playing this morning. The Holy Ghost is singing. You don't even have to leave your place. No man's hand has to touch you. Just get down where you are and start humming. If you hear it in the spirit, make some noise. If you need to holler, just holler. If you need to dance, just dance."

I was shaking all over now, watching the Reverend sway from side to side and turn back and forth. He was moving like lightning, like God had taken all the years away for a moment, like his feet were on holy ground. And maybe he was. Today, Ron Jenkins had been the burning bush for all of us.

Reverend Wilkins walked the aisles as everyone, including me, started to hum. A lady I remembered from the Buds of Promise Choir when we were kids started to sing.

"Deliver us, O Lord . . . With a mighty hand and your loving grace, bring us out of bondage, let us see your face!"

Her voice was incredible. Zeely had always sung the lead parts, but that sistah had obviously been singing at home. Reverend Wilkins shouted as she stood and kept singing. The words came easy, as though we were learning the song as she sang it.

"Yes! That's it. The deliverance song. Do you hear it now? Won't you come? Don't let the enemy keep you quiet. God seen it all anyway. The booty calls. The drinking. He knows that too. Won't you come? The drugs. The lies. He knows that too. Some folks in here didn't even sleep in their own bed last night."

"My God." A man with a grey beard climbed over the pew in front of me and ran to the front. I pulled myself up to my feet.

"With your loving grace, let us see your face . . ." she sang on in a voice that must have made even the angels smile.

"Uh-unh huh . . . Y'all ain't hearing me . . ." Reverend Wilkins grabbed a glass of water from somewhere under the pulpit.

"We're going to lay it all down right here. Your offering won't change it, your singing won't change it, your fronting won't change it. But God can change it. And he will. He's waiting down here to build you a house. Won't you come?"

When the mother of one of my worst students squeezed past me, I followed her. I'd thought this thing was going to be just between me and God, but this was bigger than me. Way bigger.

15

Zeely

"So Jerry just walked in on the two of you?" Grace diced an onion while I looked for the olive oil. Her cabinets were in need of serious organizing.

I tried to think of an appropriate, yet honest word. Ron had just asked me about us getting married before Jerry stormed in, and this time, I was the one to hesitate. In the space of a few seconds, I'd closed the door on a lifetime of love. And I had no idea why. "It wasn't like you're making it sound. We were both decent. Just . . ."

"Compromised? From what you've told me, it sounds like Ron was ready to do what you've said he never could—get serious."

I found the oil and slammed it down on the counter. The whole thing with Grace counseling me was getting old. She was usually right, but I still didn't like it. "He's already serious. About Mindy, okay? He proposed to her—twice. Once for himself and once for her baby."

"And you accepted Jerry's proposal for the sake of your baby. Everybody is trying to make decisions for the greater good, which works well for politics but I'm not so sure it works for romance. You love Ron. I don't care what your mother said about you and Jerry being meant for each other. I think she was an amazing woman, but she was human. She could have been wrong."

I shrugged and started grating a block of gouda cheese. "She probably was wrong. Who knows. The thing is, she's been right so far. Everything I've tried to do my own way just doesn't work out. I thought I could trust Ron with my heart before, and it turned out that—"

"You guys were kids. Ron's not a racist, you know that. He's human. If someone had asked you the same thing back then, you might have hesitated. You didn't tell me that Ron was white, that he was Red from when we were young. You barely mentioned him when I moved back here. Why was that? Was it because you were worried about what I might think?"

My finger burned as I accidentally raked it instead of the cheese across the grater. "I have never been ashamed of Ron or of loving him. It's just that we've been a secret so long, it's like I don't know how to make it public. We've always been hiding."

"You don't have to," Grace said, adding green peppers and zucchini to the steaming wok. "We're grown now. Act like it. Call it off with Jerry. There's no sense playing these games. I can't be sure, but I feel like he's acting out of obligation too. He's trying too hard."

My shoulders slumped. She had me there. Jerry treated me like I was community service or some kind of good deed. He didn't realize it, but it was true. He'd loved Carmel in front of me. I knew what love looked like, and it wasn't falling asleep on my couch every weekend.

"I think he still loves her."

There. I'd said it. The feeling had been haunting me for weeks. I thought about how Carmel had looked when she was taking care of me, how quiet she'd spoken. She'd come a long way from the fast-behind cheerleader I remembered.

Grace piled the vegetables onto our plates. She took the gouda from my still hands and sprinkled it on top. Veggie stir-fry and cheese was our new comfort food and, like everything else in our lives, didn't make much sense. She put the food on the counter and took my hands in hers.

"I think so too. I hate to say it, but Jerry and Carmel still come off to me as a couple. Just like you and Ron. Maybe I'm missing it. I don't know."

"I don't think you are, but if you're going to go there, what about you and Brian? You two are a couple if I've ever seen one. What's up on that front?"

It was a cheap trick, deflecting the conversation like that, but I felt like a wounded animal being poked with a stick. I was the one who made good decisions, made investments and planned the future. Now I was acting like some teenaged girl, caught between my past and my future and unable to choose. Grace had a reason to keep her distance from Brian. She'd been hurt.

So have you.

I wrapped my arms around my waist, hugging myself. I'd been hurt, true enough, but no man had assaulted me, I'd done the hurting myself. A sob came up in my throat, but I swallowed it down. Crying wasn't going to change anything.

Grace put her arms around me. "Father, I thank you for Zeely. I thank you for her strength, for her power, for her will to endure to the end. I ask you right now to be her strength, to remind her that in our weakness you are made strong. Give her ears to hear what your Spirit is saying, what her own heart is saying. Give her a perfect love that casts out all fear. Let her know that she isn't alone, that you are here. That I am here. Let her know that I love her. In Jesus' name, amen."

There in Grace's kitchen, fragranced with lemongrass and fennel, something broke open in me, something black and cold. My back curved and my arms opened as I hugged my friend back. On another day, I would have felt compelled to pray for her too, but all I could do today was receive. "Thank you," I whispered into her shirt. "Thank you."

She gave me one more squeeze and took a step back. I was grateful. There was only so much of this touchy-feely business that I could stand. We sat down to our plates.

"So, did you get someone to cover your exercise class?"

I took a mouthful of the food. Glorious. "If you want to call it that. I've actually given over the class to one of the ladies who has been with me since the beginning."

Grace stopped eating. "You? Not dancing?"

I smiled. "I didn't say that. I'm thinking about trying out for the Dayton Contemporary Dance Company again or at least trying to work with the girls in their developmental group. My life would have been so different if I had stayed in that, but Mama didn't think it was important. Education was all that mattered. And it did matter, God knows where I'd be if I hadn't finished college, but I think that Joyce was right too. Every person has to have a passion, something that makes them go farther than they think they can. Dance is that for me. For you too."

"Um hum," Grace said between bites. "I don't think I realized that until I heard Ron's sermon."

I shifted in my chair. Grace wasn't the first one to tell me about Ron's recent impromptu teaching at Mount Olive. Everywhere I went, people were telling me about it, asking me where I'd been that morning. The only person who hadn't mentioned it was Ron.

"I've decided that Ngozi, or my version of it, are my wood and stones, my materials to build something for God. And if I'm not the one to build it, perhaps God will build something for me."

Grace spoke with a confidence that scared me. I'd once known God with such assurance. Perhaps I could again.

"So you're going to do it? Ngozi, I mean?"

"Not exactly."

"What then?" I'd been so angry when Joyce first suggested that Grace bring back the dance troupe. It was her place though, it was who Diana—Grace—was. God knows she'd paid the price for who she was. The enemy had done everything but take her life to keep her from fulfilling it.

"We are going to do it, you and I, if you're willing. It's going to be a mix of praise dance, African, and contemporary. I'm calling it Rhythms of Grace. After the Scripture—not me."

I smiled. Matthew 28, in the Message Bible, invites the reader to come and learn of Jesus, to walk with him and work with him and watch how he does it, to learn the unforced rhythm of grace. Seeing the light in Grace's eyes now, I felt like we were kids again. A song began to beat along with my heart, the pulse of a drum.

"I hear it," I said softly, surprised at the sound of my own voice.

"What?"

"The music. I hear it inside me like you and Daddy do. And it's drums, like when Brian plays. Except—"

Grace had dropped her fork. "Yes?"

"The song . . . It's the 'Wedding March.'"

16

Ron

It had been years since I'd been to Mother Riley's home, but like her, it hadn't changed much at all. The plaid couch held me in the same embrace that I remembered almost twenty years earlier.

She sat a cup of tea in front of me and a warm biscuit on a china plate. "Sorry there isn't more. I'm old and don't eat much these days, I'm afraid. I still can make a good biscuit though. Not as good as your Eva's mind you, but almost."

I sighed and smothered the biscuit with gooseberry jam. My manners dissolved as I took a bite and sighed. "It's just as good."

Mother Riley laughed out loud. "That's what I always loved about you. No pretending. You just don't have it in you. At least not back then anyway. I don't know what done happened since then, but for God's sake, be yourself. The world needs more honest, God-fearing folk. Now tell me, you ain't been to my house in nigh twenty years. What brings you?"

There was no fooling Mother Riley, no matter how old she was. "I saw my mother."

The old woman nodded but didn't look surprised. "Marie? Yes.

I see her from time to time. She shows up at Mount Olive more than you. We were shocked when she first came, but she's in and out. Sometimes, when I go out to drive to church, she's standing at the end of the drive. I just pick her up and take her on. And feed her, of course. You know I've got to feed her."

I wasn't sure what surprised me more, that my mother knew where Mother Riley lived or that Mother Riley was still driving herself to church. "You're still driving? What about the church van?"

"What about it? All the young folks have gone on to other places. Nobody wants to drive it. I don't drive much, just down the street to the church and back, and only when it's too cold to walk. I told 'em that I'd drive that van myself, but they won't let me. They think I'm too old. I say that you're as old as you feel and I feel fine. It's some of you young folk that I'm worried about. Speaking of, how is Sister Joyce? I ain't been over to the hospital in a few days. At least you do keep up with *her*, I'll give you that."

"She's not doing too well, I'm afraid. We've had a few close calls, but we're trusting God to preserve her."

The old woman laughed. "Boy, please. Let her go."

"What?" Mother Riley was a prayer warrior and a great woman of faith. Her words caught me off guard.

"You heard me. Joyce done lived a hundred lives through all of you children. She done give you all some of her lives too. Some folk can do that. They's like a cat, always landing on their feet. But in the end, there comes a time when they need another one of them lives and they ain't got it, 'cause they done give them all away. Your Joyce is like that. She done good on this earth, made her life count for something. Folk like that don' need to be preserved. They ain't afraid to die. It's the folk that sit up and don't do anything that need more time. That woman done lived and loved hard as she could. Her Maker will be glad to have her. Let her go and tell her to save a spot for me in her dance group. I'm going to be right up there beside her soon. Maybe this time next year . . ."

The biscuit turned to glue in my mouth. She nodded and handed me my cup of tea. I'd never heard anybody talk about dying like that, never thought of it that way. I guess I always prayed for people what I would pray for myself—more time, more life. I was one of those people Mother Riley was talking about who had yet to make their marks on the world, one of those who hadn't given any lives away. Finally, I understood what Joyce had been trying to tell me for the past year, what she'd been trying to tell all of us.

"Just run your leg, baby," Joyce had said to me one day last year, when she found out that the cancer was back. "Do your time the best you can. The people who came before, they sacrificed so you could be here, so you could do something. They gave themselves away. There comes a time when we all have to do that. If we don't, it's like we never lived."

I'd been so angry at first and then so confident that nothing would take her from me, the last piece of my patchwork family.

You have your mother.

I had *a* mother, but I didn't have my mother. I'd never known how to have her, not really. And until I got to the bottom of what had made her the way she was, what had made my father who he was, I might never have her.

"So is that it? You came to ask me about Marie? You could have asked me about that at church. Is it about Birdie? 'Cause if it is, I'm glad to put my two cents in. Y'all done 'bout drove me nuts. All these years. I'm trying to live to see a baby from you, but you won't stand up to that Terrigan boy and tell him what's what—"

"That isn't why I'm here."

"Well, forgive me then. I spoke out of turn," she said, pulling her shawl around her shoulders. "Don't make it no less true though."

115

No, ma'am. It doesn't.

"I came about Sadie, my father's grandmother? I don't even know her last name for sure. I've searched the records at the courthouse—"

"You ain't gone find it there. Not right off anyway. I know about Sadie. I thought you did too. You mean to tell me that you became who you are without knowing? Now that goes to show you, there is a God. Folks can deny it all they like, but He's always there, working—"

I cleared my throat.

"Sadie. Oh, yes. All of us grew up knowing about her. She grew up in South Carolina, I believe. Her daddy was an Irishman, some of where your red hair comes from, I suspect. He came to this country and made a way for himself, bought land, bought slaves. One of them slaves was Harriet. They called her Hattie. Folks say she was one of the prettiest gals in the state. She was a mulatto. You know what that is?"

Unfortunately. Brian had made sure that my Black History education was more than adequate. "Yes, she was mixed."

"Uh huh. I believe she might have even been a quadroon or an octoroon. She was as white as the master's wife, they say. Anyway, that Irish man took a real liking to that girl. Old folks say he even loved her, though I don't know how you can love somebody and own them, do you?" She didn't give me a chance to answer. "Anyway, folks saw that he was too attached to that gal Harriet, and they told him to get a white wife. He did too. She thought the sun and stars rose over Master and set herself on having his son right away, like her mother had told her. What she didn't know was that when Master wasn't in the Big House, he was with Hattie. When the missy fell pregnant, Hattie was pregnant too."

I tried to breathe, to figure out where the story was going, but I couldn't. Not at all. So I listened, with every part of myself.

"Hattie worked even though she was pregnant, especially once the Missus realized what was going on. On the night the Missus was due, she called Hattie to attend her. The old doctor was there and he took one look at Hattie and knew that it was her time too, but the Missus wouldn't hear of it. She made Hattie stay." The old woman took a deep breath and a bite of biscuit. She had me on the hook and meant to enjoy it.

"Hattie held out until the Missus had her child, a red-headed boy, born blue and breathless. To the tune of the Missy's wails, Hattie kneeled down and birthed her own children, two of them, both girls, healthy and strong. For all the pain she'd been through, Hattie had joy in her heart at the sight of her girl children—that is, until she looked up and saw the desire in Missy's face. Hattie didn't have much strength, but she gathered her babies in her arms and turned away . . ."

Mother Riley paused again, staring off in the distance as a tear trailed down her cheek. I wanted to scream, but I kept silent.

"I'm sorry. This part always chokes me up. Hattie tried to run with them babies, but Missy wouldn't let her go. She took one baby by the foot and snatched it away."

My fingers gripped the arm of the couch. "She took the baby?"

"Yes, she took it and said it was hers. If the doctor hadn't recorded the truth in his notes, no one would have ever admitted it. All the black folk knew, but for eighteen years that baby lived as a white girl in the Big House."

"And then what happened?"

"One day, Sadie found out who she really was."

17

Grace

Mid-winter moved in like a second wife—nice at first, but ready to make big changes. Ice mixed with the snow and everything seemed frozen, stiff in time. It would have been easy to just stay home until the New Year. It would have been easy and expected. But since the day of Ron's sermon, I was neither of those things. As of today, I was something more, something new. A dance teacher.

"Welcome to Rhythms of Grace," the words lingering on my lips like the taste of strawberries.

Seventeen students stood in the gym in front of Zeely and me, none of them the kids we'd expected. They looked surprised to be here too. Brian had tried to talk me out of starting the group.

"It's too soon," he'd said under his breath last week as he passed me in the hall. Since my last visit to his home, we were talking more now, but probably not as much as he would have liked.

I'd reached out and clasped his hand as I passed by. "It's never too soon to do the will of God."

Though he heard the truth in my tone, he'd still looked worried. Looking out over the room, I was too. For all my fears, looking into the soft eyes of these children who by day seemed so impenetrable, I knew that my fears—or Brian's—couldn't be enough to keep me away.

I smiled at the class. "Have any of you danced before?"

Their hands remained at their sides, in their laps, and under their chins. With only a few days' notice before the first class, I hadn't expected a great response. Evidently these kids needed something new, something fresh. So did I.

A boy wearing shorts and black lipstick shrugged. "We don't know anything."

I nodded and pulled out the CD I'd burned the night before. "Good. You won't have any bad habits to break." I looked over at Zeely, who gave me a firm nod.

"Let's get started," I said.

That was yesterday. Now my legs screamed with pain as I walked the aisles in Jerry Terrigan's Algebra class, but it was a good pain, a hurt that was going to give birth to something. All the kids were talking about it.

My body would adapt to the daily dancing soon enough. I hoped my soul could get used to the memories that rose up to meet me every time I leapt across the floor. One day soon, I'd fly high enough to get over it. All of it. Until then, I just had to keep showing up, keep believing. Brian had given me a good example in that department. His silent persistence both thrilled and terrified me.

The students passed their completed math exams to the front of the class.

"Thanks," I said as the papers were handed to me, reassuring the kids with my eyes that I really was okay. Things were getting back to normal, but sometimes, like now, they looked at me with great concern. A few had asked me this morning if I really should be dancing. I told them the truth: that I wasn't sure, but that I had to try.

I wondered how Zeely was holding up in Brian's classroom across the hall, especially with Ron now at the school. Ron had his own classroom now, American Government and AP History. The kids loved him as much as Brian, but I didn't run into him as often now as when he and Zeely were getting close again. Now she was getting close with Jerry, and despite my reluctance to accept it, Brian and I were getting closer too. Slowly, things were returning to normal. A new normal.

Sean was the only student who I really hadn't resumed my bond with yet. I couldn't shake Brian's initial insistence that Sean had some part in the break-ins at my place. Brian seemed to believe otherwise now and was even talking to the police on Sean's behalf, but I didn't know what to believe. Being naïve had gotten me into enough trouble. While I would extend every help to Sean I could, I didn't want to be stupid either.

As though reading my thoughts, Sean stared at me and then smiled a cautious smile.

I waved at him.

The boy sitting one row up from Sean broke our silent communication. "What'd you get for number three? X to the fifth?"

Sean shook his head. "Naw, man. X to the fourth. The other one cancelled out. You didn't simplify it all the way."

The boy sucked his teeth. "I see it now."

A smile creased my face in spite of the pain in my thighs, the fear tickling the back of my throat. Maybe Brian was right, maybe I had the boy all wrong . . .

Behind me, something—no, someone—smelled of honey. I took a deep breath and turned to face the door. There stood Brian, looking regal yet broken. I tried to explain that now wasn't a good time, but Jerry waved me off as he put the tests in a folder. "Go on, Ms. Okoye, I've got things in hand here."

A month ago, the kids would have erupted in laughter or made some sarcastic comment as I stepped into the hall with Brian. Now they held their breath as I passed, willing the two of us together. Only Sean kept his eyes on me when I went by his chair and stepped into the hall.

Starting the dance class had come easy. Dealing with Brian's love still eluded me. "Seriously, this really isn't a good time. Call me later," I whispered. Whether Jerry said it was okay or not, I didn't like handling my personal business during class time.

"I know. It's never a good time." There was a sharp truth in his words, but his tone was as sweet as his scent. A smokiness underneath the aroma made me want to rest my face on his chest. Vetiver. That was new.

"I just wanted to talk to you more about your case. I think I may have found a connection that we can follow—"

"Let's talk later." Before that Sunday at Mount Olive when I'd wiped up the floor with myself, this would have been great news, all I wanted to hear. That day, I'd finally let my sweet baby go. I'd done what I could, filled out the papers, updated my contact information. If it was meant for my daughter and me to come together, we would. If not, well, there was this school and the dance troupe, the wood and the stones. I couldn't make room in me for anything else. Anyone else.

"I know you're trying to help. I appreciate it. I talked to some people who do this for a living, reunite adoptive families. They told me that my case was a difficult one. I don't want to send you down a bunch of rabbit trails trying to fix this for me. It is what it is. There isn't always a happy ending."

Brian looked crushed, but he recovered quickly.

"I think you should pursue this. In fact—"

The bell rang, forcing us back to our classrooms where we belonged. I'd missed this, the ringing of bells and changing of classes. It forced along days when time stood still inside of me. I wondered how long it would be before I let myself be alone with Brian outside of school again. I'd certainly felt good standing close to him today. I had to be careful though. He seemed so powerful, like nothing could hurt him, but I knew that I could hurt him, that I was hurting him. The love he wanted was still packed in boxes on the floor of my heart. Moving into my new self might take longer than even he could wait.

Back inside the classroom, Jerry stood on one side of the door and handed out the tests and scratch paper. I accepted backpacks and cell phones. We had a simple system that curbed cheating and stopped a lot of talking. Neither of us minded what students did once the lessons were done on regular days—well, at least Jerry didn't—but test days were different. I handed one of our basic scientific calculators to one of Sean's friends in exchange for his fancy one. In some of the higher classes, Jerry allowed the calculators and even encouraged their use, but not at this level. All that would come later. This class was about learning the basics.

As the students settled in their seats, I turned all the phones to off and arranged the backpacks. The students, some of them who'd come to Imani doing math on an elementary level, attacked their tests at once, pressing pencils hard against the paper. I watched them and considered my own tests. Being in this building, where I'd lost and found so much, was a test in itself. Brian's test was having a conversation without the mention of love. So far today, he was passing. I wished he didn't have to, but love cost and it wasn't fair to promise it unless you could pay.

"You Americans talk about love, but to many of you, it's just words," my first husband, Peter Okoye, had said to me on one of our first dates.

Though Peter and I hadn't agreed on what I consider the highest love—the love of God—I had to agree with him. Though I wanted to run behind Brian and sniff his sweater, to ask him why he smelled like sweet smoke, like the incense of my prayers, I couldn't promise him my heart. It was too tightly packed, a place with no room to sit down.

For people like Jerry, who knelt beside a student's desk now giving rapt attention, love came like breathing. For me, it was more like bleeding. Respect I could do. Trust? That was a leap. Love? Maybe a month ago, I thought I could get there . . . before I realized how naïve I really was.

I grabbed the folder of the tests from the previous period and waved to Jerry. "I'm going into the hall to grade."

He nodded and gave me a thumbs-up. We liked to give the students their tests back the next day, especially in the lower level classes. The second day at the latest.

The first student's test went quickly, even with the time I spent mourning the questions the student had left unanswered. The next one, Sean McKnight's test, went just as quickly but for the opposite reason—he'd gotten every one correct. As I reached for another test, someone tapped my shoulder.

"Miss O?"

Sean. How had he walked up so close behind me without me noticing him? I could be so spacey sometimes. I flipped his test over quickly, but he didn't seem to be focused on the tests at all. His eyes were fixed on me.

"Yes?"

"I heard about your dance group. I think that's cool." He twirled his hat on one finger.

"How are things going with your music?"

He took a deep breath. "I'm waiting to hear back about the record you helped me out with. You know, the scholarship for the studio time? It looks like I might get a contract. I'll always appreciate what you did for me."

I should have jumped up and hugged him, screamed with joy even, but I didn't.

"That's great. We are all so proud of you."

I wanted to say more, but the words seemed lodged in my throat. Like the bubble gum that Sean so often won from Jerry in class and dropped the wrappers all over school.

And all over my house.

A smile was all I could manage. "I'm so glad it worked out. Keep me posted."

"I will." He turned back toward the way he came but didn't leave. Instead, he crumpled the hall pass in his hand.

I stared down at the answer key and went back to correcting papers. I had dance practice as soon as the next bell rang. I tucked my pelvis in preparation.

"Miss O? Can I ask you one more thing?"

I froze. This was getting creepy. "Yes, Sean?"

He looked behind him. "Can I get in? Your group, I mean. I'm not a dancer, but I could sing. I play the drums a little. Not as good as Doc but maybe—"

I gripped my pen. Was this it? The "thing" we'd all been waiting for that would turn Sean around? I'd always thought that would come through Brian. I hated to admit it, but maybe it would have to. I paused, waiting to hear from God. All I could hear was the sound of my own screams. "Maybe next semester, okay?"

Sean's smile faded. His shoulders collapsed.

I stuttered a retraction. "I mean, I don't know—I'd have to—"

"It's cool. Forget I asked." He slithered down the hall the way he had on the first day of school. That seemed like a lifetime ago. I'd forgotten how bowed he was then. It was the last period of the day and I needed to get the tests graded, but people came in front of papers. I'd have to take them home. I turned to follow him, but the hall was empty.

"Lord, I want to save him—to save them—but I can't figure out how to do that and save myself too," I said into the stillness.

"You can't."

The words, sweet and spicy, took my breath.

This was Brian's planning period. I remembered it well from the short time we'd taught together before he asked that I be moved to Jerry's class. Things had been intense between us, even back then, before we knew so much about each other. Well, mostly he knew so much about me. Sometimes, I couldn't figure him out for anything.

He rested against the doorframe of his room, wearing khaki pants and that sweet-smelling cable knit sweater.

Goodness, he smells good. Even from here.

Brian got right to the point. "We can't save them and save us too, but God can. You and Joyce taught me that. It's not without risks though." He crossed the hallway and kissed my forehead. "Sometimes things are lost in the battle. Priceless things."

In a move that surprised even me, I circled his waist with my arms and ran my palms up his back, over the ribs of his sweater. I'd wanted to do that since I'd seen him at breakfast. "I know. It's just so hard . . ."

He pulled me close and tight, then let me go. "Have dinner with me tonight? I want to talk to you more about what we discussed earlier."

I pushed away and crossed my arms. "Maybe next time. I've got dance."

"Don't overdo it." He rocked back on his heels.

"Zeely's helping me. We take turns teaching different parts of the dance. It's the hours we spend doing the choreography that I think is working me."

He laughed. "Working you, huh? Don't be surprised if I show up in that class one afternoon."

I lowered my head. "To play the drums? The kids would love it."

"Not to play. Not yet. I get lost when I play for you. I'm coming to dance. No tight outfits though. I can't get with that."

Thank God.

The way the wool clung to his chest, outlined his shoulders . . . I didn't want to think about what was really under there. The counselors at the hospital had expressed concerns about my sexuality after so much trauma. I guess it was all still intact. Or coming back.

"I'll look for you, so don't just say that you're coming." Didn't I always have an eye out for him, even if my hands pushed him away? "I'd better run and get back to class or those kids will beat me to the gym."

Brian smiled and opened the door to my class for me, his hand on mine. "One day, you won't have anywhere to run."

I grinned like a schoolgirl and walked away, wiping the truth of Brian's words from my eyes.

18

Zeely

I tossed a towel over my shoulder and locked the gym door. I'd had it: no more music, no more movement. Only the roar of my thoughts buzzed in my head now. Grace and I were silent for a moment as we walked down the deserted hall. Without the echo of voices, the swell of bodies, this building seemed naked, as bare as a mother's heart without her child.

"They looked good today," Grace said, still catching her wind from our last run at the end of class.

"I wouldn't say good, but definitely better."

"True," Grace said, lifting her shoulders. "It'll come." She paused to push her bag up on her shoulder. "Sean came to me. He asked about being in the group."

My lips tightened. I hoped she'd told him no. I'd once loved Sean like he was my own, but with all the mess he'd been into these last two years, I just didn't trust the boy. It seemed like wherever he was, there was trouble. It didn't help that Jerry was always worrying about him and Monique. I think he'd proposed to me so that we could be a family, a place for Monique to be his little girl again. Instead, she'd decided to be Sean's wife.

"And you told him no, right? He hasn't shown up so I'm guessing that's what you said."

Grace paused for a minute and let her bag slide down her shoulder to the floor. "I told him no, but for all the wrong reasons. This isn't supposed to be about me."

And yet it was.

"You're human. And in truth, we have already started. The group is starting to gel. It would change the dynamics—"

"No." Grace shook her head. "What if Joyce had applied those rules to us? She let me come in off the street and start dancing."

"Exactly. And look at the mess it got you in."

The words left me before I could really hear them, really understand their implications. Only when I looked into my friend's eyes did I see the damage.

Grace gave me a strained look and picked up her bag and started walking. I followed. As we turned the corner, I heard voices.

Familiar voices.

The male voice was young and full of hurt. Shame.

"Why did you do it, huh? You told me to go to Miss Okoye's house. That if I did it you'd leave me alone. I went to jail, Miss Wells. You knew I'd get in trouble!"

"Sean, I didn't mean to—"

"Shut up! I've had enough. Everybody at this place is just fake. Nobody cares about me. Not anymore. Even my girl is scared of me. You made sure of that."

Grace and I should have stayed hidden, kept still, but we didn't. We couldn't. When we edged around the corner with our speeches ready, nothing could have prepared us for the gun in Sean's hands. My towel dropped to the floor.

Sean had Lottie Wells, the crazy art teacher who'd accused Brian and threatened Grace, against his chest in a headlock. I held my breath for a second. Why did trouble always seem to find me?

It doesn't matter, Lord. There's only one way out. Your way. Help me.

"Let her go, Sean." It was Grace talking, though her voice sounded a lot like Joyce's, like a memory.

Sean's face set into a stern, shadowed expression. Speeches wouldn't get far with him today. "Stay back, Miss O, or I'll shoot her. I promise I will."

Lottie squeezed her eyes shut, but she didn't look as scared as she should have been. Maybe she was in shock. I doubted that Sean would pull the trigger, but I'd thought the same thing about myself right before Mal went down.

Numbness flowed over me. Sean was so smart, but so dumb too. This would be the end of the line for him. Ten, twenty, life. And that would be just for having the gun, let alone firing it. It could have easily been the same for me.

"Sean, you don't want to do this. Trust me."

He laughed at me. "Oh that's rich. You get to shoot up the town, but I don't want to do this? Please. Just stay where you are."

I did just that, but Grace didn't. She took another step toward them. This wasn't going well.

"Lottie, did you send Sean to my house? Did you hire him to break into my place?" Grace asked. She'd been watching too many forensics shows. These were questions that could be asked when all the weapons were put away.

Even with a gun to her head, Lottie had the nerve to smile.

Sean tightened his grip on the teacher's throat. "Answer her! Tell her how you got me into this mess."

Mascara smudged Lottie's eyes. Her lips curved downward. "I tore up your place. Not him. That was going to be the last time."

My heart felt like it was going to beat right out of my chest. I tried to stay calm, to breathe. "The last time? You broke into Grace's place and then set this child up to take the fall for it?"

Lottie smirked. "He was dumb enough to do it."

"Aw, see . . ." Sean cocked the gun.

Grace took another crazy step. "Don't, Sean. This is about me. Let me help you. Let her go. Take me instead."

Lottie looked surprised. Sean loosened his grip a little while he considered it. I thought about Daddy and wondered if I'd ever play Scrabble with Ron again. Lottie was as big a head case as this child with the gun.

Grace had been stunned by Lottie's confessing to the break-ins, but she seemed intent on giving herself in place of her. "Lottie, God is going to take care of you later. What matters now is Sean and getting him out of the mess you—well, all of us—have gotten him into."

I wished now that Grace had accepted Sean into the dance group. He'd have been too tired for this foolishness. I sure was.

With a sigh, I put down my bag. I couldn't let Grace put herself in this situation again, not even for Sean. She'd been through enough.

So have you.

I held out my arms to him. "Come on, sweetheart. Let her go."

Sean loosened his grip on Lottie's throat. "I asked her to tell Miss O the truth, that I couldn't do it, that I never even went inside her place, but she wouldn't. I just wanted y'all to know I didn't do anything . . . I wouldn't have. I only went to your place that night to make sure she didn't do anything crazy to you, Miss O." He lowered the gun a bit, then lifted it again.

I started praying. This one was going to require more than I could muster.

Grace, however, seemed up to the task. "Going to my house wasn't a good idea, Sean, but you trusted Lottie. A teacher no less."

"Oh please. He came because he wanted to," Lottie said.

Sean raised his gun in response. I frowned. Did Lottie want Sean to kill us all? "Be quiet," I said, trying to keep calm.

Lottie frowned at us. "I ain't. You both think you're all that because everybody wants you. The princess and the preacher's daughter. You're going to get yours though after what you did to my brother—"

I stumbled back. "Your brother—?"

Lottie smirked as Grace's eyes widened.

It couldn't be.

"X. Malachi Gooden. The one you shot. He's my half-brother. We got the same daddy."

19

Brian

Even after an hour of helping kids after school, my back still tingled from Grace's fingers.

This waiting. It's driving me nuts.

But every time I prayed, the answer was the same. Wait. I'd have to hit the gym tonight for a serious workout.

I gathered my things, making a list in my head of what I had to do. First to the hospital to visit Joyce, then to the Christian bookstore to pick up a Bible I'd gotten inscribed for Sean, and finally the gym instead of working on Grace's case like I'd planned. She was right. I should leave that alone. I couldn't fix everything.

But you can fix something.

Maybe I could. Maybe if I could reunite Grace with her child, things would change for both of us. It was as close to finding my own mother as I'd probably get. My stomach clenched at the thought of my mother, the woman I'd hated, loved, and wondered about for so long. What kind of woman could give up her own child?

A woman like Grace.

Pastor Rodriguez's words from a recent sermon turned over in my mind.

"Have faith to believe beyond the past and hope to trust for tomorrow. But love in the present like there has never been a before and like tomorrow will never come. It's time to forgive and move on. It's time to love," he'd said.

I wasn't quite there yet, not with my mother. Maybe for Grace and her child it could be different. One of my locks snagged on the clasp of my briefcase. I pulled a crochet cap out of my pocket and tucked my hair into it. Ron called it my rasta hat. He was still around here somewhere, or at least I hoped he was. I'd rode in with him today.

After a cautious peek into the hall for any kids who might be waiting to prank me, I took one step outside the door. Just before I reached Ron's room, Jerry Terrigan slid into the hall, turning his already-worn dress shoes further over onto their sides and almost knocking me over. I was about to get mad when I saw the fear in his eyes.

"What is it?" I prayed it wasn't Joyce. Not yet. I wasn't ready. The whole school had been on pins and needles since the principal's announcement of her stage 4 cancer. Even I was praying for a miracle.

"Sean. Gun. Zeely and Grace," he said, his scarf dragging the ground as he ran for the gym.

I'd had it wrong. That wasn't grief in Jerry's eyes. It was terror. I dropped my briefcase and ran, screaming for Ron as I went. "Red, Sean's got your girl. Come on!"

Jerry looked back at me crazy. I hadn't meant to say that, but whatever. It wasn't like it was a lie.

Ron was behind me now. I could feel it though I didn't see him yet.

When we got to the stairwell, I hopped the rail and dropped like a rock. I landed on my bad leg, but nobody would have known it. Jerry was down the steps like a tap dancer with Ron close behind.

I tried to think through how this could have happened. At least there weren't any other kids in the building.

You pushed him too far.

I shrugged off the thought. Sean had pushed himself too far. All I'd ever done was help him. I was only concerned with one person now, and it wasn't Sean. I motioned for Jerry to get behind me as we neared the gym. For a big man, he moved quietly. I had to give him that.

"The janitor said Sean was down here with Lottie, Zeely, and Grace . . . and a gun. The police are on the way," Jerry whispered. "I thought he was doing better. He was upset when Grace wouldn't let him in the dance group though."

I held up one hand as we approached the next hall. Already, I could hear Grace's voice.

"Is that what this has been about, Lottie? The charges you filed against Brian, breaking into my house? You were helping Mal, your brother?"

There wasn't time, but I wanted to scream. Lottie was Mal's sister, that sweet girl who'd told me to run when the police were coming all those years ago? The girl who'd called Joyce to save me? It couldn't be.

She didn't sound innocent anymore. "Please, trick. This isn't about Mal. It's about me getting what I deserve. What I need. And I will get it—I'll get him," Lottie answered.

I tried to make sense of the conversation. What was Lottie doing here and who was the "him" she was talking about?

Surely not me.

Ron gave me a look that confirmed my worst fears.

The gunman himself spoke next as I tried to peek around the corner to check his position. "Look, both of y'all shut up, okay?"

I was with Sean on that one. Those women were doing too much talking for some folks with a gun on them. Like Joyce, they took these kids for something they weren't—afraid.

Anxious to make a move, Jerry stepped onto my heel. I winced and pushed him back a few inches just as Sean's elbow became visible. His arm trembled a little, moving lower all the time.

He's wearing down.

I held up three fingers. Jerry set his jaw. Ron gave a short nod. Sean's elbow sagged further, the gun at his side.

I put up one finger. Then two.

Grace spoke again. "It's simple. Just let Lottie go and take me—"

Then I forgot the fingers.

"Now!" I blasted around the corner ahead of Ron with Jerry charging in behind us. Grace backed into the wall, covering her face. I grabbed for Sean, but he jerked the gun away, pressing it against Lottie's temple.

A curse rose up inside me. Why hadn't I finished the count? How far away were the police? I was going to get us all killed. All I had left now was what I should have started with—words.

"Sean, put the gun down."

"Get back, Doc. You too, *Dad*," he said to me and Jerry in a bitter voice. Ron had told me that Sean and Jerry's daughter Monique were married now. Jerry didn't seem too happy about it.

Great. He hates us all.

Sean took the gun from Lottie's head and panned it toward us. His grip didn't waver.

Neither did my voice. "I know you don't want to do this, son. We can work it out—"

"Son? Yeah, that's funny. You always trying to fast-talk somebody. Step aside. All of you."

I locked eyes with Ron, whose gaze was evenly divided between Zeely and the stairs we'd come down. The three of us were the only things keeping Sean from the stairs.

Sean waved the gun to where he wanted us to go. "Move it. All of you."

"Take it easy." I stepped back one tile at a time.

Grace tried not to look at me. "Sean, I told you. Let Miss Wells go. Take me."

Zeely screamed. "No! Don't—" Why was she doing this? The police were near. I could hear them.

"Be quiet. Everybody be quiet," the boy said as he pushed Lottie away and took Grace in the same choke hold. Lottie dropped to the floor, gasping for breath.

Ron and Jerry tried to help Lottie up. I helped too, pulling her by the hand, but my eyes were on Sean, now easing toward the stairs with Grace. Zeely was calling after them too.

This couldn't be happening. I'd let somebody take Grace.

Again.

"Let her go, Sean!" I screamed.

In response, Lottie kicked me. Right between the legs. My knees buckled as I stared at her, wondering how she could have changed so much.

The sirens were here now, but it seemed too late.

Zeely lost it behind me. "Why'd you do that, Lottie? He's trying to save your behind too."

Lottie laughed. "He doesn't care about me."

She got up and pushed past me, going right for the kid with the gun. As we all watched in disbelief, she slapped Sean. Right in the face. He stared at her, stunned.

"Give it to me," she said, wrestling the gun away from Sean. To my horror, she turned it on Grace.

Like some kind of animal, I lunged toward them. Instead of the bullet I expected, I felt Jerry barrel into me and Grace.

"Move!" Jerry screamed as he crashed into my shoulder.

A pop hissed from the gun. Then another. We went down, Jerry and I together. I tried to catch him, but he fell into Ron's arms. Blood and gunpowder soured the air. I tugged off my sweater and pressed it against Jerry's wound. I heard the gun hit the ground, but I didn't dare reach for it. I had to hold on to Jerry. He had to hold on too. He just had to.

Zeely dropped to her knees beside us. "Jeremiah? Jeremiah!"

The police arrived, swarming the room. It was only then that I realized Sean and Grace and the gun were gone.

20

Grace

*I'm back at home. I have a picture of my baby but I
can't show it to anybody. They said it was best not to
hold her. They gave me her hat and my wristband too.
I put it all in the cedar chest Grandma gave me for
important things. I hope the baby is happy with her
new family. I'm not happy with my old one.*

Diana Dixon

I'm not sure why I thought about the notebook as Sean and I
fumbled down a back hall into the library. Easy, calm thoughts
would have been better, a beach scene or a greeting card poem, but
all I had were thoughts of Jerry bleeding on the floor downstairs,
my lost baby, and the crash of drums.

And the gun, of course. There was that.

Sean locked the door and took his hand from my neck. It hurt
to breathe. It hurt even more to think. A minute ago, I'd been the
heroine in this little exchange. Now I felt like the fool. Lottie was

Malachi's sister. She and her brother had both done their best to do me in. Why had I put myself in this situation to save her? I felt like slapping Sean and myself.

"I hope I didn't hurt you. Especially after all you've done for me," he said quietly as if reading my thoughts.

He'd hurt me, but not physically. I struggled to breathe, to speak. "Sean, why would you do this? Things were just starting to look up for you."

The boy rolled his eyes. "Things get better for me? Naw. I thought so, but he couldn't let that happen—"

"Who?"

He gave me a look as if I were the dumbest person on the planet. "Doc. Who else?"

My breathing slowed even more. I'd never forget the anger in Brian's face when the police found that gum wrapper in my place the night that Mal took me. Still, what did Brian have to do with it? And what did any of that matter now?

I reached out for Sean. He didn't move. We sat like that, looking at each other, for a long time. I could see in his eyes that we both shared one thing—loving Brian. And it was killing us both.

The phone rang on the desk behind us. Sean snatched up the receiver and held up a finger for me to be quiet. We'd both seen enough movies to know how things would go from here. Only this wasn't a movie. It was terribly real.

"I ain't coming out. You're just going to kill me anyway."

I heard footsteps in the hall. I tried not to think about Brian and whether or not he was among them. I prayed they'd gotten Jerry to the hospital.

If he died down there, because of me . . .

I'd never forgive myself. Zeely would never forgive me either. She might not forgive me if he lived. And rightly so. It was a foolish thing I'd done. I hadn't thought about how much worse this made things. Sean was right. He probably wouldn't make it out of this room alive. I could only pray that I would.

"No!" Sean slammed the phone down. He rubbed his head and paced through the library tables.

"What? What did they say? Sit down. Talk to me. Dr. Mayfield cares about you, you know. He knows how smart you are. Sometimes people are hard on the people they love."

He looked at me the way Zeely does sometimes, like I was the craziest person he'd ever seen. Maybe he was right. Here I was with my life in danger for the third time since I'd come here—and I was still talking about love.

"He ratted me out. He promised he wouldn't tell about his car, but he did. And then he added a bunch of lies too. He told them I broke into your place. That was Miss Wells. I came to make sure she ain't hurt you, but I didn't go in there. I promise you. When she didn't come out, I left. I told her—" His words choked off in his throat.

Have mercy.

"Sean, look at me. He said all that because they found something of yours at my house. If Miss Wells threatened me, you should have told someone. This wasn't for you to fix."

"I had to do something. You believed in my music and everything. Nobody ain't never believed in me like that. Miss Wells don't know you like I do. She say you just like her, but I know different. Even Justice knows it. She lights up whenever you're around."

Justice. Sean's little girl. He frowned at the mention of her name, as though he hadn't considered what this would mean for her. We both knew what it would mean—dead or alive, he wouldn't be seeing her for a very, very long time. The decision to pick up that gun had made so many other decisions, clicking like locks all at once, shutting away pieces of his already fractured life.

He shrugged as though there hadn't been another choice, as though the choice had been made for him. For the first time, I wondered for a moment if he wasn't right.

"Anyway, that's what happened. She even offered me some money to come. I just thought she was tripping. You never know with Miss Wells. She's so crazy. Always was."

The phone rang again. Sean covered his ears. He doubled over. "You get it this time. They want to talk to you."

I picked up the receiver, praying I wouldn't say something to the police to make things worse.

"Sean, you there?"

The voice on the line caught me off guard. "Brian?"

"They patched me in. They thought maybe he'd talk to me."

"Not likely."

"Are you okay?"

"I am. He's not. He's talking though. I think I can bring him out. Give me some time."

Another voice, mechanical and precise, spoke on the line. "Ma'am, let us bring him out. This is what we do."

Across the street, I saw something move through the window. A chill went through me. A sniper. They'd called in the big boys. This definitely wasn't a movie. And Sean wasn't the bad guy they thought he was. "Let me try. He won't hurt me. One hour," I whispered, barely separating my lips.

The man's tone was final, like someone reading an obituary. "Thirty minutes."

The first fifteen minutes went pretty well. Sean started to open up to me—with gun in hand, but still I kept him talking. Everything was going okay until something happened that I never could have expected in a million years: after he admitted that the mother

141

raising him was his foster mother, he pulled something out of his jean pocket and tossed it to the floor.

"My real mother? I don't know her. Never did. All I've ever had of her is that."

I started at the dirty mess of pink and yellow yarn on the floor. Another person might have asked what it was. I didn't have to ask. I knew: a badly crocheted baby bootie made with a J needle even though the pattern recommended an F. The yarn was pastel rainbow—or at least it had been once—because the nuns told me not to be so sure it'd be a girl.

I knew because I'd made it. Those same hands went around my neck now.

"It can't be," I said.

Maybe it wasn't. Maybe some other girl in some other maternity home with some other wrong crochet hook had made that. Somebody else. Not me. I'd had a girl with knowing eyes. Sparkling eyes like my daddy's . . .

I bent over at the waist then, unable to straighten myself. I lifted the dirty bootie and gave it to Sean. The soft, worn yarn tickled my hand. It hurt as though I'd been pricked by a thorn.

He took it. "Miss O? Are you okay?"

I shook my head. I couldn't even pretend.

"No, I am not okay. Who gave you that? Where did you get it from?" My voice sounded like someone else, someone who scared me almost as much as Sean. It was Diana's voice.

"My mother made it."

A crazy smile spread across my lips. It's-not-him-it's-not. It. Is. Not.

"My real mother."

This other me, this girl-woman, who'd come and gone a lot lately but never really spoken up, had more to say. "Tell me."

Sean licked his lips. He sniffed once and pulled out his wallet. He retrieved a pink page, worn and folded many times. He opened it on the table in front of us.

I dug my nails into the insides of my wrists, wishing that the librarian had left a knife behind. As I recognized the loops of my teenage script, I died a thousand deaths.

> *Dear sweet baby,*
> *I am so sorry that I can't keep you. You have happy*
> *eyes and I think we would be good friends. They say*
> *I have nothing to give you, that it would be selfish to*
> *keep you. I don't want to be selfish, even if you are*
> *so beautiful. I used to be a dancer. I think you'll be a*
> *singer. You screamed even louder than me when you*
> *came out. They say someday you'll understand why*
> *I couldn't keep you. I hope so. Maybe someday I'll*
> *understand myself. I'll love you forever.*

We recited the last lines together.

> *With love,*
> *Your mother*

My fearless gunman, my girl who was actually a boy, my baby who took my one blessing—"I think you'll be a singer"—and built a dream on it, smiled at me.

"It's you? It was you all the time?"

The room blurred as I reached for him. I had both hands on his cheeks now, Grace's hands and not Diana's. Satisfied finally, she'd taken her wings and flown from me one last time, leaving us alone.

"They never let me hold you. Said it would be too painful. They didn't even let me know you were a boy. I just thought—"

He was crying too. "Yeah. My worker said it was my eyelashes. Said they curled up like a girl. I ain't no girl though."

"I know," I said, pulling close this boy of mine. I put my forehead to his, staring into his face. My baby's face. "It was you all the time," I said, unable to find any words better than his. I knew now why I had always turned away from him: my father's eyes, golden brown and open wide, my mother's inky lashes and naturally arched brows. The last time I'd seen those eyes had been when I snuck out and visited the nursery. Those eyes that had looked so wise and certain, unblinking and unafraid.

Mama, I found our baby. And he's beautiful.

My hands traced the edge of his nose, the curve of his ears. I rubbed my fingers through the grooves between his braids.

"I was so sure that you were a girl. My mother said you had a man-head though. Wait until I tell her . . ."

He tugged away from me, leaving my hands dangling at his waist. I had squeezed that skinny boy half to death, held him like I'd wanted to back at that hospital.

"I'm so glad it was you. So glad that I don't have to die wondering." He closed his eyes, then opened them again. "Thank you, God."

Reality crashed into me. How many minutes had passed by? I ran to the window and put down the blinds, praying the shooter hadn't already locked on his position. "NO! Wait. We can work this out. Somehow . . ."

Sean shook his head. "Dr. Rogers saved me. Doc Mayfield tried to save me. And now you. But some folks just can't be saved. Like Doc says, everybody ain't gone make it. No matter how hard you try. Take care of Justice for me. Don't let her forget me. And tell Monique please don't be too mad at me. I just couldn't take it no more. And now, knowing it was you, finding out, I think it was the

144

right thing. Somebody finally told me something. I know something about who I am."

I wanted to grab him and throw his lanky body across my lap and sing him a lullaby like I had when he was inside me and he used to dance across my belly. Every part of me started to ache, all at once.

I squeezed his hand and leaned in toward him. "Hush, little baby, don't say a word. Mama's gonna buy you a mockingbird—"

"Thank you." Sean leaned into me and closed his eyes.

A buzzer rang that sounded like the school bell during the day. The library doors pushed open. Men in black body armor rushed into the room. The first was pointing yet another gun in my direction, specifically at Sean's head.

"Freeze!" the man shouted.

I lunged in front of Sean like Jerry had done for Brian. I put my hands in the air like I'd done the crime. I'd finally found my baby. They couldn't take him from me now. I could explain. They'd have to listen. "Don't shoot! I'm not hurt. Please. There's been a misunder—"

"Step away from the suspect, miss," the man in black said. I could see his gloved finger perched on the trigger.

"Wait!" I opened my arms, released Diana's wings in front of them, letting all my bottled tears and burned prayers fill the room. They couldn't take him. Not without taking me too.

"Step aside, lady!"

I shook my head, grabbing the desk in front of me. The gunman nodded toward the door. Uniforms swarmed on us like hornets, their fingers stinging, clawing me away from Sean.

"Please don't . . . he's my son! My baby . . ."

Their bodies swallowed my protests, pinning me to the desk. At my feet, two officers handcuffed Sean on the ground. He gave no resistance. I yanked away from the grips of the men and kneeled on the ground beside Sean's head.

"I'll try to get you out. And I'll visit you. I promise."

He looked away from me. "Tell Monique I'm sorry."

I nodded, my face flooded with tears. "I will."

"Tell Mr. T I didn't mean to hurt him. Tell Doc too." His voice echoed as the policemen pushed him through the crowd.

I ran behind them, wanting to jump on the backs of the men and force them to release my boy. To release me. Didn't they know how long I'd waited? How many Mother's Days I'd ignored? How many nights I'd dreamed of finding my child? Someone grabbed me, stopping me from chasing after them any further.

"Thank God." Brian leaned toward me, his hair covering me like some kind of veil.

I pummeled his chest with my fists. "They took him. They took my son!"

21

Zeely

They recognized me at the hospital, but had the courtesy not to act like it. Except for one nurse, young, with curly black hair.

"Back already?"

I paused, both appreciating and resenting the woman's courtesy. "No, I'm fine. I'm here with—there was a shooting at our school." I had no energy for long explanations.

The nurse sighed. "Oh yes. Carmel's husband. Three doors down."

Carmel's husband.

"Thanks."

The nurse managed another smile before trudging away. I didn't return it. I couldn't.

I arrived at the room with jumbled thoughts. I'd been sent to the hospital also, in a separate ambulance. My blood pressure had been high and my breathing erratic, but they'd finally cleared me so that I could come and check on Jerry. In that time, he'd gone from being my fiancé to who he really was, who he'd always be—Carmel's husband.

No matter how much time we spent together or how close we tried to be, they were always between us, Carmel and Ron, keeping our respect and admiration for each other from growing into the love that we both kept waiting on. Though I'd been by his side when he was shot and his blood had stained my clothes, it was Ron who they said I cried out for in my distress. It was Carmel who'd rushed to Jeremiah's aid when he got here. I considered just calling a cab and going home, but Jeremiah would not have done that to me. Lately, he'd been there for me so often . . .

He wasn't always there for you, Zee. I was.

Swallowing back a response to God invading my thoughts, I stepped over the threshold into Jeremiah's room. There was a curtain pulled around his bed. A nurse appeared from behind it and she wasn't wearing the smile of her colleague down the hall. She pulled the curtain shut behind her, almost forcing me out of the way. "Are you family?"

Not yet. It's complicated. "We, uh, work together—"

"Sorry. Family only." The nurse's pink scrubs looked too bright all of a sudden, especially when the curtain inched forward and I saw the three figures huddled around Jerry's bed—Carmel, Monique, and Justice. Jerry's real family.

"Let her in," Carmel said in a voice so quiet it seemed as though she were screaming. "He'd want her here."

I wasn't sure whether to duck under the curtain or run all the way to the school and jump in my pink Cadillac. I chose the former.

The nurse reached for my arm, her pressure firm but insistent. "Carm, you know I can't do that."

Carmel stood and pushed back the partition separating us. "Please."

The woman's resolve seemed to fade. "Just for a few minutes.

He's stable, but he needs rest. And quiet." She shot me a threatening look. "Understand?"

I nodded, watching the nurse until she was out of the room. Though she didn't seem to like me, as soon as she was gone, I longed for her to return. I approached the bed slowly, wishing I hadn't come. No matter how many rings I wore or how many church services Jeremiah and I attended together, the reality of Carmel's love for Jeremiah—and the flimsy arrangement of our endearment—had never been so apparent.

This was their place, their man. I did not belong.

And yet, Carmel showed compassion for me once more, lacing her fingers in mine. I'd envied Carmel for so long, even hated her at times, thinking her to be the harlot who had come between me and my beloved. Now in the eyes of Jeremiah's daughter and granddaughter, I could see how I appeared to them. It was all I could do to stay on my feet as Monique glared at me.

I'd used Jeremiah to secure a family for my own baby, the one I'd lost, the one I'd bought, an abandoned egg from a lab. In all of that, I'd never thought about these children, now staring back at me. They'd obviously been thinking about me.

Lord forgive me. Forgive us.

I released Carmel's hand. This was too much and we all knew it. It was Monique, the result of all our confused love, the baby Jerry had kept while I'd thrown mine away, the baby who now had a baby of her own, the baby who was angry, who broke me down. For the first time, she forced me to really see her. To hear her.

"Did you have to come? Can't we have anything?" The girl's hair plastered to her face, wet from crying.

"Hush, Monique." Carmel brushed Jeremiah's cheek, swollen to twice its normal size from the tubes up his nose. "She had to come. The same as we did. She loves him too."

I stepped back, eyeing the ring on my finger, the elephant in the room. Did I love him? Or was Jeremiah only a symbol of love? All my life, my mother had dangled him in front of me, the victory, an acceptable union, what was best for everyone.

Everyone but me.

Was what I felt when that bullet had hit Jeremiah a match for Carmel's pain? Or the pain of Monique, who not only had to deal with her father being shot but knowing that her own husband had been a part of it?

Invading my questions were thoughts of another man, a redhead with a noisy truck and an empty stomach . . . I'd made so many mistakes, things it seemed I could never undo now. I popped my knuckles. "How—how is he? What did the doctor say?"

Carmel shook her head. Her eyes were full of undeniable love. "He'll be fine but it'll take time. It's not the physical healing that worries me. It's the rest of it. I can't believe Sean did this . . ."

Monique shoved the baby high on her hip. "He didn't do it. Dr. Mayfield said so. The police said so. Miss Wells—"

"If he didn't have the gun, it wouldn't have happened." Carmel sighed, lifting Jerry's hand. "It doesn't matter, at least Daddy will be okay. Thank God for that."

Daddy.

I took another step back.

Jerry stirred in the bed. He cleared his throat, but his eyes remained shut. "Carm, that you?"

"Yes, OJ, I'm here. We're all here." Despite her words, she must have forgotten about my presence. She stroked his face. Kissed his hand. The three of them crowded toward the head of the bed while I stood in the shadows at the foot of the bed. I was done when Carmel called him OJ. Omega Jeremiah Terrigan. I'd never called him Omega. My mother said to focus on Jeremiah, the prophetic part

150

of him, not Omega, the ending. Carmel, however, had somehow learned how to appreciate him from beginning to end.

I'm here too, Jeremiah. I'm here too.

Jeremiah smiled a blind, broken smile, still unaware that I was in the room. I wished I'd worn my usual pint of cologne.

"Scared you, didn't I?" Jerry whispered, reaching for Carmel's hand.

She collapsed over the side of the bed and onto the wires attached to him. "Scared me to death."

Jerry tried to laugh, but choked instead. "Scared me too. I'm so sorry. For everything . . ." He took a deep breath.

"Don't talk, rest—"

"No, I need to say it. I don't ever want to be without you, Carmel. Without the girls. When I thought it was over, you were all I could think of . . ." He fell silent as if he'd never spoken. Monique clutched her mother's shoulder.

That was my cue to go, to run to the Caddy and speed through the snow until I got to Ron's place, to run in and refuse to leave until he forgave me, to let him know that if I got hurt, I'd say words to him like Jerry had just said to Carmel. I tried to go, but I'd left all I had back at that school, in the gym, on the steps, on the bloody floor . . .

This must be what dying feels like.

Strength returned to me. Courage inched up my arms as my feet started for the door. I turned back to the bed, my eyes skipping from Jeremiah's bandaged chest to the women he loved, huddled by his side. Stepping quietly so Jerry wouldn't hear, I slipped the ring from my finger and pulled Carmel's arm. She didn't turn away from Jerry, but extended her arm. I pressed the ring into her palm and closed her fingers.

Then I ran.

151

Carmel came after me, her voice breaking from the emotion. She looked ashamed as she stepped into the hall, embarrassed that in the wake of her husband's love, both she and Jeremiah had forgotten about me.

"Wait! He's in shock. He didn't mean those things. He loves you, he's just out of it. It's your ring. Keep it. Please."

I shook my head, wiping away my own tears. I could finally see why Jeremiah had chosen her. It was more than the short skirts and desperation Carmel had worn when we were in college. Despite my church songs and modest hemlines, Carmel was the better woman. She was woman enough to love hard, even if it meant she was left with nothing. Now she would have everything, starting with the ring that should have been hers all along.

"The ring is yours. And so is he. Always was." I turned and walked down the hall, into my future.

22

Grace

The students looked wounded too. I rubbed the scratch on my shoulder from the tiles in the library. This time I agreed with everyone about needing more time to heal. This time I wished I could have waited before returning to work—another week perhaps, to let my mind and body repair. But I couldn't. The state proficiency test wouldn't wait for me to heal. These kids wouldn't wait either.

This was what Joyce had asked me to come here for, this was why I'd been assigned to teach with Brian in the first place—because the success of Imani Academy, the success of these kids I'd come to love, was in question. Joyce had known even then that the cancer would keep her from making it through the semester. What she couldn't have known is how coming back to help her would tear us all apart.

Or maybe she had known. Maybe this was the only way it could have gone down.

If you've ever loved me, please come.

That beautiful old woman who never really looked old knew how to get what she wanted. Maybe one day, some way, I'd learn how to get what I wanted, what I needed. For starters, I needed my son and for more than the short visits we shared as often as they allowed it. Since there was no changing that, I needed for these kids to pass this test.

My heart broke as I looked over the hurting faces, weary of the violence and loss that had torn through our school. Some of the students had never recovered from Joyce's announcement that she was dying, let alone all the rest of it. I couldn't blame them for that, I'd taken Joyce's illness hard. I still was. I hadn't visited her as much lately as I should have, mostly because I didn't want to upset her.

Still, it was hard standing here hoping they'd remember algebraic inequalities, looking away from the real inequalities, the empty chairs of our best math students, Monique and Sean McKnight.

Then there was the empty seat beside me. Jerry would have been in rare form today, reminding the students of how hard they'd worked to get here. Sean would have been something to see too, preparing for what we'd all predicted would have been the highest math score in the school's history. I tried not to think about where he'd gotten his talent for math. While I'd done a decent job of teaching math since being reassigned from language arts—math was my minor, after all—making things add up had never been my strong suit. Malachi had been a physics major in undergrad.

"Come on, guys. I know this has been a rough time. Trust me, I know. But we can't let this stop us. Let's review before the test tomorrow. Please? If you can't do if for yourself, do it for Mr. Terrigan."

One boy, a close friend of Sean's, jumped to his feet. "Study for what? So we can be smart in jail? They might as well come and lock us up now."

I felt like screaming with him, at him, but I pressed my lips together instead. He was a kid. He had no idea how much I'd lost.

None of them knew and they couldn't know, not ever. In this room, I was a teacher. In this room, there was no place for me to bleed. There'd been blood enough.

"Sean is in jail and Mr. Terrigan is in the hospital. It's true. And they're in those places because of a choice. A poor choice. All of you have a choice too. Life or death. I know I'm not supposed to talk about God, but this proficiency test is the beginning of many choices He'll offer you: life or death, succeed or fail. It's multiple choice. I'm here, scars and all. And I'm going to do my job. I can only hope that you'll do yours."

I turned quickly so that they wouldn't see me cry. So that I wouldn't crouch under the desk like I wanted to. I turned and wrote two problems on the board, both from other parts of the test than what we'd been studying all day. With trembling fingers, I pointed to the first one. "Can anyone solve this?"

The students stared at me, through me, as though they were waiting for me to crack so they could too.

Lord, please. Help me. I can't lose them too.

"You subtract the exponents and combine like terms," an unfamiliar voice answered in stilted English.

I dropped the chalk, as if I'd seen—no heard—a ghost. The voice was male and the accent Nigerian. After so many years of trying to translate the conversations of my late husband's friends, I could even make out the tribe. Ibo. Peter's tribe. The stranger walked in and wrote his name on the board.

Ifyangi Umagekwe.

He turned to the class. "This is my name, but I do not expect you to say it. You may call me Mr. I. U. I know your principal Dr. Rogers quite well. Months ago, she asked that I help prepare you for the proficiency test. I'm a little late, but here I am. Mr. Terrigan is out, yes?"

155

"Yes. You're right on time." I moved to the table at the side of the room, thinking about how hard Joyce had planned for this, for everything. She always had a backup. I never did. I couldn't have been happier to see Mr. I. U. He seemed familiar and capable, someone neutral to keep the students' minds off all that had happened.

The new substitute paced between the rows handing out packets of papers. "This is a practice test. You have fifty minutes to complete it. No talking. No questions."

I went to my desk and grabbed the pencils for the practice test I'd planned to give later in the day. Now seemed like a perfect time. I grabbed a stack of scratch paper too and headed down the next row behind the new teacher. I met Mr. I. U. back at the front desk. At first, he said nothing, choosing to watch instead as pages turned in front of us, to listen as pencils pressed hard against the future. Maybe the disaster I'd so feared, letting Joyce down, had been averted. If so, I'd likely have this man to thank for it.

I extended my hand. "Thank you so much for coming. They were really down today. I was worried."

"It is no problem." Though he answered me calmly, the teacher's dark eyes flitted up and down the rows, daring disobedience, while his voice stayed pleasant. "Everything will be fine. The Lord is never late, eh?"

I didn't trust myself to answer. Lately, God had been making some very ill-timed entrances into my life, but who was I to complain? Though so much had been lost, so much taken, still so much remained. I nodded, staring at the man's cheeks, round and brown as my husband's had been.

He took out a pen from his pocket. "What is your name, miss?" he said, in between his visual security details.

"Grace. Grace Okoye." The words bounced back over the months, reminding me of another day, another introduction on the first day I'd met Brian. Sean had been mixed up with a gun and all the wrong people that night too.

At my answer, the man dropped his pen, but dared the students to stop working when they looked up from their tests. Instead, he lowered his own voice to a whisper. "Okoye? Is it true? From Cincinnati?"

When I nodded, he lifted his hands. "Praise be to God."

A few students looked up, irritated by the man's volume, but Mr. I. U. summoned a stiff face and pointed to the booklets in front of them and spoke again, resuming his whisper. "I am sorry that I could not attend Brother Peter's funeral. I was still in Nigeria myself. In fact, I was scheduled to be on the same flight as he, but I was detained by illness." His eyes were moist.

Brother? What did he mean? I'd known most of Peter's friends. Or at least I'd thought I had. Who was this man? "Were you related to Peter?"

Mr. I. U., who now insisted I call him Ifyangi, gathered my hands in his. "Relatives? Peter and I? Far from it. In fact, in Nigeria we were not close. We were united in Christ alone. He was one of my best deacons."

I snatched my hands from his grasp. Peter, a deacon? Christ? What a cruel thing to say. Somehow I managed to take a seat at the desk. I shoved myself back in the seat until my dress pressed through the slats, pushing to make room for more, only there was no more room. Not even for me.

"I'm sorry," I said in my best you-will-not-hurt-me voice. "You must be confused. My husband was not a Christian. In fact, he never set foot in a church all the years I knew him."

Mr. I. U.'s expression clouded. His voice rose again. Too loud. "Peter knew Christ. He said it was you who convinced him. I begged him to bring you with him to our services, but he said you had your own commitments. He spoke as if you knew."

Once again, an audience of students drank in my mistake of a life. I'd chided them to focus and now I was providing another distraction. I wanted to stop the conversation, to ask if we could discuss it later, but it was too late. I was hungry to know, to understand what this stranger was telling me. It seemed too good, too crazy, to be true.

Doesn't everything?

As the man went on, I ripped through the drawers of my sub-conscious, probing every corner of my memory. I sucked in my stomach, trying to restrain the grief rising from my belly. There was no place for it. No more room. "He was always home when I got home from church. I would have known . . ."

"Our church met on Sunday evenings."

"He had soccer—"

Mr. I. U. laughed. "We met at the soccer field. After a short game, of course. We have since found a building." He sobered, leaning toward me. "I prayed with him to receive Christ myself."

A girl in the third row murmured to the person behind her, then scribbled an answer on her paper. With the agility of a much younger man, Mr. I. U. moved through the desks and ripped the note from her hands.

"Life is 90 percent discipline and 10 percent intellect. Do not let anything in this room distract you, myself included. You have forty more minutes."

When he returned to the desk, I transported to another place, another time, sifting through things that hadn't made sense at the time: the Bible Peter had bought me for Christmas, the way he'd stopped changing the Christian radio station in the car . . . My head fell forward as I tried to squelch the joy rising in me, the laughter trying to escape my lips.

"I'm finished." A student's voice broke my madness.

I looked up at him, and smiled, almost giggling as I went to take his paper. In the midst of all this pain, God had held something sweet for me, something beautiful. Something I'd thought I needed when Peter died but God had known would only do in this moment.

The boy began to chuckle too when I took his paper. Soon the laughter spread to everyone, even the stern substitute. I laughed until I cried, and then I stepped in the hall and ran to the faculty lounge. There alone, my tears became a scream, a scream stuck in my throat since the day Peter died, since the night Mal almost killed me in the snow, a scream of relief at knowing that even though my life had come undone, God was still tending to the stitching.

I was just seeing the underside.

23

Zeely

There are times when you need your girlfriends. There are times when you run from them too. When I found myself with a new haircut, standing on Grace's porch, I was tired of running.

For the last month or so, I'd worn nothing but my best wigs and imported hair. Not that I'd had much of a choice, with Jeremiah showing up all times of the night, pushing his fingers under my scarf. Little things like that—how much it bothered me when he tried to touch my hair—should have let me know that I didn't mean it, that I didn't really love him, but I hadn't wanted to see it. I hadn't wanted to admit that sometimes nothing is better than something, especially if the something isn't really yours.

I hadn't wanted to see any of it, but Grace had seen it. She'd seen it and hadn't rubbed it in my face. She'd seen it and whispered love to me when she should have been hating. She'd seen it and taken me where I'd belonged the whole time—back to Jesus.

And now, it was time for me to do the same thing for her. At the very least, I'd come to sit and listen, to twist her hair with honey

160

and coconut oil or whatever wacky mess she had in her bathroom jars. I was here to just be and to let her do the same.

I knocked again. It felt strange not to push my way in, giving a critique of things like usual. Today wasn't about that, I thought, raking a hand through my own cropped curls. Nothing like a new style to help me forget the real adjustment, the switch back to my former status—alone.

When Grace didn't respond to my knocking, I pressed the bell, wondering how long we were going to play this game. Since my friend had gone back to refusing to answer the phone, I'd had to make a house call. The curtains revealed darkness inside, but the car in the driveway told a different story. She was here. She just didn't want me to be here with her. And considering my sometimes not-so-nice behavior, I couldn't blame her. Peeking through the window, I caught a glimpse of light. A flame. I squinted and made out a leaping flame in one of the candle sconces I'd mounted on Grace's wall.

She's going to burn the house down.

I loved candles too, but I also knew how raggedy these condos could be. I'd never leave a candle unattended in mine. But then, Grace would never try to marry someone she didn't love. We had different priorities that way. I toggled the bell again, and when Grace didn't answer, I acted on instinct and turned the knob. It turned.

Okay, so the candle is the least of our worries.

I stepped inside, eyes straining to adjust to the dimness. A few blinks later, I bumped into the kitchen counter, then the microwave, which almost made me pee on myself when it dinged in my ear.

"Zee, will you bring me that plate?" Grace's voice came from somewhere in the back of the house.

I snorted, angry that she'd been so sure it was me and shocked that she was using the evil, cancer-causing microwave that she usually used for a clock. I was the one who nuked my food. This was too weird. "I'll get it, but I'm not happy about that door being unlocked and how calm you sound about it. You're a trip. I could have been anybody."

"I knew it was you."

"Hmph." I punched a button on the microwave. A Styrofoam carton from the local barbecue restaurant spun to a stop. I took a good long sniff and reached in the drawer for two forks instead of one. The smell told me what was inside: a date plate from the Rib Hut—a slab of ribs, spicy greens, and macaroni and cheese, the real kind, eggs and all. The kind of food Ron called me for in the middle of the night for weeks after eating at my table. The kind of food that Grace would never eat under normal circumstances, not in a million years. But the past few months had been anything but normal. And a pot of good greens had been known to cure many an ill.

"Grace?" I flipped on the light in the bedroom where Grace usually slept. No one.

"I'm in here."

The bathroom? Now that was just nasty. I gripped the Styrofoam container, praying for ears to listen. I turned the knob and almost dropped the food. Surrounded by candles, Grace sat knees-to-chest like a beige mermaid. She reached for the plate as if this were everyday stuff. Maybe it should be.

I perched the container on the edge of the tub, suddenly not so sure about the need for my fork. "You could've answered the phone." I moved to the toilet, thankful for the padded cover and the knowledge that I'd been the last one to clean it.

Grace gulped down a forkful of macaroni. "I didn't feel like talking. I still don't. But since you're here, answer this for me. Did you ever think that Peter was a Christian?"

"He did seem different at the end. He even remembered my name. How—"

"His pastor is subbing for Jerry."

Who knew? "Well, that's good, isn't it? At least you know where he is. Maybe he listened to you after all."

"He listened. Poor thing. I preached at him all those years. If only I'd loved him as much as I'd preached to him."

Though I was uncomfortable, I was glad I'd come. The proficiency test had taken a lot out of us, and this weekend was the first time any of us had to think straight in far too long. As usual, Grace had a lot to think about. Me? I was still stuck on the same things: he loves me, he loves me not . . . "You did love Peter. You loved him the best you could."

"Maybe." Grace grabbed a tall plastic cup from the corner of the tub and splashed it down her back.

Without meaning to, I grabbed the food and slammed it shut. I just couldn't take it. "Can I take this out of here? I'm sorry but you're driving me nuts. You know how I am about food and bathrooms. They just don't mix."

Grace grabbed a rib before I ran back to the kitchen with the warm food.

When I got back, she was still holding the rib, so I took that too. When I took a bite of it, I knew we were both in a bad way. I could only hope I hadn't caught some disease.

It made Grace laugh so it was worth the risk. Something else, something sad swallowed her laughter. "I saw Sean again."

I tried not to frown, but I wasn't successful. It was bad enough that Grace had insisted on going to the jail instead of the hospital after the shooting. True enough, Lottie had actually fired the gun, but Sean had been wrong with the whole thing. Real wrong. But I'd vowed to try to listen and not judge, and so far I was batting zero. I had to try harder. "How'd it go?"

"Better than I thought it would."

"I still can't believe you went to see Sean after what he did . . ."

Grace looked at my now clean rib like she was finally ready to tear into it, only it was too late. "It's complicated."

I thought back to my visit with Jerry at the hospital. Talk about complicated. "Jeremiah came around for a minute. At the hospital, I mean."

"What'd he say, call the chaplain and let's get married now?" Grace rinsed her hands under the faucet.

"Not exactly." I folded my arms. "He said he wanted Carmel and the girls and that he never wanted to be without them again. When his life flashed before him, it was them he saw. Not me."

Grace blew out a few candles and got out of the tub. She dried off and wrapped in a robe I didn't recognize. On the lapel, I made out a small monogram. *BM*—Brian Mayfield. How had she gotten hold of that?

Don't judge. Just listen.

She must have seen me looking at it, because Grace shrugged and explained that Brian brought it to her at the hospital after Malachi attacked her. "I wouldn't see him, but he kept bringing me things. I keep saying I'm going to return it, but it's very comfortable."

I laughed as she tightened the belt and headed for the kitchen. "I see that."

The date plate had probably come from Brian too. Though the menu was regular fare for me and Ron, for crunchy granola folks like Grace and Brian, it was a once in while thing. The vinegar from the greens drew saliva into my throat. "Can I have some?"

"Have the rest." Grace said, lifting the container and handing it to me. "Get yourself a fork."

I pulled out the one I'd stashed in my pocket. "I got one for me too, just in case."

Grace shook her head and flipped on the lights. She stood behind my bar stool for a moment and then kneaded my shoulders like only Joyce could have. She smelled of shea butter and sandalwood. It was a comforting scent, though nothing I'd ever wear. Her words were comforting too, even if they weren't true.

"Jerry's had a lot going on, Zeely. I'm just now realizing how much. Did you know that Monique and Sean were—married? And the little girl, the smallest daughter, Justice, she's actually their baby? No wonder he didn't balk at taking that bullet. He's been through it."

I reached over and flipped off the light so she wouldn't see me cry. "I knew. You're right. Jerry has been through it. And he went through it with Carmel. Not me." I took another bite of macaroni before putting my head down on the counter. Grace sat down and held my hand. It started to rain. We sat there in the dark kitchen, listening to our lives and our lies run down the window.

After what seemed like forever, Grace got up and put water on for tea. She handed me her favorite mug, the one with the sunflowers.

"She let me in, you know." I pressed my thumb into the center of the china flower.

"Who?" Grace asked.

"Carmel. Visiting was for family only, but she got me in."

Carmel's name was just flowing off my tongue now, but I couldn't remember the last time I'd actually used her name. She was always mentioned in clipped tones and pronoun phrases like "She came to the school" or "She called his cell." But during my past two trips to the hospital, once for myself and the other for Jeremiah, Carmel had become human to me again. A woman. One of us. Just by using her name, I'd invited her into the safe place between Grace and I.

My friend grabbed my hand as though she felt it too. I went on, telling her the rest of it.

"When I saw them together, I knew that that's how it should be. She kept insisting that Jeremiah loved me . . ."

"I think he did. That he does." Grace paused. "In his way."

She didn't have to try to sugarcoat it for me anymore. I could take the truth. I had to, even if it meant I'd be alone. When I got out of my hospital room, Ron hadn't been waiting this time. Since the day I'd met him, he'd always been waiting. And now I'd lost him too.

"It isn't me that Jeremiah is in love with, but the idea of fulfilling a destiny. Come to find out, even that part of it isn't true. When Jeremiah went to Daddy for his blessing, my father wouldn't even give it. He asked Jeremiah who told him that he was supposed to marry me. Now that I think about it, Daddy never did say it. It was always my mother. And Jeremiah's. The ramblings of old women. Nothing more."

Grace let go of my hand, like she was thinking something through. "Are you sure?"

"I'm sure. The question is, are you sure?"

"About what?"

"About telling me whatever drove you to eating ribs in the bathtub, whatever you've been itching to tell me since I got here."

"Girl, I'm fine. Or at least I will be. That stuff about Peter shook me up—"

"Hmph. That stuff about Peter helped you out if you ask me. It's this mess with Mal and now Sean's foolishness that's got you on the edge."

Grace gave me a wild-eyed look at the mention of Sean's name. She crossed her legs, started shaking her foot.

I took a deep breath. This was bad. Really bad.

"Did you sleep with him? Brian, I mean."

She was crying now. Crying too hard to speak. She shook her head. This was really bad. I slipped off my chair and stood behind her, kneading her shoulders as she'd done mine.

Grace reached up and covered my hands with her own, sobbing so hard that I could barely make out her words.

"Sean-is-my-son."

I closed my eyes and squeezed Grace's shoulders. She would probably have a bruise, but she didn't cry out. I should have been holding a chair. A table. Something that couldn't break off in my hands. Only when she let out a little breath did I realize that it was her body my fingers were digging into.

Tears raged down my face. "Sean is your baby?"

She nodded and turned to me. We hugged like two lost children. I was so happy and so sad at the same time. She'd found him, but she'd found him too late.

"I thought it was a girl!" I said.

"Me too."

"I was so mean to him sometimes. I didn't know he was yours. It shouldn't have mattered though. He was someone's child. I should have—"

Grace wiped my face. "You were afraid of him. I was too. I was mean to him too, Zee. We're just going to start over. At least he's still alive."

Yes, at least you have that.

This was a great time for my own telling. I searched for the words, but found nothing true enough to say. It wasn't my moment, it was too big to try to fill.

Grace sank down onto the carpet and curled up at my feet. It was too much, all of it. I could see that now. I could feel it.

"Just leave me, girl. I'll be okay. Just go," she said from somewhere under her robe.

167

I leaned down and pulled her up instead. Once she was in my arms, I started to sing.

"A-aa-ma-zing Gra-ace. How sweet the sound . . . tha-at saved a wretch like me . . ." My voice, powered by both sorrow and joy, bolted from me bigger than ever. I felt ten feet tall, riding a chariot.

Grace blinked back her tears . . . and started to dance.

"I-I once was lost . . ."

Dancing too, I stretched my leg overhead, pausing for full extension as we entered the throne room. The holy place.

She sang with me. "But now am found. Was bli-ind bu-ut now . . . I see."

Our voices poured over the room as we flew between the furniture, wings extended, as Joyce would say. I could almost feel roots pulling up, bitter roots that had buried themselves in our souls.

"When we've been there ten thousand years, bright shining as the-e sun . . ."

The abortion clinic. The pain. I twirled in the air. *Ron's words. The miscarriage. The bullets* . . . I spun again and again, my arms lacing upwards.

Grace moved past me, arms outstretched, her hurts dangling from each of her fingers. *The rape, the maternity home, the labor, the loss. Signing the papers.* She bowed at the waist, reaching . . . *Brian's love.* Her fingertips brushed the floor.

"We've no less days to sing Go-od's praise, than when . . ."

Ron. I leapt again, my legs scissoring this time. My arms swept out, then dropped to my sides. *Jeremiah.* I shuffled backward the length of the futon, drawing in—pulling a rope too heavy to hold. I had to let him go too.

"We'd first begun." Grace finished the song as I landed in one final arabesque, the last amen to our prayer.

Grace clapped slowly. "That was magnificent. I haven't heard you sing in too long. I forget sometimes how good you are. Amazing, just like the song."

I lifted my head. "Thanks. I can say the same of your dancing. You need to cut loose like that in class sometime. That was strong. Real strong."

Strong enough for a breakthrough.

"Hush, girl. It wasn't all that."

It was more.

I followed Grace back to the kitchen. She poured both of us another cup of tea and complimented my hair. That meant a lot coming from her. We were pretty opposite in our ideals of beauty, but we were rubbing off on each other. Grace was wearing pink toe polish pretty close to my shade.

"This looks so good on you. For real. Did you do it today?"

"I did. I went straight to the shop from the hospital. I like it too. I've been pretending so long I forgot who I was."

"You? Pretending? You're one of the realest people I know."

I arched my back into a stretch. "Grace, if I'm the realest person you know, I feel sorry for you."

"You know what I mean. You're comfortable with yourself."

"Nope. I thought by behaving like a wife, I'd become one. Creating my own destiny, walking in the promise and all that jazz . . ."

Grace nodded. "I guess there's nothing wrong with believing."

"There isn't anything wrong with believing God. The problems begin when you start believing you." I took a sip of my tea. I'd tried something different this go around, peach blossom with a hint of vanilla and bergamot, loose, using the tea ball. Incredible. I'd even used some of Grace's honey. She seemed excited about that but tried not to let it show.

"It's local. Wildflower. Good for the immune system."

I brought the tea to my lips. "I don't know about all that, but it's good."

We laughed carefully, like patients afraid of popping their stitches.

"So what's going on with Ron? Now that you're sure things are over with Jeremiah, you two can be together, right?"

If only it were that simple. "Well, think about it. How would you feel if a guy showed up and said, 'That other chick dumped me, so now I can be with you!'"

"Oh, that would be messed up."

"Exactly."

Grace sighed. "So it looks like we're both in the same place again—single with no prospects."

I had to smile at the way that sounded. "That sounds like a weather prediction—black woman with a chance of depression."

Grace almost spit tea on the counter she laughed so hard. She turned to reach for a napkin, but stopped to look at the purple-black sedan creeping up the street. It was Brian again, doing one of his check-ins that usually happened when Grace stopped answering the phone.

I reached for my keys. "You've got more than a prospect, girl. You just don't know what to do with him."

24

Brian

I'd tried to stay away from Grace's, but concern won out over courtesy. She might send me away, but I had to be sure that she was okay. I'd had a meltdown of my own when I had found out that Sean was her son. She seemed to be taking it well. A little too well.

I pulled into the drive slowly. Her car was covered in snow, still white and fresh, unlike the snow up and down her street, grimy with exhaust, black with shoeprints. Grace could be amazing that way, untouched in the middle of so much mess. And then other times, like now, when she unplugged the phone and pushed me away, she was someone else, someone taking all the bad things upon herself.

Her yard looked like a white blanket with a cement border. I could see where a small set of footprints had tracked through the neighbor's yard and up to the front door. That meant Zeely was here too. I thought about leaving since Grace wasn't alone, but the thought left as quickly as it had come. It took a lot for me to love somebody, but once I did, I loved hard.

I stepped onto the porch and raised a fist to knock. If she didn't answer, I wouldn't stay. I had some things in the car and I would leave them. I didn't want to though. I wanted to see her. Before my knuckles struck wood, the door opened and Zeely squeezed past me with only one arm in her coat and the other hanging to the side.

"See you guys later," she said, wearing a sheepish grin that wasn't at all called for. I didn't know what she thought had been going down between Grace and me, but she was wrong about it. All wrong. For now, anyway.

"Later," I said softly, wondering if Grace had told her about Sean. If not, I certainly wouldn't be the one to tell her. I hadn't even told Ron. It didn't seem right. Grace would tell people when she was ready.

Zeely punched my shoulder as she passed. "Be good now. Don't y'all be out here rolling around in the snow or anything. The angels are watching."

I lowered my head and laughed a little bit. It was all I could do. It seemed like a lifetime ago that Zeely had come upon Grace and I right here on this porch, or maybe rolling off of it. It had been our first kiss and, since then, our last. But like Zeely, I'd never forget it.

"Hey, you," Grace said, as she appeared in the door . . . in my robe. She didn't look like she usually did when she unplugged the phone: hurt, vulnerable, angry. There was peace in her eyes and something else too, something grown and sexy that made me wonder if Zeely shouldn't stick around. We'd been shot up and beat down, true enough, but God help me, I still wanted what I'd wanted the first time I saw Grace—all of her.

Down, boy. Don't go there.

Yeah, it was like that now. I had a lot of respect for Quinn, being able to stay a virgin. Being a Christian man, especially when you've fallen in love with a fine—though emotionally unavailable—woman,

172

was more difficult than I remembered. I'd had a wife when I was going to church before, and I could see now how that made things simpler. Maybe difficult was better. It kept me on my knees. As much I wanted to get close to Grace, I wanted to get close to God more. Even if that meant that Grace and I were still holding hands a year from now.

Don't do me like that though, Lord. Please don't.

I guess I must have zoned out for a second, because Grace reached out and pulled me inside. "Are you remembering our tumble in the snow too? If you are, it's not happening again. That mess was cold. Get in here." Her voice seemed to sparkle.

I was more than happy to accept her invitation. As she took my coat, it was all I could do to keep from reaching for her. The house smelled of peaches and tea—the loose kind. Even from here, I could smell the honey in Grace's hair. Instead of burying my hands into her curls and kissing her mercilessly like I wanted to, I laughed a little myself, remembering how fragile new love—and new faith—could be.

"You're in a better mood than I expected. At my expense, perhaps? I see Zeely's got jokes now. Is that contagious?" I smiled at the thought of it.

Some of the humor drained from her voice. "We were just kidding around. It wasn't really about you."

I rubbed my beard. So much for that. "I won't stay long. I just wanted to see how you were doing."

Grace led me into the kitchen and poured me some tea. Orange pekoe. I knew no one else but Joyce and myself who kept it on hand. I'd only mentioned it being my favorite once. That Grace had remembered made me hopeful. These days I clung to most anything.

She left the room and returned in a tank top and shorts that looked as good as my tea tasted. I couldn't touch, but it was nice to see what she'd been hiding under all those coats and sweaters for the past few weeks.

As she sat down next to me, I tried to ignore the ripple of her new muscles and the return of her old ones. Her back was getting cut again, especially in the shoulders. I downed the tea though it was hotter than was safe, and then slammed a fist to my lips. This wasn't what I'd come for. I didn't know what to do with this Grace, strutting around in tank tops and shorts, sitting close to me in her kitchen drinking tea.

The Grace I knew would have met me on the porch with a Bible, in the snow, mind you. It had taken a promise of Zeely's presence to even get her to my house for dinner the first time. The woman I loved would have been dressed and ready for church tonight, where I'd been on my way to before coming by here. It was a Friday night service hosted by the couples' ministry. I wasn't part of a couple, not really, but I wanted to be. These days I went to everything at the church anyway, even the children's Christmas play practices. I got something out of that too.

When Grace leaned over and kissed the small of my neck with that fruity smelling lip gloss that I remembered from our porch encounter, I knew that something had to give and somebody had to go. Though she looked all right, this was some other stage of grief and pain, one I had a lot of experience with—the comfort stage. While it apparently took the form of candles and tea for Grace, for me it had been liquor and ladies, not a good combination. I knew that I could kiss her now and she'd yield to me, but I didn't want it like that, not for either of us.

She'd prayed so hard for me, stood so firm. She was up now, standing in front of me, coming in to kiss me, on the lips instead of the cheek as she'd done ever since the hospital when I said I loved her. And I did love her. I loved her enough to see that whatever she needed tonight, I wasn't the one to give it to her.

"Love me," she said in a whisper that echoed through me like thunder.

It would have been so easy. So good . . . but so wrong too. Though her words asked that I love her, Grace's eyes said something else—*help me.*

I can do all things through Christ Jesus.

I smiled. It wasn't me she needed, but Christ. I was about to love and help us both. "I do love you, don't you know that? Now get dressed. Get your shoes on."

Grace laughed at me and shook her head. "Get dressed for what? I'm not going anywhere. It's freezing out there."

And it was burning up in here.

I grabbed Grace's hand and took her to the stairs leading to her bedroom, stairs that I often climbed in my dreams. But in reality it wasn't time for that. I checked my watch. 6:51. We could still make it if she threw on some jeans. Her beauty was simple, one of the things I loved about her. "You are going somewhere. Come on, throw on something. We're going to church."

25

Zeely

I peeled off my clothes and lay across the bed, trying to process what Grace had told me—that Sean was her son. I was happy for her, though it was likely he'd be put away for a long time. At least she could see him, watch his chest rise and fall, see how his eyes crinkled in the corners when he laughed. There had always been something familiar about Sean, something in his eyes that reminded me of times and people that I wanted to forget. It was Brian he reminded me of most, tall and wild, hair going everywhere.

Tears tried to come up, but I pushed them back. I could be happy for Grace, even though I'd never hold my baby, who would have been a few years younger than Sean now. It seemed I would never hold a baby at all. I'd risked everything on that hope and lost everything too.

Like I had every night since I'd given Carmel Jerry's ring, I reached for the phone and dialed Ron's number. And as he had every night that I'd called, Ron refused to pick up. I knew he was there because the machine didn't pick up. That meant he was on the phone and he only talked on the phone with two people: me and his girlfriend Mindy. For the longest time, it had really only been me. Mindy had been his girlfriend in name only.

But the night Ron had called to say that he had something to ask me as Jerry appeared at my door with a ring and a proposal, I'd done a horrible, practical thing. I'd accepted Jerry's marriage proposal. Ron was always around but at a safe distance, with a plate or a board game between us. I figured that what he had to ask me was how many ham hocks to put in a pot of greens.

So instead of love, I'd taken the offer of a life, both for myself and the child I'd carried. It was selfish and stupid, something I realized now. When Ron left the hospital after I lost the baby, he'd been broken. I saw it in his eyes. What his eyes hadn't shown me was that his love for me was broken too. And now, when I wanted to do what I always should have done and shout my love for him all over this wretched town, I had a sinking feeling that, for the first time since I'd seen him staring at me in the choir stand back in the day, he wouldn't be happy to hear it.

Maybe if he couldn't be in love with me, I just needed him to mourn with me, for our baby, for our shoulda-coulda-woulda love. Something. I'd always hated when those relationship gurus on TV talked about closure, but I needed some right about now. I let Ron's phone ring five more times and hung up, disgusted with my own desperation.

There were no papers to grade since we'd just had the proficiency retake, which left cleaning, taking a much needed nap, and the mail. That last thing, the mail, was piling up in a basket on my counter, covering a square peach envelope with handwritten calligraphy on it. It was addressed to Miss Zeely Ann Wilkins and nobody but my dead mother called me that anymore. It could have been a bill collector with great taste in stationery, but I doubted it. In my heart, I knew what the letter would say or had some idea, and I just wasn't ready to face it. I might never be.

Read it.

I peeled myself from the comforter and walked to the bundle of envelopes, most of them long and thin. There was the square one in the middle though, the only splash of color in the pile. I scanned the return address for the confirmation of my fears and quickly found it: M. Bent and R. Jenkins.

Ronald Jenkins.

I opened the invitation—as I'd suspected, that's just what it was—and a sheet of vellum fell away, revealing more flowing script. The words confirmed what I'd feared most, that like me, Ron had decided to hide behind a lie instead of love.

The outside of the invitation had been the first lie, a picture of two young children, two white children with blushing cheeks, kissing. The biggest pain hit me with the caption on the scene—to the other people who'd received it, it had probably been cute. I read it again.

First kiss.

I wished that Ron and Mindy's first kiss had been their last, instead of this. Anything instead of this. I forced myself to read the inside too, to take in all of it and face up to it. *Save the date. We couldn't wait. Ron and Mindy forever . . . from the first kiss.*

I dropped the card, unable to read further. There was no need for me to know what day my world would end. Knowing today's date would be close enough. Though I'd walked around with Jerry's ring on my finger, I didn't want to think of how heavy the stone must have weighed on Ron's heart. I didn't want to think about how deep a little bit of paper could cut into me either.

Cut into us, the family I'd always wanted but now would never have. And I had only myself to blame.

26

Grace

The worship rained down like fruit from the wrong grocery store—juicy to my ears at first, but then came the bitter words, *sacrifice*, *surrender*, in an endless refrain. It seemed as though I'd given up everything already and unlike the heroes and heroines in the Bible, I'd received no reward. Pain was all I held in my hands these days, that and the thin thread of Brian's love, which I tested on every occasion. I could hardly look at him now, knowing what might have happened tonight, what I'd wanted to happen. I tried to convince myself that I never would have gone through with it, not after so long, so much.

That, too, was a lie.

The music pressed in on me, urging the lifting of my hands, the raising of my voice. I didn't give in. I fumbled through the songs, singing some parts, remaining silent on others, with verses vowing more than I could promise. I rationalized my piecemeal praise until Brian let go of my hand and lifted his weathered palms to the Lord.

I started crying then, but vowed to hold it together. I had to.

This wasn't even regular church. It was a couples' service and this, well, this was more intimate than the touching I thought I'd craved. Both with God and with Brian, it was too close.

And so I held it in, keeping my eyes closed and my arms pressed close to my sides. I held it in until I heard the seat of Brian's chair flip up, until I peeked and saw his body bowed like a kneeling child. I'd like to say that he was crying too, but it's not the right word.

I was crying.

Brian was weeping.

I'd always loved the short verse in the Bible that brought Jesus closer to me than any of the healings or miracles. Just two words: Jesus wept. And now this man who'd once cringed at the sight of my Bible on the desk at work forgot that he loved me. He forgot that I was even there. He forgot because his first Love had come into the sanctuary. I'd felt it too, but my heart was cold, trained by too many years of church services where people wanted to get home for the game or go out to lunch.

Brian's faith was raw and real. Nobody put their hands on him and knocked him down or tried to force him to "be in the Spirit." He was just there, baring his heart before his Savior, his voice breaking in tender prayer. It was a rushing river, that prayer, swimming beneath the music, rising now and then for air.

"Heal me, Jesus. Help me. Help . . . both of us."

I felt something then, a hot something against my neck as if someone was pushing me into the warmth of God's glory. I looked around but no one was there. The other couples were pews away and Brian's hands were consumed with his praises. The warm kept on, tickling across my neck while I watched Brian turn from me and stretch out on his face almost under the pew, still crying out to God.

Though Brian was a world away from me now, Jesus was close,

so close that I was sure that if I listened hard enough, I would hear a beat brewing somewhere in me, a song of deliverance, like the one that Zeely had sung for me today. That had been a beginning, an opening, but somehow this, this warm, wide something would be an end. And finally, I wanted it more than I was afraid of it. My hands lifted from where they'd been fastened at my sides and went straight over my head. The heat flowed down both my arms, over my elbows, down my spine.

Warm like oil, joy flooded me, running straight down to my toes. With purpose, I stepped over Brian and into the aisle and began a dance I'd never done before—a dance of betrothal, a dance of love.

An hour and a lot of tissue later, we helped close down the church. Brian and I were both drained and not quite sure what to say. That I should thank him for how the evening had ended in contrast to how things could have gone seemed obvious, so I started there.

"Thanks for bringing me. I really needed that." I relaxed against Brian's leather seat, remembering our first date. I'd almost passed out when he called from his cell phone saying that he was outside my house. I should have known then that I was in for a ride. Not for the first time, Brian's persistence had blessed me and kept me safe. I couldn't help but smile.

"I needed it too. I hope I didn't hit you or anything. Things got a little crazy there at the end. I'm not used to worshiping like that in public. I guess I just really needed to let God lay hold of me tonight." He flashed a smile of his own.

I touched his cheek. "I'm sorry I've been so grumpy. As the kids at school would say, I have issues."

"Who doesn't? With what you've been through, I have nothing but respect for how you're handling yourself. It's me that needs work. I want to try and love you now, fix things for you now, and it's not the time for that. It's a time to heal. That's why I'm here so often. I don't know how I survived so long without going. I must have been a bear."

"Well . . ." I laughed. He did too.

"See? No apologies. We're even. I wish you would have called me though. Isn't that what friends are for?" He reached for my hand.

I squeezed his fingers. "I was so angry. Hurt."

"I know. I liked the teaching tonight. Philemon isn't a book I've read a lot. I'll have to read that again tomorrow."

I nodded. " 'Charge it to God's account.' I'm going to remember that. I have a hard time forgiving people sometimes. Even myself."

Brian downshifted, thankful he hadn't bought an automatic. Shifting gears gave his body and his mind something to focus on. What did Grace think she has to forgive herself for? He gripped the steering wheel, trying not to think of what Mal did to her. To both of us.

Vengeance is mine, says the Lord.

"I think we're all too hard on ourselves sometimes."

"Or not hard enough." My fingers went limp.

Brian took a deep breath. "You hungry?"

"Not really. I had a date plate from the Rib Hut. Zeely finished it off."

"No way! You didn't leave me any?" Brian elbowed me across the armrest separating us. "That stuff would kill you, but it is so good . . ."

"If you really want some, we could get another. But you wouldn't have wanted that first one, trust me. Zeely and I picked all through it." I left out the part about eating ribs in the bathtub. That just didn't sound right, even to me.

He smacked his tongue against his teeth. "No offense to Zee or anything, but I was thinking we'd pick up a fresh one anyway. That's more sharing than I want to do." He turned to face me at the red light.

What a smile.

"Feel like stopping by the hospital to see Joyce on the way? Jerry too."

"Jerry is family only. Zeely stopped by today."

"They must have done that after my visit earlier. How's he doing?" Brian sighed. "I still can't believe the guy took a bullet for me. For you. Thank God he lived. The cross is enough of a sacrifice to swallow."

"He's stable. Carmel and the girls were there too."

"Hmm . . . how'd that work? A little awkward I would think."

"A lot awkward. I think Jerry and Zeely are quits for now."

He brightened. "I'm sad for ole Jer, but he and Carmel are good together. Besides, maybe Ron finally has a chance with Zee. Except—"

"What?"

"Nothing. Something I'm trying to talk him out of." He shook his head. "Those two need to get together and get this over with. I warned him back when we were kids not to start on Zeely . . . but you know how that goes."

I laughed a little. "I know just how that goes. I wonder though—"

"About what?" He pulled into the hospital and parked in the first open space, and then turned, giving me his full attention.

"I'm wondering why anybody listens to other people's warnings about the people they . . . love." I stopped smiling, thinking about all the bad things Mal had told me about Brian, when he was the one who wanted to hurt me. Sometimes it was so hard to know who to trust.

You just listened to the wrong guy.

Brian provided his own wide grin before lifting my hand and kissing it. "A warning wouldn't have helped me. I was as good as gone from the moment I saw you."

Brian gave me a crazy look when we got to Joyce's room. Empty. For a bestselling author and nationally known speaker, he was completely at a loss for words. Me, I just started running, holding my chest, willing my heart to start thumping. We were all on the call list, and Brian and I had spent the night here on a close call once before.

She isn't gone. Not yet. It's a mistake. A stupid, crazy mistake.

Brian followed and then passed me in pursuit of a nurse who turned down our hall. Though he reached her first, my words came out faster.

"Joyce Rogers. Where is she?" I screamed the words, pointing back at the room.

The woman shrugged. "Gone."

Everything went still inside me. "Gone?"

The nurse shrugged. "Yep. She got dressed and snuck out a few hours ago."

Brian let out a long breath. "I thought you meant—Forget it. How can she be gone though? I just talked to the doctor this morning."

I nodded. "How could she sneak out? She can hardly sit up. What'd she do, call a getaway taxi?"

The nurse walked to the room and took the chart off the wall. "Another patient reported seeing her with an elderly black man wearing a clerical collar—"

Brian groaned. I sighed. Reverend Wilkins. Zeely's father.

"Thanks." He grabbed my hand and ran for the door.

The nurse cupped her mouth with both hands, calling behind us. "If you find her, try to convince her to come back. She's going to have a rough night. It might be her last."

27

Brian

In all my years of attending Mount Olive Missionary Baptist Church, I could never remember going to the pastor's house. Eva, Ron, and I had passed by and even stood outside, but in my mind it was a holy place, a place one didn't go without invitation.

Tonight was different. I wasn't invited, but I was going in.

"Brian Mayfield? Is that you?"

"Yes sir. It's me. May I come in?" I didn't bother to say why I was coming. The Reverend likely knew. Nor did I stop to wonder why my childhood pastor still called all of us by our full names as though we were still children in Sunday school.

The front door swung open easily instead of creaking like I thought it would. The house smelled of orange oil and peppermint, just like the vestibule of the old church. Though I loved Tender Mercies, that smell and this man's voice would always mean Jesus to me.

"Where is she?" There was no point in wasting time. I meant no disrespect, but I couldn't play games here.

The Reverend, still nimble and stylish in his way, looked frail and weak. Whatever had gone on tonight had taken a lot out of him and not just physically. It would have taken a lot of prayer to get ready for this one. I could use a bit more myself. Instead of answering, the older man simply pointed upstairs and turned away from me.

I swallowed back my anger. No matter how old I was, I couldn't stand here and scream at Reverend Wilkins. But I wanted to. I couldn't believe this foolishness. Not only had he brought Joyce home, he'd let her go upstairs. It'd be a job to get her down without hurting her. As I ran up the stairs, I turned back to him. "Why'd you do it? Why'd you bring her here?"

The pastor looked up from a chair he'd collapsed into. "She would've done the same for me."

"I doubt it." I'd already topped the stairs and started for the bedroom when the Reverend started up them. He caught up with me a little too quickly, placing his strong hand on my shoulder.

The old preacher fixed his eyes on me. "Joyce stood with me many times in my life, especially when my wife died. It's the least I can do for her now."

One look inside the bedroom revealed what he'd done, all right. Joyce looked like a child instead of the steady-minded principal the community had come to know and love. I watched from the door as pain contorted her body. I tried not to cry out as she jerked as though guided by a puppeteer. Her ankles whipped behind her knees and back again. An arm shot out, then up.

The Reverend flew to her side, whispering something to her and holding her bony hand. It helped for a moment, but seconds later, even the old preacher had to watch helplessly as the hurt coursed from Joyce's toes to her fingertips.

I stroked my beard. This dance, this death, was something I'd seen before. First Eva and then Karyn, my wife . . . The first time

I'd kept waiting, kept hoping that mercy would come. Now I knew better. This could go on for hours. I couldn't watch it again. If she had stayed at the hospital, they could have at least managed the pain . . .

"We've got to get her to go back, Reverend. She has to take something. She doesn't know how bad it can get."

The preacher shook her head. "She knows. Trust me she does. It's time though, all the same."

Joyce closed her eyes and melted into the agony, almost welcoming it. I tried to turn away, but he didn't. I watched the throb turn into a flame burning through her veins. She threw her head back and screamed. The Reverend slipped off the bed onto his knees, knowing better than to touch her at this point. She travailed like a woman in transition.

A woman giving birth to herself.

Her limbs quivered once more, then stilled.

Grace, who I'd forgotten about for a moment, clasped my hand. She'd wanted me to come in first, in case . . . I was supposed to give her a signal. I guess she just came on in when I didn't return. Her touch gave me strength, reminded me of the worship and prayers from church tonight, though that seemed like a lifetime ago now. Joyce had stilled and fallen into a thick sleep as life colored her cheeks again.

I motioned to the pastor. "Help me get her into the car. Quick, before it starts again."

"No." Joyce raised a finger in the air. Her voice crackled like dry timber.

"No?" I frowned. "I'm supposed to just sit here and let you—let you die?"

Her lips flexed into what would have been a smile if she'd been able. "Yes."

Why did she have to be like this? Always in control, even to the end. At least we could take her to the hospital. A hospice even. Anything but this. "I can't leave you like this! You can't stay here."

A warm hand touched my wrist. Grace's voice. "We should pray." Her voice shook with the reality of the moment.

"Yes. Please." The Reverend nodded too. I bowed my head, but despite my outpouring to God earlier, my heart refused to kneel. Instead I did what I could and focused on the sound of Grace's voice, shaking with tears.

"Let your healing love flow over this place, Lord. We know you have the power to heal. To do a mighty work . . ."

Joyce moaned, then spoke in a hoarse whisper. "Don't pray about me. Pray for me. Pray me a good journey." She paused as a pain went through her. "I'm not afraid. Don't you be afraid either." Each word seemed to suck her under.

I clutched the sides of the bed, looking at Grace and the Reverend as though they'd lost their minds too. "Come on. Help me. We cannot let her die like this! It is not acceptable."

The Reverend's voice rolled in. "She made it her ambition to live a quiet life, Lord. To love folks. It'd be to our advantage for her to stay with us. It's to her advantage to come to you. Have your way, Lord."

A pit of silence opened before me, waiting for me to step into it, to pray. For a moment, I was too angry to speak, and then, all the things rushing through me ran over the side, bringing me back to the throne of grace. "Lord, I wish I could take this as easy as the others. To just give up and say it's okay." I sighed. "I can't. Not this time. It might be selfish, but . . ."

I leaned over and kissed Joyce's hair. For so long I'd been looking for my mother, defined my life through what I'd do when I met her. I realized now that Eva, Joyce, even Thelma, our childhood lunch lady who still looked out for me . . . they'd been all the mother that I needed. Sometimes you just have to love the people in front of you. And God knew, this woman had loved me. She'd loved me when no one else had. "I can't give her up without a fight. I won't. I need her. We all do." Even as I said it, I knew it didn't make sense. It wasn't like Joyce was coming back to work or something. I realized that most of what I said had been about me and not about her.

I stroked her hair, looked into her eyes. Joyce looked so pale without her makeup, so cold. Her veins peeked through her skin like a blue highway.

A shaky hand reached up and touched my cheek. Joyce sniffed, her eyes full of love. Whatever else I wanted to say dissolved with her touch. "Amen."

As if that word had taken all her strength, Joyce's hand slapped against the bed. She bought her air in costly bursts, choking to breathe. The next wave. It was here. And yet, she was still fighting. For me.

"Sit—down." She looked at me, and then turned to the others. "You—two—go." Somehow, she forced out the words.

The Reverend hesitated. Grace nodded, pulling the older man along. "It'll be okay. We're not going far." They headed out the door.

I sat on the edge of the bed, analyzing how to get Joyce out the door without causing further injury. And then down the stairs. Had the Reverend carried her up? A formidable feat for a man his age.

"I crawled." Joyce's air came easier this time.

My fists clenched. "Why in God's name are you doing this to yourself? Let me take you back." Pain stitched across my forehead. "Please."

Her fingers, like raw bones, lighted on my shoulder. She fought for a long breath. "Thank you for coming. For loving me."

Tears rushed in, stinging my eyes. "Thank you for loving me." My voice started strong, but ended in a whisper.

"Listen." Her left foot arched. Her gaze flickered to the ceiling. She seemed to force herself back to the room. Back to me. She reached under the pillow for an envelope with letters sprouting from its mouth like flowers. Roses. It smelled like them too. "Eva was a good friend. Too good. My cousin on the other side."

Cousin? Eva? My foster mother, the woman who'd raised me and Ron? I stared, trying to decipher her meaning. Joyce had never visited our home. She and Eva were friendly enough at school functions . . . Sometimes it'd seemed like they'd all conspired against me. Thelma too. "You know, don't you? You know who she is. Please tell me. Who is she?"

Joyce closed her eyes for a moment. "Who?"

"My mother!"

Joyce tried to sit up, but her elbows buckled. I caught her, eased her to the bed as if the sheet would slice through her skin. I chided myself for raising my voice.

Before passing out, she willed herself to say a sentence that I'd been waiting forever to hear, only not from her.

"I am your mother," she said, closing her eyes with finality.

I sat still for a few seconds, too shocked to move. Then threw back the blanket, tore at the sheets, and pulled Joyce to my chest. "No! Wait!" I hadn't found her only to lose her again. I couldn't.

An ambulance wailed in the distance.

Grace. Thank God.

I still had a chance.

28

Grace

I clutched my sides, wondering if I should have come to the hospital. I'd thought I wanted to be here at the end, to see it all. Now I wasn't so sure. A tall woman, her skin the color of sassafras tea, wedged into the chair next to me. Her voice sounded like an out-of-tune violin. *Twang.*

"Do you thank she'll make it?" she said matter-of-factly.

What a question. "I hope so."

"Hmm . . . me too. She's my cousin, ya know. Never met her 'til now. Hate to lose her before I get to know her good. I'm from the colored side."

I listened as the lady covered three states and four generations of hardworking, hard-loving people. *Brian's people.*

While her voice droned on, I watched Brian, huddled in the corner with Thelma and the band of prayer warriors she'd brought with her. I could hear his voice above the others.

"You knew, didn't you, Thelma? About Joyce being my mother." Brian's voice sliced through the noise.

My heart ached for Brian as his long-lost cousin the storyteller went right on with her tale.

"Um hum . . . Then she fell slap out. The rooster crowed and she died right there. Can you believe that?"

"Nope." I couldn't believe any of this.

Brian's voice rose again. "But what about my father?"

I closed my eyes. I wanted to run to him, kiss his face. Instead I watched as he sank into his chair, his head in his hands.

The rooster lady tapped my shoulder. "Looks like Joyce's boy is having a hard time. Why don't you go sit with him, darlin'? He ain't been right since they took her back."

I nodded, maneuvering next to him. That was easier than trying to tell her that, though he'd known Joyce all his life, Joyce's boy was meeting his mother for the first time too. His hair flailed as he rocked back and forth. He didn't seem to notice me as I sat down beside him.

Thelma touched his shoulder. She stared at him from raccoon eyes, black from crying. "I thought she'd tell you before—before—"

Why did people always think lies were going to protect anyone? Would anybody ever tell the truth? I shook my head and reached out for his hand. He jumped at my touch, then smiled. His eyes calmed from hazel to brown. Though we'd talked about the change in color before, it startled me. He hadn't done that for a long time.

"Thelma, I know you did what you thought was right. But there is something you can do for me now." He pulled my arm under his like a broken wing.

"Food? I can do drummettes—" Thelma dug into her purse and pulled out a pen.

Brian shook his head. "My father, Thelma. Who is my father?"

The lunch lady withered. "She never told me. I don't know for sure."

Brian squeezed Thelma's hand. "Tell me what you know for not so sure. Please."

"I don't know . . ." She stared at me.

Why was Thelma looking at me? If Brian could handle the truth, I could too. What could be worse than knowing that the woman he'd searched the world looking for had been right under his nose? It was as bad as discovering I'd been teaching my son all semester. "Tell him," I said. "Please."

Thelma shrugged. "I only saw Joyce with two men. One was Timothy Wilkins, the pastor over at Mount Olive, and the other . . ."

"Yes?"

"Trey Dixon. Grace's daddy."

The room swam before my eyes. I'd come to support Brian. To be there for him. But this . . . Could he be my brother?

God help me. Send somebody. Do something. I'm going to lose it.

"Grace?" Brian tightened his grip on my hand.

I forced myself to pull away.

He tugged at my hand. "Please. We don't know . . ."

"Don't we?" I gave a final pull and braced my forehead in both hands. "You've always reminded me of Daddy." Dancing eyes. Playful mouth. A king to reject the princess. "It was too good to be true. The whole thing. I should have known."

"No. Let's just wait and see—"

I jumped up, shook my head. Could this be a way of escape—the way God wanted it? Anyway, I was tired of losing, and that's what loving always led to. But why would Joyce try so hard to push us together if we were related? Had she meant family love, when she told us to love each other? It sounded like something more . . .

Brian pulled me to him with a hungry, desperate look. "So this is it. Just like that? After everything?"

"I guess I'll send you birthday cards or whatever sisters do—" I stared at my feet. Unless . . . Would the Reverend know? My mother? No. She wouldn't go around town asking for family trees. My mother never seemed to like Joyce much back then . . . Was it because of this or because of the dancing?

I smiled, remembering the only time my father had ever stood up to my mother. The day the ballet teacher told me not to come back until my hair stayed in a bun and my behind stayed in my leotard.

"Just twenty pounds," the woman had said, so blonde and thin. So pale.

I hung my head, waiting for my father's agreement. He grabbed my hand and walked out instead. A wonderful day. My mother never had a kind thing to say about Joyce. Was it because I admired my teacher so much, or something more? I wasn't sure if I wanted to know.

A doctor peeked into the waiting room. "Mr. Mayfield?"

Brian took a deep breath. "Yes?"

"She's asking for you. Come quickly. It won't be long."

29

Ron

Mother Riley wasn't surprised to see me. We had a standing date now, almost every Friday night since things had gone bad with Zeely. Some weeks I got more biscuit than story, but it was starting to come together, just as I was falling apart.

"And you're sure you're all right? That boy ain't hurt you now, did he?"

"No, ma'am. I'm all right. What I need more than anything is more of the story. When we quit, I think Sadie had come north."

"Oh yes. You know when they found her out, the boy she was engaged to wouldn't have her and the white folks was in an uproar. It was Hattie who hid her away, remember that? Hattie and Sister."

Yes, Sister. The other twin. "And what happened to her after that?"

"Sister came north too. She was supposed to go to Wilberforce University. She met a white man though and passed on over. She married him, had a few babies. Some of 'em's still around here. That fat man on the city commission always yelling at people?"

I held on to the couch. "John Bent? Of Bentek? The lawyer?"

Mindy's father?

Mother Riley sipped her tea. "That's the one. He comes from Sister and 'nem. Now back to Sadie. She came up here only having lived with white folk. Sister was supposed to look out for her, but I reckon Sister felt like she'd done enough looking out for folks since she'd been Sadie's maid when they were growing up. So Sadie did what she knew and married a white man. It took about a year for word from South Carolina to get to her husband about who she really was. By then, they had a baby boy, Ronald."

I closed my eyes. "My grandfather?"

Mother Riley nodded. "One and the same. Though he never knew much of Sadie once it came out that she was a negro. They ran her off to the black side of town, where people thought she was crazy. Only one man believed her story—John Parker. They were friends, people say, and eventually they fell in love. They had a whole slew of yellow babies. Your Eva is from some of 'em."

All I could do was stare. Eva had really been related to me. No matter how distant the connection, it had been real. That was good to know, that something had been real. "Is that why my mother hated Eva so much?"

"No, that's why your daddy hated Eva so much. He'd been taught to. They didn't want anybody to know about the black branches of their family. The truth had gotten out once and ruined your grandfather. The old man had always blamed Eva and her people for it. So your mother hated because she loved a man who hated. It's crazy, but that's how it goes sometimes."

As I tried to sort through what I'd been told and prepare for the next leg of the story, I heard a knock at the door.

"That sounds like Birdie. You'd better get it," Mother Riley said, clearing off the table.

"Sounds like? How can you tell?" I was up and moving to the

door, though I seriously doubted that it was Zeely. No one knew that I came here, and despite her calls, I don't think Zeely would have cared if she did know.

"I can hear all those bracelets jangling, and she still knocks like she did when she was little, like she's about to knock the door down."

True that.

When the door opened and Zeely rushed inside, I couldn't do anything but shake my head. At first, anyway.

"What are you doing here? Shouldn't you be at the hospital with your man? Or is he your husband yet?" I shouldn't have said that, nor did I mean to, but that's what came out of my mouth.

Mother Riley looked up from the trash can where she was scraping my plate. "Umph."

It was only when Zeely didn't answer with a snappy comeback of her own did I realize that she was crying and that her hair, what was left of it, was her own.

"It's Joyce," she said, whimpering through her fingers. "Grace said that Joyce and Daddy left the hospital so she could die but Grace and Brian are taking her back. I couldn't find you. Then I saw your car and . . ."

Her words dissolved into my shirt as I pulled her to me and grabbed my keys. I gave Mother Riley a quick nod. "Thank you," I said to her on the way out the door.

"No problem," she said. "Tell Joyce goodbye for me, and if y'all really want to thank me, get married and get me a baby 'round here before spring—"

The front door crashed against her words.

30

Jerry

My eyes fluttered open. The hospital room, the tightness of the bed, surfaced before me. Someone tucked a sheet over my toes. I strained to see who was taking care of me while I dipped in and out of sleep. At first, my eyes refused to focus. "Who's there?"

"Good morning. Or should I say good evening? You've slept most of the day." Carmel leaned over and stroked my chin. "How do you feel?"

"You *are* here. I thought you were . . . it seemed like a dream." I closed my eyes, savoring the warmth of her hand versus the icy hospital bed. Something cold struck my skin. Metal. I pulled Carmel's hand to my face. It was a ring. Zeely's ring. I frowned, confused as everything came back to me. "How did you get this? What—"

"That first day, when you came to after the shooting. She was here."

She wasn't. "No!"

She was. "Yes."

"What did I say exactly? I remember something about not being able to live without the girls." I shook my head, rustling the stiff pillowcase. "And you . . ."

Oh no. I'd meant every word of that, but I hadn't wanted Zeely to hear it. I'd wanted to speak to her alone, when we were both stronger.

"Was she upset? Crying?"

Carmel sat next to the bed. "No crying. She didn't say much at all. She gave me this and left. She did have a crazy look on her face."

"Probably thinking of Ron and how she should have married him a long time ago. I don't know what either of us was thinking. Funny how mixed up things can get."

"Ron? Do you think? A few times when I saw them together, I wondered . . ."

I nodded. "They have it." I took Carmel's hand. "We have it too. I've just been too busy looking at the wrong things. Amazing how a bullet can clear your mind."

Carmel dabbed the corners of her eyes with her scrubs. "Let's not ever let things get that confused. I can't go through this again. When they called me—"

"I'm sorry. Brian and I ran down there like the Mod Squad. I guess we got a little carried away." I tugged at her hand, pulling her forward.

She leaned over the bed, her lips a breath away. "A lot carried away."

Pain shot through my shoulder. I groaned. Carmel let go and raised my bed to a comfortable position. "See there. Trying to get frisky and hurt yourself. Just rest."

"Okay." I sighed, noting the difference in how the ring fit on Carmel's finger. Zeely needed a wad of string to keep it on. We'd planned to get it resized for weeks but had never gotten around to it. That should have been a sign in itself. On Carmel's finger, the stone rested exactly as it should. A perfect fit.

Carmel settled back in her chair, and slipped off the ring. She put it in my hand. "Don't look at me like that. Besides, you didn't give me this ring. Zeely did." She folded my fingers around it. "A few words said in anguish won't solve our problems. You're going to have to tell me more. And counseling. Lots of counseling." Softness touched my arm. "Not now. When you're better." She stood to go.

I grabbed her wrist. "Now is a good time to get started. I might not remember it later. I know you're on your job—"

"I got off hours ago."

I tried not to think about who was keeping an eye on the girls. I guess if Monique was old enough to have a baby, she was old enough to watch her.

"Okay, well, I know you're tired. I am too. Sit down for a minute. I need to tell you something."

Carmel shrugged and sat down in the chair next to my bed.

"Yesterday, in my time with the Lord, I read about the Gibeonites. Know the story?"

She narrowed her eyes. "The people who pretended to be from far away?"

I nodded, eyebrows arched. "That's right. Later, when David was king, there was a famine for three years. No food. Nothing."

She frowned. "That's a long time. I don't want to go hungry for three days."

I laughed. "In my case, make that three hours. Anyway, when they asked the Lord what was up, guess what he said?"

"I have no clue." Carmel shrugged.

"Because of the Gibeonites. Joshua gave his word they'd be safe and Saul killed them anyway."

"But why did God punish David instead of Saul? I don't get it."

"I didn't either. But somewhere between that bullet and here, it came to me. Covenant. It's part of God's character. He has to uphold what he enters in to. That's where you come in."

She smiled. "Me?"

"You. The wife of my youth. The Scripture that came to me in the ambulance." I cleared my throat. "'The Lord has been witness between you and the wife of your youth, to whom you have been faithless, although she is your companion and your wife by covenant.'"

Carmel's breathing shortened into a pant. "Is that in the Bible?"

"Malachi. Chapter two, I think." I observed her more closely—the sweat edging off her forehead, the flush on her face. "Carm, are you okay?"

She shook her head, hid her face. "I can't believe this."

"Did I scare you? I know we'll have to work on some things. Go to counseling—"

"It's that Scripture. Covenant. Everything that you're saying. I had a dream . . ." She stared out the window.

"Probably indigestion. It doesn't mean anything."

"It wasn't. It was real. Different. There was a voice—your voice—reading. It sounded like the Bible."

I pressed the button to lift the top of the bed. "What did I say?"

"Something about a wayward wife. A woman who left the husband of her youth and ignored her covenant. A woman whose house leads down to death."

I took a deep breath. "Proverbs chapter two. Somewhere near the end." I held out my hands. "Come here."

Carmel touched me gingerly, careful not to graze my wounds. She sobbed on my good shoulder. "I'm so sorry. I hope this didn't happen because—"

"No. God has nothing but good plans for us. We stepped out of his protection. Outside his covenant. But not outside his love. Even if I'd married Zeely . . ."

She shook her head. "So close. And I didn't say a word when you told me—"

I rubbed her back. "I know. I'm sorry. I thought I was doing the right thing. I was trying to uphold a covenant then too, just the wrong one—the covenant of man."

"Me too. All our marriage I believed it. I never thought of myself totally as your wife."

I sighed. "That's a good place to start. We'll pray about it. Talk about it. No pressure. Like I said, God loves us. He's not mad at you. Or me."

Carmel nodded. "I guess I know that. I just want His love and His blessings too. This past year . . ."

Nerve endings awakened all over my chest. I squeezed my eyes shut and let Carmel go. Medicine must be wearing off. I pressed a button on my IV. Numbness flooded up from my toes.

"We have His blessings, babe. If we didn't know any better, that would be one thing, but we know what's right. It's time we started acting like it."

"True—" Carmel's head snapped toward the door. "Did you see that?"

I peeled my eyes open from a long blink, fighting the sleep overtaking me. "What?"

A small, brown figure ran by the door. I blinked. "Was that—?"

"Zeely. And Ron before her. I wonder what's up. They passed right by here." She looked right and left, then back at the door.

I gripped the rail, already in the throes of sleep. "Joyce."

31

Brian

The lines on the monitors were flat. Joyce's chest was still. And yet, I fixed my eyes on the nurse, waiting for her to do something to bring my mother back to life. I had so many questions and it looked as though Joyce might take the answers with her. Grace seemed convinced that we were related. Everything was bitter and sweet all mixed up together. I'd found my mother, but it'd been too late.

Why didn't she tell me something? All that time . . .

The nurse finally spoke, forcing me to deal with what I already knew. "I'm sorry but she's gone."

I rubbed my hand through my hair, wishing I could comb my thoughts, arrange the nurse's words into something understandable. I looked around for Thelma or Zeely, hoping that one of them would try to raise Joyce from the dead or something. My faith wasn't as strong as theirs, but my need was greater.

"Gone?" I asked no one in particular. "How can she be gone?"

No one answered.

Ron and Zeely slid into the room in a crush of shirt and skirt, both of them out of breath. My brother, the only brother I'd ever known, ran to join me at the bed. He'd known about the cancer long before I did. He'd taken Joyce to appointments and picked up her medicine. In some ways, he was Joyce's son too.

He looked stricken as he spoke. "I came as soon as I knew. Zeely found me—"

Someone moved behind me. Grace maybe? Somehow I doubted it. I kept my focus on Ron. "You're too late," I said in a flat voice.

Zeely fumbled in her purse, finally coming up with a bottle of anointing oil. I turned to face her, relieved to see that someone still believed, that someone hadn't given up.

One word passed my lips as Zeely pressed her thumb into Joyce's cold flesh.

"Gone?"

Gone.

She took one look at me and covered her face. The bottle in her hand fell and shattered, spilling across the floor.

The nurse pushed a button. "I need a cleanup in here." She grabbed Zeely's hand. "Watch your step."

Ron spun me around. His tears spilled into my shirt, down my chest into my heart. We clutched each other, hanging on for . . . for what? For life? What was that? Ron shook his head. "I knew it was coming." He sniffed. "We talked about it. She said it would be like this. I thought I was ready . . ."

I looked up at the ceiling. "I knew I wasn't ready. Not before. Especially not now." I looked over at Grace, huddled with Zeely in the corner.

She stared back, closed her eyes. Closed me out.

The nurse, so quiet I'd forgotten her presence, reached under a chair and pulled out a packet. "I spent a lot of time with Miss Rogers. She taught me a lot of things in the time she stayed here. Things about myself and about all of you . . ."

Ron turned around. Zeely lifted her head in the corner.

The woman stepped over the oil spill and handed a letter to each one of us. "Brian."

I took it, tucking my finger under the edge and ripping the seam.

My Grace is sufficient for you. Your power can only be perfected in weakness. Don't quit until you attain Grace.

I shoved the envelope in my pocket. I leaned over her body, already growing cold. "You just don't know when to quit, do you?"

The nurse brushed past me, handing out the other letters. She skipped over the next two envelopes, marked Jerry and Carmel. I looked down at the woman who had loved me from afar, believed in me up close—all the mother I could have ever hoped for. I kissed her fingers and pressed them to her lips. "I love you."

Grace's eyes met mine; she held her unopened letter with two fingertips. I watched, waiting for her to open it, but she just stood there. Why wouldn't she open it? I sighed.

Because it says the same thing yours did, and she doesn't want to hear it.

The Reverend thanked the nurse and slid the envelope into his Bible. I staggered to a chair and hung my head, my hair draping almost to the floor. Ron's feet appeared in front of me. He had his letter in his hand. "She wants me to preach her funeral. I don't think I can."

I lifted my head knee-level and smiled. Now that made sense. "Do it. She's watching, you know." We both chuckled. What a life Joyce had lived. How she'd touched us . . .

Zeely tapped my shoulder. I turned to face her, to face Grace.

"Brian, Grace, there's a note on the outside of my letter. I have to open it with the two of you." Zeely reached for my hand. I took a deep breath and gripped her palm. I wanted to be home in my own bed under Eva's wedding quilt. I'd had enough of letters, of dying. Just enough. Yet somehow, I was curious too.

"Go ahead," I said. She was dead. It was over. Nothing else mattered now.

Zeely nodded. "Okay, here goes." As she opened the envelope's seal, Grace shook her head and took back her hand.

"Grace?" Zeely's voice sounded still and small, more a plea than anything.

I closed my eyes, knowing that she was going to run anyway, knowing that she might always be running, from the past and from the future. Our future.

The clatter of metal made me open my eyes, just in time to see a tray of surgical instruments hit the floor. Everyone stared at me to see if I was going to chase, but I didn't run, not this time. I stood in the doorway and listened to Grace's purse squeak against the wall as she ran away from our destiny.

I couldn't blame her either. On another day, I might have run too.

32

Grace

I'd made up my mind—I was leaving Testimony. I wasn't sure where I was moving to, someplace close enough to visit Sean, but far enough away to keep from running into Brian.

Brian.

When his love had been available, I hadn't been sure I wanted it, but now that us being together seemed impossible, I knew I couldn't stay. Whether Brian was my half-brother or the love of my life, it was too much.

And then there was that other question, the one that wouldn't leave my head: could my father have had an affair with Joyce? That thought was unbearable too. Joyce had meant so much to me. In some ways, she knew me better than my own mother. She'd honored parts of me that few people ever saw, much less understood. Even after her death, with all her letters and last wishes, she was still pushing us, pushing me toward something painfully beautiful, something that nothing could stop.

Until now.

I was stopping it. No matter how good you are, how saved you are, there's a place where everything breaks. I'd been here before, sitting in a gown in group therapy. I didn't plan to go out like that this time. This wasn't the usual chips and dings of life, the cracks down the side of coming to terms with my issues. No, this was the breaking of secret hopes I thought I'd given up on: a godly husband, a baby who no one would take away, a community of love and gratitude. One day, while I was sniffing Brian's hair, my heart had messed around and betrayed me, my soul had breathed a prayer without my knowledge. And now, all of it was broken.

I had no more tears. As much as I'd miss Joyce—and I would miss her—there was a relief in her passing too. This was it. The end. What I'd come here for.

If you've ever loved me, you'll come . . .

I had loved her. I still did. And I had come. Now, it was time to go.

Packing seemed simpler this time. There was none of the nervous shoveling into bags that I'd done when I came here, leaving Malachi Gooden, who I then thought was my last chance at marriage and family, behind. Now Malachi was in jail, both for my kidnapping and assault, and for my rape years ago, if it fell within the statute of limitations. I'd come here sure that singleness was God's gift to me. I'd leave praying that one day I'd be able to see Brian without screaming on the inside.

Until then, I'd gather books into boxes, cloud knick-knacks in too much tissue, and wish my heart could be packed away for safekeeping.

I heard a car outside, but kept packing. I didn't dare stop.

Zeely rushed in without knocking, as though she were coming home from a long day.

"What are you doing?" she asked, her voice quiet but angry.

I should have told her. Should have called her. I should have, but

209

I couldn't. Still, I was glad now that she'd come, though it would make things more difficult. Better that she hear it from me. "I'm moving."

Zeely touched my arm. "Running won't change it. You might as well stay."

Stay? Here? With him? "Columbus probably. That's where I'm heading anyway."

"What about Sean?"

"I'll write. Visit as much as I can. I saw him today."

"What does he think about it? The move, I mean."

I tore off a length of tape with my teeth. I slid the tape along the edges of the box and smoothed it with my fingers. "Sean doesn't know yet. It won't really make a difference. I'll commute to school until the end of the semester. It's less than an hour."

"And then what? It's almost Christmas."

"And then, I don't know. The school will probably fold anyway."

Zeely folded her arms across her chest. That discussion was off limits and I knew it. She narrowed her eyes at me. "She appointed you to the board, you know. The lawyer came after you left. I can't believe you'd do this—walk out on me, on all of us, over a man." Her nostrils flared.

Guilt wouldn't work. Not this time. "You might as well fix your face, Zee. I have to go. It's not just him. It's everything. Don't look at me like that. I still believe. I know God is here, even now. I'm tired though. Weary. Battered." I placed another book in the box at my feet. I knew I'd loved them: Joyce, Brian, Zeely, Sean . . . Until now though, I hadn't known how much I loved myself.

"I wish I could make you understand, Zee, but I don't have any words left. I don't have any tears either. I'm just . . ."

Zeely wrapped herself around me. She was so small, but so

strong. Strong enough to carry all of us, but I wondered who was carrying her.

I AM.

"I still don't understand what's gone so wrong between you and Brian. When I left here the other night, things seemed fine. More than fine. I know losing Joyce is hard and finding out that she was his mother is even harder—I don't know if I'll ever get over it—but I don't see why you have to leave. Do you want to talk about it?"

Talking. Always more talking. "What's the point?" My counselor from Cincinatti told me straight on the phone that she'd probably end up applying the Baker Act and putting me straight into the hospital for three days from the way I was talking, so I'd hung up on her. Now I wondered if I shouldn't call her back and take her up on that.

I'd tried to talk to Reverend Wilkins, but he was busy putting the funeral together and heading out of town for some unknown reason. I'd gotten up the nerve to call my mother and ask if Brian and I could have had the same father, but she'd slammed the phone down in my ear. Not that I blamed her. I'd just needed to know.

Now I wasn't so sure if it mattered. Some things just don't work out. Maybe the gift Brian and I gave each other was the ability to love again. I didn't believe that, not yet, but for now I was sticking with it as a theory.

"Why do you hate about me the same things you once loved? Stop trying to change me, Diana. Just believe . . . in us and in your God." They were Peter's words, but I heard them in my heart now as clear as when he'd spoken them so many years ago. Peter had rarely called me my given name. It had startled me. As I had then, I turned away from the truth in his words.

"Have you prayed about this?" Zeely held my wrist lightly.

I turned to the wall. What was that supposed to mean? Didn't she know that my every breath, every movement was a prayer? That only God was holding my body together, keeping me in my right mind? I wanted to say all that, but instead I just shrugged.

I'd once been so strong, so deep, so wide. Grounded. Six months ago, I'd been the one at the front of my old church praying for people to be delivered. Healed. Now I spent my days burying, packing, trying to recover, trying to find the answer the Bible said I was supposed to have ready, the reason for my faith. Finally, I answered Zeely—and myself—truthfully.

"I didn't pray like I should have. Too scared, I guess."

Zeely nodded. "Me too. I'm terrified."

I paused, relieved that somebody was being real, even for a second. Still, it seemed strange to hear this from Zeely, always ready with a good hairpiece and a vial of anointing oil. What did Zee have to be scared of? "How about we pray for each other?"

"Deal." My friend stood to her feet, looking around the room. "I can't believe you've only been here since school started. Seems like I unpacked this stuff years ago."

"I know."

"If you really decide to go, I'll help—packing, moving, whatever. I'm here."

Yes. That's what I needed now. Just be here. "Thanks. Sorry I'm so needy." I tucked a wisp of hair behind my ear.

In weakness there is strength.

Zeely smiled. "Needy? Girl, please. Remember how I was when Mama died? You sat in my room for three days without saying a word. You fed me. Took me to the bathroom. Remember that?"

Wow. I had done that. It seemed right at the time. "I do remember."

"That's what friends do. They stay through the hard things.

Running is easy." She took the box I'd taped shut and ripped it open again before setting it on the floor.

I reached for the tape, clueless for a response. The truth stuck to the roof of my mouth, too difficult to say. My father had run away from Testimony after he found I was pregnant by my rapist, ashamed of what people would say about his princess, ruined by a stranger on a fall afternoon. Running away from this place, this man, this life, was the hardest thing I'd ever do. My shoulders shook but no tears came out, no sound.

Zeely took the box from me and slammed it down. "Just stop it, will you, before they have to take both of us to a padded room! Goodness, girl. See, look. I'm crying already."

And she was. I couldn't believe it, but she was. The only time I'd ever seen Zeely cry was at church, usually when she was singing.

We paused, held hands.

"What about Ron?" I asked softly.

"He's marrying her. I got the invitation."

I closed my eyes. "I'm sorry, Zee. So sorry."

She nodded and covered her mouth as though that would stop all the tears she'd been choking down from coming up. It didn't. Not at all.

Like a broken ballerina, Zeely's body extended over a box of my china, her pink blouse snagging on the cardboard. She was crying hard now, coming apart at the seams. I should have hugged her. I should have understood.

I should have, but I didn't.

"Girl, if you don't get up from there, I know something. What are you crying like that for? So you lost Ron. We've all lost. Joyce is dead. Jerry's nursing a bullet wound. Shoot, Brian might be my brother. Suck it up."

I did not just say that.

213

"Suck it up?" Zeely bit her lip to keep from slapping me and I knew it. I was glad too, because she would have beat me down. I was too tired for a fight and yet I'd started one. And I wasn't done yet.

"Look, I'm sorry about the miscarriage of your rescued egg, the end of your fake engagement, and all your little virgin drama. Like you always tell me, we're all going through."

Another tear snaked down Zeely's face. She didn't wipe it away. She took the masking tape from me and kicked away the box of books at my feet.

"You can't get away that easy, Grace. You can't run me off that easy. I'm the queen of that technique." Her words were steady but clipped.

I was starting to cry now. I grabbed for the masking tape, but Zeely tossed it across the room too.

"Stop it! I'm going. I have to. I need to. You don't know how I feel. You can't know."

Zeely wagged a pink nail in my face. It was broken at the tip. She rubbed her thumb across her nose like a kid itching for a fight. "You want to get in it? Let's get in it, since you think you know everything. I am not a virgin, and that's not the first baby I lost. I killed the first one. Killed it! Right down there in Dayton."

I stumbled over the boxes and grabbed her by the shoulders, then the neck, and pulled her to me. It took a few seconds to get my breath, to find my words.

"Was it—Jerry's? Is that why you kept waiting for him?"

She pushed away from me and laughed then, an ironic twisted laugh like some villain on a cartoon. "That would make too much sense now, wouldn't it? No, it wasn't Jerry's. It was Ron's baby. He was my first." Zeely sat on a box, caving with it as the sides gave way. She hung her head. "He was my last too."

214

I was too stunned to put her in a headlock again. I felt like I'd just run a marathon. Here we were, grown but still trying to set the bones of all our skeletons, all our secrets.

Down on my knees in front of her, I took Zeely's hands and pressed them against mine. It was a reflex, something I usually did during intimacy with men, but it seemed right. Just one of those things.

"Did you tell him, Zee?"

She pressed back against my palms before pushing my hands away. "He knows." She wiped her eyes. "I don't know how, but he does. I wanted to tell him, went to tell him before I did it. My roommate from Central drove me down to UC, but when the boy told him that he couldn't be a lawyer with a black wife, just a black mistress, Ron didn't say anything. He had to think about it, Grace. Mama warned me—" Her voice broke off.

"You're not being fair. He was a kid. You both were. Your mama— God bless the dead—and mine put us in so many boxes that it's taken us a lifetime to unpack ourselves. This isn't 1969, I don't care how crazy Testimony is. If you love that man, you can't let him marry somebody else. If you love him, you have to tell him that too."

Zeely pushed the broken box aside and sat down on the floor. "Maybe you should take your own advice if it's so easy."

Though we'd been so close a moment ago, Zeely and I now seemed worlds apart. She could see the back of my head, the bottom of my soul, and I could see the same of her. Neither of us really wanted to know what was there. Not yet anyway. "I'm so sorry."

Zeely laughed again. "You're sorry? I'll always be sorry. I've always been sorry. Every day I go to school knowing that one of those kids could have been mine, should have been mine . . . At least you can see your son. I can never have my baby, not in this world."

She hugged her knees and I hugged her. We held steady for a while until my love came down, until my best tears, the ones I didn't even know I had left, came down. We dropped back on the floor together, arms tangled, tears mixed. One of our elbows hit the remote. The stereo, not yet packed away, clicked on, playing an instrumental track I'd been using to choreograph a dance.

Once again, Zeely supplied the words. "Hail, hail Lion of Judah . . ."

I rolled away from Zeely, echoing her, both with my mouth and my body and then I got to my feet.

Zeely raised her hands to the ceiling. "How wonderful you are . . ."

My hands went up too after I shoved a box out of the way to make room. There was a time to be born, a time to die. A time to be broken and a time to mend. There was a time to mourn even, but we'd done enough of that.

Right now, it was time to dance.

33

Brian

I pulled into the shopping center in a daze. Numb. Though I thought I'd been alone before, I'd still had an unknown mother out there somewhere, someone who still might have a bad day on my birthday or whisper a prayer for me.

Now I knew what it really meant to be alone, orphaned by all that had been. Ron had done a good job of trying to convince me otherwise, sticking to me like glue since we left Joyce's hospital room. He'd been tracking down his own family tree, with all his beautiful, mixed-up branches. I'd encouraged that, and now his stories were all I had. I was left with a corpse of a family: a dead mother, a father I'd never know, and perhaps a sister I wished was no relation.

And yet, Joyce had told me to love Grace.

I was angrier at her for that than anything. There were all the times when she could have easily told me the truth—those hurt too. It might have been better if Joyce had never asked me to come and help with the school at all, if she'd left me in the tower of pain I'd erected. It didn't seem right that I'd climbed down and put myself out there for this.

It's not her you're mad at, Brian. It's ME.

It was true. Not for the first time, I was mad at God. This time, though, I had the sense not to vocalize it, not in the mood I was in. The fear of God was alive and well in me. My questions didn't stop though. Until heaven, I'd never know why God had let it all come to this—evidently then, I'd have what was required for me to understand it all. For now, I was sitting in my car outside of Tender Mercies Church, praying that the pastor would keep his word and be waiting for me. Right now, I couldn't handle another disappointment.

The church had put up their Christmas decorations since my last visit. The décor was simple, garlands of white and gold around a simple wooden cross. On another day I might have smiled at its understated beauty; today, I trudged into the church office with no expression.

The secretary, a graying redhead with a pair of the kindest eyes I'd ever seen, did the smiling for both of us. "Hello, Brian. Go on in. He's waiting."

Brian. It sounded so good to hear that. Since Joyce died, there'd been a rush of calls from old colleagues and false friends—"We're so sorry, Dr. Mayfield"—it was nice to just be Brian. This church felt comfortable to me now, a complete flip from my first visit when I'd been locked out of the sanctuary. Pastor had loosened up on his rules since then, but he was the one thing about the church that still caught me off guard sometimes. I stepped into the pastor's study slowly, not knowing what to expect.

He, on the other hand, knew just who he was dealing with as he waved me in and pointed to a seat right across from him. "Brother Mayfield. Come in."

None of that Brian stuff for him. Good enough. I stopped at the chair he'd indicated, drinking in the vibrant colors in the room before taking a seat. Two red-white-and-blue flags, one American and one Puerto Rican, waved above the pastor's desk. South American art decked the walls. Brazilian worship music seeped from the radio. A prayer shawl from Israel hung on a hook under a vintage Mickey Mouse clock. The smile I'd been lacking emerged. I'd found someone as weird as I was.

Pastor Rodriguez chuckled. "See something you like?"

"All of it."

"Good. Me too." The man leaned over his desk wearing what I called a "Florida shirt," usually worn by old men anywhere south of Orlando. It had a different effect on the pastor though. He actually looked younger in it. "I am sorry to hear about the principal. Dr. Rogers? She was a good woman. I knew her. Is that what you want to talk about? Not that I want to rush you, you understand, just trying to see where we're going."

Everywhere unfortunately. I sucked my teeth. "We can start with that, I guess."

The man of God smiled, his brown eyes shining. "How about we just start at the beginning? You've got the rest of the afternoon."

34

Zeely

The worship Grace and I had shared washed away my grief, leaving only my quiet determination behind. With newfound energy, we shoved Grace's boxes back in their groups—bathroom, kitchen, bedroom. If she insisted on moving again, at least she could be organized about it.

A rasp tightened in my throat. I paused to rub it. Too much singing. I should have stopped myself, but I couldn't. We'd done an entire CD of tracks. Tomorrow would be all lemon juice and whispers.

"You must be all sung out, Zee. I thought Donnie McClurkin was going to show up and add you to his choir." Grace slapped my knee.

"Please. Donnie and 'nem would laugh me out of the place," I said, my voice cracking. "Hand me my purse."

She found it in the kitchen by the stove, where I must have kicked it somehow. That would explain the reason my toe was throbbing. "Here."

I dug into my purse for an envelope and handed it to Grace. "You left this at the hospital."

"Joyce's last wishes. How could I forget? Not that I had enough pulling at me in the land of the living or anything." She pushed it aside. "Thanks anyway. Did you read yours yet?"

"I'm supposed to read mine with you and Brian, remember?" I cleared my throat, but it didn't help much. "You left the hospital before I could read it. Now you're trying to jet out of town. I'm going to have to think of some way to get us all together before you leave."

"Good luck with that." Grace grabbed another box. She seemed thankful that I'd accepted her decision to leave but there was still worry in her voice. She didn't have to worry about me. I'd done what I could to keep all the kiddies together. Playtime was over. All I wanted was to do what Joyce asked and then she and Brian could move to Mars if they wanted to.

"Come on. It's what Joyce wanted. One last time? For me?"

Grace held her head as if it was pounding to the beat of one of the songs we'd listened to earlier. We both knew that if she saw Brian again, there'd never be one last time.

She was blushing just thinking about it. "I can't."

"You mean you won't," I whispered.

"Pretty much."

There was no sense in fighting about it. If I were close enough to Ron right now to smell his motor oil and hot sauce, let alone that Cinnamon Binaca Blast . . . it would be all over. Grace and Brian had it just as bad. They just moved a lot faster than Ron and I had.

As if reading my mind, Grace asked, "Is Ron going to do the funeral?"

I nodded. "It'll be hard, but he'll do it. I'm pretty sure. He could never tell Joyce no when she was alive. I doubt he'd start now."

Must be nice, always doing the right thing.

Grace agreed. "He's a real saint. When he preached at Mount Olive, he had me mopping up the floor."

Hmph. He'd had me mopping up the floor a time or two. And it wasn't at church.

"Ron isn't perfect. We all mess up. We got one thing right though." I stood and stretched. All of my body was starting to hurt. "I don't know if you heard with everything that happened with Joyce, but the kids passed the proficiency."

"All of them?" She squeezed her eyes shut.

Thank God.

"Yes. It's not official of course. It'll be a while before we have it on paper, but I have a friend who has a friend on the inquiry committee. Almost all of them passed. In all subjects."

I smiled, and then frowned. "All except Sean."

"He'll be fine. He can get his GED in there—"

"It's not the same. You know it isn't." Nothing would be. Not ever.

I sighed. "Everything is so much the same it's sad. No matter how much shooting and dying and foolishness goes on in this crazy little town, some things never change. Like school on Monday. Do you really think you're just going to pack up that raggedy car of yours, ride off into the sunset, and show up for work on time next week? I mean really, what are you going to do?"

"The same thing you're going to do when Jerry gets out of the hospital and when Ron gets married." Grace unscrewed a candle-holder from the wall.

I stared at the floor. "I don't know what I'll do then."

"Exactly."

35

Brian

"That's some story, Brother Brian." Pastor Rodriguez leaned back in his chair.

I rested back too, exhausted by the tale. And I'd only told the half of it. The pastor didn't have all afternoon for my drama and neither did I. "So what should I do?"

"About what?"

"About me. About Grace. I've been trying like crazy to find Reverend Wilkins and settle this, but he's dropped off the earth since Joyce died. The guy's been stuck in that church for thirty years and the one time I need him, he vanishes. Can you believe that?" I forgot myself and propped myself up on an elbow on the pastor's desk. He didn't say anything, but I straightened up anyway.

"Is that why you came to me, because you couldn't find Pastor Wilkins?"

Warmth flushed my face. "No. I chose you from the start. Rev. and I know each other too well."

The pastor nodded. "Impartiality is always good. I don't mind playing second fiddle to Reverend Wilkins."

I stiffened. "You know him?"

"I know him well. In some ways. We have lunch once a week. He has much to teach me about loving God and loving people."

"I didn't mean to tell you his business. I didn't think you knew him . . ." The same problem. I never stopped to think. I barreled into things and couldn't understand why they kept exploding in my face.

"You haven't betrayed any confidences."

I stared across the desk, trying to read the pastor's eyes, the intentional tone he'd just used. What did that mean? How well did this guy know Zeely's father? I wasn't sure I wanted to know. "Well, enough about Rev. I'm trying to figure out the next step for me. What do you think I should do?"

Pastor Rodriguez leaned forward. "You found your mother. The information you need to clear things up with Grace is unavailable, so you can't move on that."

"You make it sound so neat and clean. What's left?"

"What's always left, the main thing. Forgiveness. You need to make a trip to the jail."

I should have seen this coming. Several times since the incident with Malachi, I'd considered visiting him at the jail. Each time I'd decided against it, not sure if I could trust myself. Sometimes the ambassadors of Christ could do more damage than good. I'd been on the other side of that and didn't want to be responsible for being the guy who beat somebody down with a Bible out at the jail. Still, it showed me that Pastor Rodriguez was just who he represented himself to be, a real man of God. Those meals with Reverend Wilkins must have been potent.

"A visit to Mal, huh? Is that what you mean? The Reverend said that too. I guess I'll do it sometime, but I'm not ready yet. I know that for sure. It's going to take a lot more of your sermons before

I can face him and keep my composure. We could have all ended up dead . . ."

The man across the desk shook his head. "You're getting ahead of me. It's not Malachi that I was referring to at all. It's Lottie—Charlotte Wells. That's who you need to see."

36

Grace

Elect Jesus king of your heart.

I stared at the bumper sticker on the back of the van in front of me, turning away before the driver looked in her mirror and caught me staring. The traffic light flickered red and everything went still, leaving me alone to choose anew my government—King Jesus. I'd done that, I thought, for a very long time and wasn't quite sure about the results. At least not now anyway. I reached for the radio dial, wishing for any distraction from the quiet. At the last minute, I pulled my hand back to the steering wheel.

You are altogether beautiful, my darling. There is no blemish in you.

My shaky grip let the steering wheel pass quickly through my fingers. A deep breath and lifting my foot off the gas some slowed things down.

On the outside anyway.

On the inside, things were going a mile a minute. Words and phrases that explained the way I'd felt, the way I still felt now.

Stained. Torn up. Spit out.

When the next light blinked yellow, I drove ahead, slipping through just as it turned red. Tears threatened at the corners of my eyes, but I ignored them. What difference did another tear make now? I'd woken up aching after another long night with Zeely, but then it had been a good pain. Until now.

Testimony scrolled by, barren trees, sad-eyed houses. Staircases steep and unforgiving. Though she'd been quick to forgive, I'd said things to Zeely that I hadn't meant, hurt her because I was hurting. No matter how many songs she sang or how many dances I danced, those words were out there, hanging between us.

Worse yet, there was Brian. I'd felt so strong last night. So sure. But now when I reached for the light inside me, the joy, it seemed as if ashes sifted through my hands. I drove on, mentally packing my bathroom as I drove. Had I labeled the hair products box? Those boxes were the only things in my control right now. Everything else was just . . . too much.

I will go my way to the mountain of myrrh and to the hill of frankincense.

My face twitched in the mirror. The mountain of myrrh? Myrrh Mountain condos was where I lived, where I was trying to get away from. There was no way I could stay in Testimony. Surely God wouldn't require that, not after all I'd been through.

How beautiful is your love, my sister, my bride . . .

The road blurred in front of me. Whose sister? Whose bride? Brian's? How cruel. I'd never be anyone's bride again.

A horn blared behind me. I swerved back into my lane, scanning the horizon for a place to pull over, to have the breakdown threatening for the past few blocks. Snow hit the window, melting on impact. An exit sign emerged from the swirl of white coming at me: *Testimony Correctional Center, 5 mi.*

Five miles. Five miles and then I could pull over and lose my mind.

37

Brian

Lottie picked up the phone, her expression as hard as the last time I'd seen her—when she'd leveled a gun at me. "I'm surprised to see you," she said.

I'm surprised to see me too, I thought.

Under her uncaring façade, I saw something in her eyes, something tired and vulnerable, something I couldn't ever remember seeing in her before. And yet, it looked familiar. I stared across at her faded prison uniform and the short hair sticking out from her head in soft curls. That was new too. Near her ear there was a thin spot, almost bald and the size of dime. Though she tried to cradle her head in her hand to hide it, it was hard to conceal.

I sighed, wondering how things might have been different if I'd ever seen this woman instead of the wigged and wicked woman she'd shown me before. Maybe it wouldn't have mattered, but I felt sorry for both of us as I considered it. I pressed the phone to my ear, now wishing that the glass wasn't between us. "I'm surprised to be here myself."

She nodded in understanding as if she knew that it'd taken God

Himself to get me here. Her words confirmed both our suspicions. "The Reverend came by. Prayed with me. He said you'd be by sometime. I didn't believe him."

"Wilkins? How'd the old man figure that?" I forced back a smile. That preacher would have me visiting everyone in the building if it were up to him. Maybe I'd check on Sean while I was here. Mal too.

Maybe not.

Lottie shrugged, tapping her chipped nails on the table. I tried not to think about how they might have been broken. They looked like what she'd been but I'd been unable or unwilling to see: well-painted but damaged. She coiled the cord of the phone around her fingertip. "The preacher said he had a feeling. A dream or something. You know how they are, them church folks. Joyce too."

"Uh huh." I felt my chest flex against my shirt. Joyce. My mother. I couldn't even hear her name without reaction. Sometimes I smiled. Other times, I wanted to scream . . . Like now, realizing that Lottie probably didn't know that Joyce had passed and that I would be the one who had to tell her. It shouldn't have been a big deal, but somehow it was. Hearing the words would make it even more final. I tried to think of some way to put it delicately, but Lottie asked about Joyce before I could come up with something.

"How's she doing? Any better?"

"She's dead."

Nice, man. Real nice.

Lottie slammed back against the metal chair. "And Jerry?"

"He'll pull through." At the mention of Jerry, I sucked my teeth. Here I was starting to feel sorry for Lottie, when she was the one who'd started this whole madness. She looked relieved at the news about Jerry, probably because she wouldn't be charged with murder.

Under her relief though was a half smile, a mocking sort of grin that meant she'd gotten away with it all.

I shouldn't have come.

As quickly as the smile appeared it faded. A look of remorse took its place. Another first. "I'm sorry." She drummed her stubs on the table again. "Really sorry. About everything. I don't know how things went this far." She lowered her head.

I raised mine. Did she apologize?

As if she'd heard my thought, Lottie went on. "I apologize for shooting at you. For charging you with sexual harassment. I'm sorry for everything."

I stared at her.

Her breathing, deep and ragged, was the only sound on the phone. After what seemed like forever, she finally spoke. "Aren't you going to say something?"

"Like what? I want to say I'm sorry too, but I don't know what I did. I don't know why you—you—hate me so much."

Lottie closed her eyes. "Hate you? Is that what you think? I guess I do. Did. But I love—loved you too."

Wow. Now we were getting somewhere, but I wasn't sure if it was somewhere I wanted to go. Maybe the glass was a good thing after all. "But why, Lot? How can you just love somebody you barely know? I'm just . . ." I made a fist and let it go. I could feel the vein in my arm twitch. If I didn't calm down, the one on my head would be popping next. I'd trained for conflict resolution and studied relationships most of my life, but when it came to my own relationships, I struggled to find the right words. I'd come here for resolution, but if I wasn't careful, I'd be starting another problem.

Lord, I'm just trying to get some understanding.

Lottie shifted in her chair. "You'll never understand."

"Probably not." She was really starting to scare me the way she seemed to know what I was thinking, but I couldn't let her know that. It was my turn to play hard.

Lottie frowned at me in a way that made me feel ashamed. For what, I had no idea.

"Why did you even come?" she asked. "To make yourself feel better? I don't need your pity."

I bit the inside of my cheek and forced my fists open. I'd come here because my pastor told me to, because it seemed like something God wanted too. "Obviously a bad idea. My pastor suggested it—"

"So you're a choirboy now? It fits. You've always been high and mighty," she sneered. "If only people really knew . . ."

This was the Lottie I was used to. Having her act like her usual obnoxious self would make leaving easier. I stood. There was trouble enough going around. I shouldn't have come looking for more. "I don't know how you got the idea from a few dates that you've always known me. You haven't. But I guess I should expect that from you, since you say Mal is your brother. If that's true, craziness runs in the family."

"At least I've got a family."

I waved for the guard. "Let them come visit you then."

Lottie smiled, stretching her lips beyond their limits—as though she held a bullet between her teeth and this time she wouldn't miss. I braced myself.

"My family does visit. Our son, Quinn, is on his way here now."

"Wait!" I shook my head as the guard pulled Lottie away. I banged the glass.

The man bit his toothpick in half. "Do you want her or don't ya?"

"I want her!"

The man shrugged and dumped Lottie back into her seat.

I motioned for her to pick up the phone.

She laughed.

I shook my head. No. It couldn't be. She'd toyed with me enough. To say something that crazy, she'd have to explain.

Lottie didn't budge. Instead, she pried the remaining polish from her nails, looking up at me now and then.

I tucked the phone between my ear and my shoulder and closed my eyes.

Lord, give me a sound mind. Help me make sense of this.

My mind struggled to sort through the facts. Quinn was Lottie's son. She was a few years younger than me, but . . . Impossible. I hadn't crossed that bridge until much later. Not to mention that I'd just met her last year. Or was it the beginning of this year? This seemed to be the longest year of my life, like a decade all at once. I hadn't had a year like this since—

She tapped the glass. "I spent the night there sometimes. I stayed in the back room out of the way. Invisible. Nobody noticed me. Except you. You called me Annie Mae, like the Natalie Cole song."

I dropped the receiver. My mind filled with a girl, all legs and sad eyes, hiding in the back of Mal's house. When I'd asked about her, Mal said she was a cousin. She came and went at random, never saying a word.

One day, when she ran down the hall back to her room, I'd stopped her. "What's your name?"

She stared at the floor. "Anne."

Thinking of Joyce, I raised my chin. And hers. "Anne is too plain for somebody with eyes like yours. How about Annie Mae?"

She nodded and smiled for the first time. "Okay. I like that song." The second time I'd seen her smile, that I remembered anyway, was when she told me to run out the back door and into Joyce's car. If I'd been arrested that day like her brother and the gang I'd been stupid enough to fall in with had planned, my life would have been so different . . . Could it really be her?

A tap sounded against the glass.

I looked up, trying to focus, my mind still lost in the past. Lottie stared out of those same sad eyes, pointing to the phone. "Pick it up."

I took a deep breath. Though I'd begged her to talk to me when I thought that there was no possibility of me being Quinn's father, now I wasn't so sure. I didn't remember anything but hugging that girl, maybe kissing her a few times, but from the time I found out that Eva wasn't my mother and that I was basically a throwaway, it was a drunk-high haze. One night I didn't want to remember. Things I didn't want to know.

Behold I do a new thing.

Cold plastic grazed my ear as I gripped the receiver, trying to find my voice. "I remember you now. But I never—"

"Mal went out with the gang, remember? We played cards. Got drunk . . ."

My head smacked the glass as the memory stabbed at me, then crashed through. Strip poker. She said it'd be fun. We'd show them.

They left us behind.

I had showed them or so I was foolish enough to think. Drank the liquor. Smiled at Annie Mae. She looked sad. Afraid. I apologized. Held her. She kissed me. The liquor burned inside me. She felt even warmer . . .

"No! It was a dream."

Lottie chuckled. "More like a nightmare. Daddy knew he hadn't done it. Not this time anyway. He'd already sent me there once. That's where I met your princess Grace. I lost that first one, but not this one. A boy. This time they took my baby away."

I pulled at my shirt, my jacket, my hair. This could not be

happening. This was what other men did. Irresponsible men. I'd wanted to believe that I was better. Above. To think that all this time, that big, beautiful boy was mine. All this time . . .

Only he wasn't mine, not at all. Biology laid no claim. Someone else nurtured him, loved him, watched his first steps. And yet, it was this boy, my son, who'd brought me back to Jesus, who'd laid me at the foot of the cross. And now, I was there again, digging my nails into my palms and trying not to scream. Everything hurt. Everywhere.

I tried to look up at Lottie, to tell her how sorry I was. Just plain sorry. I tried to, but my head felt so heavy, like it weighed a hundred pounds. This must be what dying felt like. What Joyce had felt like. Joyce. . . . As I pressed my eyes together, thinking of how Joyce forced Quinn on me that first year, how she'd hired Lottie . . .

She knew. She knew everything.

Pain surged in my head as the terrible truth swelled in my heart. I'd hated Quinn's father, the man who'd give away his own flesh and blood.

I was that man.

Somehow, I found the strength to lift my head though my hair still covered my eyes. The phone rested against my ear one last time as I recalled Lottie's eyes when she'd pointed that gun at me. How I wished that Jerry had let her take her best shot.

"You should have killed me," I whispered into the phone.

Her laughter grated against my soul. "I tried."

38

Zeely

I could see him from my car.

Ron could see me too—I could feel it—but he didn't move. He stood at the window of his house, looking down at my car. I didn't have to wonder what he was thinking. We'd played this scene out before, only I'd been the one in the window. He'd been the one in the car.

The only new player in our tragedy was Mindy. I'd hoped she wouldn't be here, but perhaps it was best if she was.

It seemed much colder now than when I'd left home, but I pressed on, face into the wind. Maybe it was my new haircut that left me exposed. Maybe it was my new heart. It was still fresh, just a few hours old—a revived heart, a young heart, a brave heart. Perhaps, maybe even a foolish one. I'd soon find out.

When I pushed the doorbell, I had a moment of hesitation, but at the sounds of Mindy's grating voice, I stood my ground. She was an amazing woman, really. I'd known her before Ron did. Met her at a woman's retreat in Kentucky. She'd make someone a fine wife. Just not Ron.

"Coming!" she screamed again.

Ron, I knew without stepping back to look, was still silent at the window.

The door swung open. "Did you cut it into squares—Oh . . ."

Yeah. Oh. I had a message to deliver, I was far from the pizza man. I was also beyond the pleasantries of asking her to go and get him. I stepped inside. "Hello, Mindy."

I probably should have said that she looked well or asked about the baby she was carrying, but I hadn't come here for her. It had finally dawned on me that the things wrong between Ron and me were Ron and me. Jerry and Mindy had little to do with it except to complicate things further. Whether Ron married Mindy or not was his choice, but tonight I had to get free of some things . . . once and for all.

He heard me on the stairs, but he was still looking out the window when I walked into the spare bedroom that he used for an office. The credits on a movie I knew he hated scrolled across the computer behind him. I guess this had been their date night. Mindy hadn't said much to protest me crashing it.

"Hey," I said, reaching for his shoulder.

I expected Ron to tense, but he relaxed instead and turned to face me with a weary grin.

I swallowed down my desire and smiled back. "I'm sorry for not calling first and for interrupting your . . . date, but I need to talk to you, face-to-face, right now, if possible."

He stopped smiling. "It's not possible."

"What?"

"Zee, what do you want? What else are you going to take from me?"

I was getting mad now. "Let's see, maybe the same things you took from me? My life, my love, my child. That sounds about right."

"Don't go there."

"I must."

"Please."

"It's time." I wanted to take his hand, to talk gentle to him like I'd planned, but I could see this wouldn't be easy.

"Babe? Pizza's here!" Mindy yelled upstairs.

Nope. It wouldn't be easy for any of us.

He rolled his eyes, but I couldn't be sure if it was meant for me or for her. I didn't have time to try to figure it out either.

"You should go," he said, raking a hand through his hair, which was shaggy and sexy all at once.

"Of course I should go, but I won't. I'm tired of trying to love you politely, of giving up on us because it isn't convenient. Whether we're ever together again, I need closure on when we were together. I finally told Grace what happened, and when I did, something inside me broke open. I can feel again, and as much as it hurts, it's good. And I feel you, still part of me, still hurting. I caused a lot of that hurt and I came to say I'm sorry. Can you forgive me for killing our child?"

Ron narrowed his eyes at me like he was seeing someone else, someone he hadn't seen in a very long time. I nodded, understanding how hard it must have been for him all those years, talking to the glass shell of me, what was left after all the lies. It would have been so easy to love him again a long time ago, but I couldn't. I couldn't feel anything but the ache of my empty womb, the hollow of my barren arms. Somehow, in Grace's hearing me, holding me, in the words of those deliverance songs we'd danced and sung, the bars holding me had come undone. My prison of secrets had finally crumpled.

"I forgave you that day, Zee. Right there at the place. I don't know though if I can ever forgive myself. I need you to pray for me."

He knelt down then, right there in front of me and buried his face in my waist, intertwined his fingers in mine. I couldn't move for a moment. How many times had I dreamed this—Ron with his head to my belly trying to hear the heartbeat of a baby long gone?

I heard Mindy on the steps behind us, but I was crying too hard to try to talk to her. The noise stopped and the door closed. I was thankful for that.

"Father God, here we are. You know why we're here, what we did—what I did. Restore Ron. Give him back his joy, his peace. Forgive me for leading both of us toward something that has hurt so much. Thank you for the life you gave us. Help us. Help me. I'm so, so sorry . . ."

Ron let go of my hands and pulled me close. I put my hands around his neck. I kissed the top of his head.

"I am so, so sorry."

"I know," he said. "I know."

He placed a hand across my belly. "Lord, I pray that if it is your will, that you would heal Zeely's womb. That she would once again carry a life inside her. May her every cell be whole and well. May she and her husband J—"

I put my hand across his mouth. I've never interrupted a prayer in my life, but I couldn't allow him to say it. "That's over. Just pray that I can bear spiritual children, that God will allow me to make up for the years I've spent being evil and crazy and try to make a difference in this world."

He ignored me. "May she and her husband be fruitful and multiply, bearing healthy children who will serve you all their lives."

My lip began to tremble. With a simple prayer, he'd done it. As surely as if he'd walked me down the aisle, Ron had given me away.

And now it was my turn.

I sank down to my knees beside him.

"And Lord, bless Ron and—and—his wife with healthy children. Help him to be the good father that I know he will be, in Jesus' name."

The words were few, but they'd exhausted me. I was ashamed that I hadn't been able to bring myself to name Mindy as his wife, not even in a prayer. I'd sometimes been able to talk myself out of my love for him over the years, never mind that my heart stopped every time I saw him. Like now, looking at me with those eyes that hadn't changed since the first day I'd seen him.

I reached out and touched his cheek, cupped his face in my hand. He closed his eyes and turned into my touch. For a moment, we were teenagers again.

For just a moment.

"You have to go now, Zee."

He let my hand fall to my side.

I didn't move. Not right away. I sat there, studying his face. Was he bluffing, like he did when we played Bible Trivia? Did he really want me to go or was I supposed to beg? If so, I couldn't be mad. He'd done more than his share of begging over the years. It was definitely my turn.

He was on his feet now, pulling me up. I stood as the truth sank in. He wasn't kidding. He really wanted me to go. I'd waited too late to come back to life, to tell the truth. Now there was another truth, one that hurt almost as much as the first: Ron didn't love me anymore.

"Let me walk you to the car," he said, fumbling for his slippers.

They were in the hallway. I'd seen them on the way in. I didn't bother to tell him though. I just started walking, running almost—

"Wait!"

Though I tripped down a couple steps and almost broke my neck,

I did not wait. There was nothing left to wait for. There was a time for everything under the sun. This had been our time to mend, but not our time to love. Perhaps I'd known it before I came, but hadn't wanted to accept it.

As I passed Mindy on the way up the stairs, I decided not to accept it. Not tonight anyway. They weren't married yet and God was still on the throne.

I considered going straight home after Ron's, but I didn't want to lose my nerve. There was one more person who I needed to talk to, though he was hard to catch up with these days. My father.

"Daddy? Are you here?"

I hadn't used my key to the church in a few months and was shocked to see that Daddy hadn't changed any of the locks or asked for the keys back. He scared me sometimes, the way he just didn't worry about things like that, but that was just him. The church had looked so dim when I pulled up that I'd almost left, but I saw his car parked in the back next to the door so he was in here somewhere.

"Daddy?"

Music began to play in the choir room. The sound chilled my bones. Daddy's arthritis had long since stopped him from playing, but he hadn't lost any of his skill. Though I knew each note caused him pain, I didn't want it to end. And so, I joined him at the piano and began to sing.

"Can't nobody do me like Jesus. Can't nobody do me like the Lord."

Daddy nodded. "Again. This time like you mean it."

That was the last thing I remember him saying before I slipped off into a medley of spirituals and hymns from my childhood. So many of the songs I thought I'd forgotten, but I guess thirty-plus years of choir practice is nothing to throw away.

I hit a note in "Jesus, You're the Center of My Joy" that brought a tear to my daddy's eyes. He looked over at me and sighed.

"You know how old you were the first time you sang that?"

I had no idea. "Six?" That sounded about right, though it seemed I'd always been singing at Mount Olive.

"Four. Four years old. People thought we were crazy and trying to get you on the gospel circuit. We really had nothing to do with it though. Your mother used to take you to choir practice with her, but neither of us realized that you were memorizing the songs. One night after dinner, you grabbed a hairbrush and sang the whole song through, not missing a word. The next Sunday, I went against your mother's wishes and asked the choir director to give you a solo and the rest is history."

Isn't it though?

My father's story startled me. I wondered, not for the first time, what else he was hiding. He was like a deep, amazing cavern with treasure that couldn't be reached and every now and then a diamond flies out to remind you what's in there.

"Speaking of history, Daddy, I need to talk to you about something. Something that happened a long time ago. Something I never told you."

His fingers went still on the piano. He pulled his hands into his lap. "Go on."

"I went against you, Daddy. Against what you and Mama taught me. I had sex with Ron. The summer after I graduated from high school."

He nodded. "When you were sneaking out the window? I remember."

My breathing became shallow. "You knew."

241

"Not at first, but I'm a pastor. People make it their business to let me know what's going wrong in my house, in my life."

"Why didn't you say something?"

"I was going to, but when I knew you were heading to school, I prayed on it daily, and when you got home that Christmas, well, I was going to talk to you and Ron together, encourage you to let me marry you then. He'd already asked me for your hand, but that was before . . ."

My throat went dry. "Did Mama know?"

"I think so, though she never would admit it to me. Every time I tried to talk about you to her, she changed the subject. We had other issues then. Other secrets. She was sick and trying to hide that from me."

Umph. "Well, I'm sorry, Daddy. For everything. There was more to it. I got pregnant."

He looked away from me for a moment, then reached for my hand.

"I know," he said softly. "I know."

I put my head on his shoulder. "I didn't know what to do. The Bishop's daughter said—"

"Hush now. Don't upset yourself over it. I forgive you. I do wish you'd come to me. It could have been different. So much different. It's been hard to watch you hurting all these years."

"Why didn't you say something?" I said, somewhere between a whisper and a sob.

He hugged my shoulder. "It wasn't mine to say, baby. Maybe I was afraid that if I rattled your skeletons too hard, I might stir up a few of my own."

I listened for the laughter that always followed my father's jokes.

It never came.

39

Ron

Everything in my body hurt, like I'd been in a fight. And maybe I had been. To hear Mindy tell it, it was a fight I—we—could never win.

"Will you ever stop loving her?" she said softly as we ate cold pizza in my dark living room.

It was a stupid question, one that deserved an equally stupid answer.

"Will you ever stop loving him?" I asked, lacking my usual regret when sarcasm got the best of me.

"Touché." Mindy slammed her pizza crust down into the box and rolled away from me.

"Hey, I'm sorry."

"I'm not," she said. "I'm glad. I can't do this anymore. You don't love me. You never will. You love my kid and I appreciate that. Without you, I know I'd have had that abortion, and I know now that I would have regretted it. But if I let you marry me, I'm going to regret that too. She came for you tonight. Don't you get that?"

I did get it. And it scared me to death. "She doesn't really want me. She just doesn't want you to have me. We do this. It's a sick game but we do it. I can't do it anymore."

Mindy turned on the light. I closed one eye.

"She wasn't playing a game tonight, Ron. I'm a woman. I know. You and I can keep playing house and ordering pizza until Jesus comes, but it's not real. It'll never be as real as what I walked in on tonight."

"We were praying."

She stood. "Uh huh. If more people prayed like that, there'd be a lot more babies and a lot less divorce. You all were about five minutes from going at it right there on the floor."

In my dreams.

Wow. Had I just thought that? "You know what? I don't know if anything will ever happen again for me and Zeely, but you're right about one thing: it's not fair to play house with you. Marriage is special. It's real. I've tried to make it suit my purpose, first by trying to get its benefits before making the commitment and now by using it to help out a friend. Either way, it's wrong. I'm sorry."

Mindy turned and started up the stairs. I trailed behind her. She headed for the bathroom, where she grabbed her toothbrush and a handful of hair scrunchies next to the sink. "You can send me the rest."

I held my breath. "But . . . the invitations. Your father."

"All mine to deal with. I'll handle it. You have to admit those were some cute invitations though. Not exactly true, but definitely cute."

"Definitely." I had to laugh. Mindy and I were getting along better now than we had in the past year.

"Again, I'm still in for the labor classes, the delivery—"

"I know," she said. "We'll see. I think it's time for me to trust God a little more and men a little less. If this whole thing has taught me anything, it's that I'm stronger—that God is stronger—than I ever thought."

So true.

She was downing the stairs now, shoving things into her purse as she went.

I grabbed my house shoes from the hall and followed her. "I'm not God to be sure, but I'm here if you need me. Seriously."

"I know," she said. "I'm hoping you might be busy making babies of your own by then." She pulled her key off the ring and dropped it into the basket next to my door. "You sure prayed about it enough."

So she'd heard it all. I shrugged. "I just got caught up in the moment. It's hard to explain . . ."

Mindy smiled before disappearing through the door. "Not really. My gym teacher broke it down pretty well in fourth grade. See ya."

By the time I got my legs to move and got out the door, she was already in her car and backing out my drive. She seemed in a hurry to get away and I couldn't blame her. Living a lie is a draining, tiring thing.

Back inside the house, I sat for a few minutes staring blankly before I cleared out all the pizza boxes and packed up Mindy's wretched collection of low-budget DVDs. I'd go and get a mess of greens tomorrow and clean them. It should have been more complicated, more painful than this, but it wasn't. Things wouldn't probably kick in until Mindy had the baby.

Then, I'd be hurting.

I was still pondering that when the doorbell rang again. I didn't answer it at first. Whatever Mindy forgot, she could get tomorrow. Right now, I just needed to be alone, to think. Since Joyce died, things had stopped making sense for a while, and then there were just the routines of going to work and spending time with Mindy. And now there was the doorbell, and whoever was pressing it wasn't going to give up.

So I gave in.

"What'd you forget?" I asked before identifying my visitor.

"Everything," Zeely said, standing there in the cold with a bag of groceries. "I forgot everything, but it's all coming back to me."

I stepped out onto the porch, into the snow, and gathered her into my arms and carried her inside.

I had questions but I didn't ask them. Not with words anyway.

As night gave way to day, Zeely answered those questions, but not just with words.

She danced for me. Sang to me. Prayed for me. Cooked for me. It seemed like all my best dreams happening at once, but I didn't dare interrupt to be sure it was real. Real or not, I needed it. I wanted it.

I wanted other things too, but I wasn't a boy anymore. I knew how much I had to lose and how long I had waited. Nothing, not even my own hormones, would ruin this. Drinking in her scent though, I knew it wouldn't be easy. When she woke up in my arms and smiled before opening her eyes, another question was answered too.

"Will you marry me?" I asked in the twilight of morning.

"Yes," she answered in one breath before kissing the tip of my nose.

"When?" I said, running my hands through her hair for the first time in forever and loving it.

"Now."

"Now?"

"Now."

"We need a license. A preacher—"

Zeely smiled at me. "Daddy is scheduled to meet us at the courthouse when it opens. Now go back to sleep. You'll need your energy later on."

I closed my eyes. If this was a dream, I didn't ever want to wake up.

40

Grace

I made it to the prison. I wheeled through the gate and into the first parking space before sprawling out on the front seat. There wasn't much room, but I was glad for the containment. Swirls of color burst beneath my eyelids as I let myself fall down, down, down. I waited for the crash at the bottom.

It never came.

After what seemed like forever—actually it was more like five minutes—I sat up, confused. I'd expected to be hysterical, but there was nothing. No crying. No kicking. Not even one scream.

I should have been glad, but instead I was a little let down. I knew better than to get out of the car though. In the few minutes since I'd pulled up, the snow had blanketed the car in a bright sheet of white. I found a quilt in the backseat and draped it over myself. If I was going to lose my mind, at least I could be comfortable. I blinked at the white everywhere, the purity.

You are altogether beautiful, my darling, and there is no blemish in you.

I covered my face with my hands, but the snow's radiance invaded the darkness beneath my eyelids. Light streamed all around, embracing me. Hiding me. I took my hands away from my face but didn't open my eyes.

For in the day of trouble He will conceal me in His tabernacle; in the secret place of His tent He will hide me; He will lift me up on a rock.

I raised my palms and opened my eyes, accepting that there would be no darkness here. Even though I couldn't see any light, any hope, he'd brought enough of both to go around. This Jesus who I'd sung about, who I danced for, this God who knew all my secrets and loved me anyway . . . He was here.

My voice came out softly, half singing, half praying in the language of heaven. I couldn't remember the last time I'd said anything. All day had been silence it seemed. Mourning.

For those who grieve in Zion—to bestow on them a crown of beauty instead of ashes . . .

There wasn't room inside the car, but I danced the best I could, arching my back, twining my hands. From the ashes of Joyce's death, my rape so many years ago, and my giving away the child who resulted from it, God had given me back this beauty, this access to the secret place.

The oil of gladness instead of mourning . . .

My dancing stopped then. My hands went still. Only the tears, happy tears, moved down my face as I felt a warmth, colored gold and scented with cinnamon, pour through the wounds and tears, the breaches and broken places inside me. A laugh started deep in my belly as God's healing continued to flow. My shoulders rose and fell as the glad oil I'd been missing came back to me. Exhausted, I stretched out again on the front seat of the car, thinking surely God was done.

And a garment of praise instead of a spirit of despair.

My limbs came undone, arms here and there, feet out of my shoes . . . In the parking lot of the prison where both my son and the rapist who'd fathered him were being held, God came to me and restored the virginal robes that had been ripped from me. In my mind, I stood in a cloud of incense, arms extended as my new clothes, white but spun with gold and dipped in blood, were lowered over my head. In the light, the hem first and then all of it became other colors: blue, green, orange, pink . . . so many that I soon realized they weren't colors at all, but jewels.

I opened my eyes, wiped my tears, unable to bear, to see, any more.

They will be called oaks of righteousness, a planting of the LORD for the display of his splendor.

Trees? Plants? I thought through the Bible verses in my mind: the tree planted in Psalm 1 to—

My muscles tightened as I made the connection. I'd made many baby shower gifts from the verse: birthstones for girls and for the boys? Plants. This was about my son. Psalm 144:12, the verse I'd painted and stitched many times confirmed it:

Then our sons in their youth will be like well-nurtured plants . . .

The practical part of me, the me that had changed her name to Grace and done what she had to do to make it, wanted to know just how that was going to work. My son was in jail and this wasn't his first charge with a gun. On the night I'd met him, he'd been part of a gang initiation that ended with the school cafeteria getting shot up. No judge was going to look at Sean and see a plant, an oak of righteousness. None of them would know how he could sing or that he had a daughter and had been finally coming around. Grace, my rational self, wanted to know how exactly those ashes were going to be made into a beautiful tree.

Diana, however, the fifteen-year-old dancer who'd set out one evening to take the bus to a dance recital and lost everything instead, had no questions. Diana knew that there were times and spaces where nothing made sense, where people could look at something and call it dead. Done. Over.

Diana knew that nothing is ever over until God says it is and that he doesn't keep time like we do. I folded my hands and watched more snow fall on the windshield, turning the transparent light into a quiet darkness.

I reached into the backseat for the blankets I kept in the car in case of emergency and pulled them around me. As I closed my eyes, I realized what God had made for me tonight.

A fortress.

41

Brian

"Wells!"

I snapped out of my daze as the guard called Lottie's name. Our time was up, I guess. I didn't know whether to run and thank him or insist on more time. There didn't seem to be much point in that. There weren't any words to fix what I'd done.

The guard frowned as Lottie held the phone to her ear one last time. "You got another visitor, Wells. Make it quick. This ain't a hotel."

Lottie and I stared at one another through the glass. Questions gleamed in her eyes. I swallowed hard, wondering what else she wanted to know. I held the phone but dreaded saying anything. Any words I could offer seemed like an insult.

"Goodbye. I'll come back again. We'll talk more."

She shrugged. "We won't."

She was probably right. I put the phone down and tried to get up, but my balance was off. There was someone else on my mind, someone I wondered if I'd ever be able to face again. On my feet now, I shot off another quick and rambling prayer.

Lord, let him somehow find a way to forgive me. Let me find a way to forgive myself.

"Doc?"

I turned slowly, both pained and pleased at the sound of Quinn's voice. The boy I'd so admired. The son I'd deserted.

"Hey," I said, jamming my hands into my pockets instead of reaching out for our usual handshake.

"I thought that was your car. Surprised to see you over here. I thought you were on the men's side seeing Sean with Miss O. Her car's out there too."

Grace was here too? This was a regular ghetto family reunion, everybody visiting at the jail.

How wonderful.

Despite my hands being jammed into my pockets, Quinn reached around and hugged me. "Thanks for coming to see her. I know it wasn't easy. I'm proud of you," he said.

"Th-thanks. I'm proud of you. Always." I cleared my throat and stepped aside so he could sit down. As soon as he did, I would be gone, running out of here for dear life: both mine and his.

Lottie sagged behind the glass, staring past the both of us as Quinn came in.

Quinn turned back to me. "What's wrong with you two? Are you sad about Dr. Rogers dying? I mean I am too. It hasn't fully hit me yet, but at least we knew that she was sick . . ."

Neither of us even attempted to answer.

The boy leaned over the counter. He slid the phone to his ear. "That bad?"

Lottie set the phone down in front of her and pointed to me.

Quinn stared at me. "So it's like that?" he asked.

A snorting sound came out of me. "Worse," I said. "Have a seat."

42

Grace

"Create in me a clean heart, O God. And renew a right spirit within me."

I woke with those words on my lips just in time for a call from Brian.

"Pick up," he said into the machine. "For real. Ron and Zeely are getting married. Reverend Wilkins called me a minute ago. He thought they'd need us. I haven't had the best night myself but I'll drop by and scoop you—"

"No need." I snatched up the phone then, knowing how quick Brian could be. I didn't want to look up and see him outside. I peeked out my blinds.

Too late.

This would be a good time for some of that glad oil to come back . . .

I smiled, knowing that regardless of who was outside my door, joy was still with me. God's Spirit had descended upon me so sweetly, but so violently too, crashing through all my excuses.

God showed me His heart. And mine. My true spirit. Even now,

I could hear music that sounded like myrrh smells—Zeely's wedding music.

"Grace? Are you there?"

I was . . . and I wasn't. "Yep. There's someone on the other line. Come on in. It's going to be a minute."

"You sure?"

I wasn't. "Nope, but come in anyway. I'm clicking over." I pressed the button to switch to the call waiting. "Hello?"

"Mrs. Okoye?"

It was Miss, but whatever. "Yes?"

"This is Dan Chambers from Soul Tree records. We've been trying to reach Sean . . ." Papers shuffled at the other end.

"McKnight?"

"That's it. The recording studio gave us your name as the person who rented the time for the demo we were sent? Well, if you could, tell Sean to give us a call. We've got a contract for him."

In my mind, I saw seeds breaking through ground, pressing skyward. Oaks of righteousness.

When I hung up, Brian was at my door, beautiful and breathless.

"Come on, girl. You look fine. You need help getting ready?"

If he gave me the help I needed, we'd all be in trouble. "No, just—"

Brian's eyes went wide and flashed an angry shade of green. "You were going to . . . leave? Just like that?"

The boxes. I'd forgotten all about the boxes.

I reached for him. "I can't stay. I'll keep teaching, but that's all I can take."

Brian slammed his keys on the table before straightening his sweater and walking away. "Save me a spot on the runaway train," he said.

"I will, but not yet. This isn't about us. It's about them. They've got a few years on us in the drama department. Let's hold it together for today. For our friends."

Brian nodded. "I can do that," he said, sliding down onto a box of books. "Get your coat."

43

Zeely

We saw Marie walking and offered her a ride. When she got into the car, I started to cry. All my could-haves went away. There would always be some regret, some sorrow over the winding road our love had taken, but not now. Now, there was only joy as Ron's mother reached for me with her liver-spotted hand.

"There she is. The songbird."

She didn't say anything else as we neared the courthouse, but she was humming something I couldn't make out.

When we got there, Ron talked to her for a while, explained what was going on.

"Well, I know that this is kind of spur of the moment, Mom. At the same time, it really isn't. You know I've loved Zeely a long time."

Marie humored him and acted as though he had really let her in on a secret. When his back was turned, she winked at me.

"Your daddy called the shelter and left a message. I didn't figure on getting a ride from the bride and groom, but I was going to get here somehow."

I had to laugh. My daddy, who had never done a courthouse wedding in his life—he didn't believe in such things—had called the homeless shelter to leave a message for my soon-to-be husband's homeless mother. And I loved him for it.

I did not love him for all the people lining the halls of the courthouse while Ron and I tried to get our documents in order for our marriage license. Brian had to run to Ron's house to find his passport and Grace went to my place to get the original copy of my birth certificate, but in the end, we got the license.

I wore a rumpled pair of jeans, something I'd never been seen outside in, much less get married in, but for once, I didn't care. Or maybe I just cared about something else more.

"I'm sorry you don't have a dress," Ron whispered into my hair. "Maybe we should—"

"No. We've waited long enough. I have plenty of dresses. We can exchange vows again on some anniversary. I can't wait any longer."

Ron's shoulders relaxed. "Me either. Thank you. Thank you so much."

"Don't thank me yet," I said, not caring if anybody heard. "Tonight, you can thank me." I raised my voice. "Make it quick, Daddy."

My father's voice sounded strong and full, like when he used to baptize in the river when we were young.

"We come here to witness the love and commitment of Zeely Elizabeth Wilkins and Ronald Jenkins to God and to each other. Zeely, do you promise to love, honor, and help this man as long as you both shall live?"

We were close now, close enough to kiss, but I forced myself not to. Not yet. We had to wait for something.

"I do."

"And you, Ronald—"

Ron, however, didn't make it. "I do! Love, protect, honor, pray for . . . Forever. All of it forever."

I kissed him then, though I hadn't meant to. Kissed him so hard that I almost fell down the courthouse steps. I didn't fall though, because Ron caught me as he repeated the vows my father recited. In all the faces witnessing this, two stood out: Grace and Brian. She blew me a kiss. He gave a nod. Only when I got into the car did I realize they were holding hands.

To accomplish an impossible task—bringing two crazy people together—it required an equally impossible event. My wedding.

44

Brian

I'd always secretly hoped that Ron would get his day. Knowing Zeely, I'd thought it would be all lace and long-winded prayers. A courthouse wedding? It sounded more like something I would do. And yet, Zeely looked so happy. Ron too. Their lives were finally coming together . . . just as mine was falling apart.

Grace and I had scrambled to help them get everything together and then took our places near the front where amazingly, she let me hold her hand. Quinn stood a few paces behind, out of my sight, but I knew he was there. I could smell the vetiver cologne I'd given him last Christmas. He'd seen me but hadn't said anything. That was okay. I was tired of talking and I'm sure he was worn out from listening. I just wanted to be sure he was okay.

When the crowd broke up and people started to head home, I motioned for Quinn to follow me. "Come on. I'll take you home."

The boy shook his head. "My mom is on her way."

His mom. The woman who raised him, loved him, fed him . . . He had a father too. A family. And there was no room, no need for me in it.

Maybe we shouldn't have told him at all.

Maybe telling Quinn everything had been more about my pride than what he needed. In the light of day, with Grace's hand on mine, I could see that. I just didn't want to lie to him like so many others had lied to me about my parents. I could see now just a glimpse of what Joyce had gone through when she decided I was better off where I was. "Your mom? I remember her. Nice lady."

Quinn smiled. "Yeah. She is. She's been through a lot with me. I guess she's about to go through some more."

"I'm sorr—"

He shot me a look as we pushed through a snow bank to my car. He'd had apologies enough. Grace was distracted, still trying to shout things to Zeely as the new couple pulled out of the parking lot.

"This is confusing and I wish it wasn't. Your mother is probably going to find this really hard to believe." Or so I hoped. In any other situation, I would have volunteered to talk to her for him, but not this time. He didn't look like he wanted me to either.

"Actually, I don't think she'll be shocked at all. When she met you freshman year, she freaked out all the way home. She kept asking me if you were my father or if I thought you could be. I said I didn't know, but I was pretty sure that you weren't. She even talked to the social worker on my case."

My turn to be shocked. "Why? I mean we don't really look alike . . ."

Quinn rolled his eyes at me.

Grace squinted at me. Oh well. I'd planned to tell her later.

"He's my son. Long story."

She blinked a few times and then smiled before leaning over to give Quinn a kiss on the cheek. This woman was like a rubber band. She'd go zigzag on you, but she always snapped back. And just in time. "Of course," she said softly. "That makes perfect sense."

It was my turn to smile. "Okay, well, I guess I didn't see it. Not until now. It was what's inside you—who you are—that I always felt a kinship to."

"Yeah well, Mom mentioned that too. She gave up on the dad theory, but she still thinks there's some tie between us. My dad got a little sick of the whole thing. This is going to take some getting used to for him."

For all of us.

The boy blew out an icy breath. "I guess there's really nobody to blame considering the circumstances, but I have to be honest, I'm madder at you than her. I don't know why, maybe because I know how smart you are. When Pastor started teaching on forgiveness, he must have known something." He stared at the ground. "I wasn't expecting this."

"Me either." I unlocked the car and pleaded with Grace with my eyes. The part about Lottie was the part I was going to have to take my time with. How do you explain that the crazy woman who tried to kill us all is the mother of your only child? "Let's talk in here. You don't have to freeze while you wait for your mother."

Quinn kicked a drift of snow off the curb. He looked around before getting in the car where I immediately cranked up the heat.

"If you two want to be alone, I can go in the courthouse for a while," Grace said. "I have my phone, Brian."

That would be great. "Thanks—"

"That's okay," Quinn said. "I think we should get it all out now since it's pretty obvious you're probably going to be my stepmom, so you might as well stay."

He was definitely my kid.

Grace offered him a peppermint, which made us all laugh. She was such a teacher sometimes. "Wasn't the wedding beautiful?" she said.

We both stared at her for a moment before Quinn took the peppermint and went back to the subject at hand. "It's not like I'm disappointed, you know? I'm not." He chuckled. "This is my dream actually, but now that it's come true, I'm mad . . . I never would have expected that, but I am. Maybe if I'd known from the beginning. Now it just seems frustrating. I need some time . . ."

I nodded, remembering how I'd felt finding out about Joyce on her deathbed. She'd been there all the time, but if only I'd known. So much could have been different. Or at least I'd like to think so. "We'll all need some time, Quinn. Lot's of it. I know you have a family. For now, we can just be friends. Like we were before."

Quinn didn't look convinced. "It won't be the same. We're more than friends now."

"Biologically. Anything beyond that is up to you." I flipped my lights at his mother's minivan, circling the parking lot for the second time. She pulled toward us and blew her horn. "It's also up to your parents."

"Quinn! That you in there?"

"I'm here." He opened the door and got out of the car, unfolding his long arms and legs. He looked relieved to see his mother. I was too. "We'll talk later, Doc. Right now I've got more explaining to do. Mom didn't really want me at the prison yesterday. She wasn't too crazy about this wedding thing either. She says that all my teachers have gone crazy."

She had a point. I wasn't even sure that I should be here either.

"Don't dump this on your mom all at once. She'll need some time too."

Quinn nodded and trudged away, leaving Grace and me to face our questions and each other.

"So you were at the prison too? Who did you go to see?" Her voice cracked.

There was no way out of this but through. Straight through. "I went to see Lottie. Quinn's mother."

45

Zeely

At home in my bedroom closet, there was a wedding scrapbook so big it couldn't close anymore, a swollen record of all my best dreams. On the honeymoon page there was something different in each corner: an Eiffel Tower, a Caribbean beach, Swiss Alps, and California dreaming.

We ended up at the Red Roof Inn.

And I couldn't have been happier.

"Special delivery, my queen," Ron said as he swooped back to the bed with a bag freshly delivered from Perkins Pancake House.

I couldn't help but laugh as he opened the bags. "This is ghetto, you know. Totally ghetto."

He kissed the curve of my neck. "It's redneck actually, but same diff."

I considered that for a moment and started laughing again. "Either way, this is the best pancake I think I've ever eaten."

"Right . . . you've just been holed up with a man with over a decade of sexual frustration. Do you realize it's Sunday? We've had a long night—"

"And day," I said, spearing a piece of pancake and guiding it into his mouth. And what a day it had been. When God said that he blessed the marriage bed, He didn't lie.

"Well, we do still have a little time left if you want to catch a red-eye flight somewhere. I know this is totally not you at all."

"Maybe not, but I'm loving it. Maybe I'm not who I think I am after all."

Ron shook his head. "Oh no. I know exactly who you are," he said, kissing my nose.

That tickled like crazy. "Oh really," I said before dissolving into giggles.

"Yes, really. You are Mrs. Zeely Jenkins, that's who."

I blinked at the sound of my new name. It had looked pretty on all my high school notebooks, but now it didn't sound quite right. At all. "That sounds ghetto too. The kids will laugh at us."

Ron smiled. "I hope so."

"We should have done this a long time ago."

"We could have done this a long time ago, but that's another story. I'm liking this one too much to worry about that one. We did do it."

"We did, didn't we?" I pushed my food away and pulled his lips to mine.

"Do you think it will take them as long as it took us?" Ron asked without having to say who "them" was.

"It'll take them longer. Or at least it would have . . . if they didn't have us for friends."

"Oh boy. What are you planning, Mrs. Jenkins?"

"Right now? Nothing much except staying undressed until Monday morning. After that, those two idiots get all our attention."

"All?" Ron pressed my thumb to his lips.

"No, that's a lot. Some?"

"Yes," he said, pulling me under the covers. "Some."

266

46

Grace

I didn't know if it was because Sean got a recording contract or what, but I found myself sitting at the kitchen table with a cup of tea . . . and Joyce's letter to me.

> *I knew you wouldn't read this until now. Didn't read Zeely's either, did you? At least I tried. I won't ask much of you. Dance for me at my funeral. Love Brian. And stop crying. You'll get wrinkles.*

That made me laugh until my stomach hurt—until I thought about her funeral. She asked to be cremated, God knows why, and requested that the service be soon after her death, but not right away. Maybe she wanted to leave enough time for Zeely and Ron to get married. Knowing Joyce, she just didn't want any of the surface emotion that went on when someone first dies. She'd have wanted people to think on things for a little while and be honest about how they felt about it.

Things were far beyond the surface now, I thought, listening to my son's songs. I had no idea that cold morning that those songs would be the only way I had to get to know my son. Each time I played the demo, I got to know his heart a little bit more. I even heard some of my father in him. I wished now I had talked to him more before he died, asked him subtle questions like, "Did you ever get my dance teacher pregnant with my boyfriend?" That would have been some family event.

It was good to hear some of him in Sean, not that I'd ever know my son the way Joyce had seemed to know all of us. And here she was again, asking me to love Brian. Those were not the words of a woman who'd birthed a child by my father. Or were they?

I sat among my boxes, still packed and unresolved, much like my relationship with Brian. With my back to a box full of my best china, I considered Joyce and her crew of contemporaries: Thelma, my mother, my father, Reverend Wilkins . . . They made me mad. They'd made up so many constructs for us to live in, yet given us no direction on how to go about doing so. It was like trying to live a jigsaw puzzle.

Follow ME.

That made me smile, that small voice in my heart reminding me that it wasn't Joyce I was trying to follow, but God. He knew it all, the end before the beginning. And if nothing else, I knew that God loved me. The question was, what would I do with that love?

Arms around myself at my kitchen table, I thought how I'd do it all again—well, most of it anyway. It wasn't just for her. It was for myself.

My fingers skimmed the buttons of my phone. Zeely picked up on the first ring.

"Yes?"

I cleared my throat. She sounded a little too much like a newly-wed these days. The sound of her voice was enough to make me blush. "I'll be there. At the funeral, I mean."

"You sure?"

"Nope."

"I love you." She laughed. It sounded like music.

"I love you too."

"Meet me there in the morning. At the church."

"Have y'all practiced?"

"Nope. I don't know if Brian's coming either. Have you talked to him?"

My stomach tightened like it did every time I thought about Brian. Our last time together, the day of Zeely's wedding, we'd done more than talk. Things had gotten . . . close. Except for a message from him saying that Reverend Wilkins was still out of town and a return call from me saying that my mother had no answers, our words had been few.

"He'll be there," I said, staring up at the ceiling.

Brian would definitely show up for Joyce's funeral tomorrow. I prayed that God would too.

47

Zeely

The church looked more ready for a wedding than a funeral. The flowered foyer opened into aisles of swathed tulle and lace. A resting place. I tugged at the shift draping my body, watching as well-wishers filled the aisles. Students. Parents. Neighbors. Friends. Smiles and tears showed on their faces. Some waved, while others wandered past the poster-sized photos of Joyce looking like I felt.

Ron held my hand as I wondered who would show up when I died? Would Grace dance while Daddy preached? Or would Daddy even be alive? Would Ron have to preach the sermon?

Too much to think about. Too many people I'd promised to love and never quite gotten around to it. Too many friends I'd called and called who never called me back.

What I knew for sure was that marrying Ron was a triumph that would mark all my days. I didn't want Grace to go through what I'd gone through. As Brian emerged from the hanging fabric, I knew they wouldn't need much help from us.

"I knew you'd show," Brian said.

Grace, who was walking toward me when she saw him, went

270

still at the sound of his voice. They had it bad. "I knew you'd come too."

He was close, close enough for even me to smell him. I tried to get away, but I was sort of stuck between them. Where did Ron go?

"I came for you too. I'd come for you anytime . . . if you'd let me." His hand lighted on her shoulder but was gone just as quickly.

That was my cue. I pushed through the breath of space between them.

They didn't seem to notice. I turned back to watch them, wondering if this was how it had been to look at Ron and me.

"I know. I know you would. Thank you." Grace leaned her head toward where his hand had been. It took everything in her not to kiss him, I could tell. They hugged instead. The embrace was strong and fast, but they both seemed more relaxed when they let go of one another.

I faded into the shadows. Though we'd all loved Joyce, this was Brian's mother's funeral. His loss. I had to forget myself, my feelings, and think of him.

Grace didn't have any problems thinking of him. She was smiling big and goofy, her heart opening like one of the flowers tied to the pews.

He lingered near but didn't touch her again. He didn't have to. "Your hair looks nice," he said.

Funny, I'd thought so too. A set of comb coils I'd done on her weeks ago had transformed into a matted mess that somehow worked for her. I guess she was going ahead with that dreadlock idea.

Brian's locks were covered today with some kind of scarf, though the tips dangled near his waist. When Grace reached out and touched one, I knew I should go, but I couldn't.

I could hear him speaking to her softly, adjusting the collar on his blue African suit she loved so much.

271

"I can do your locks for you. Anytime."

I went on, making a mental note of that. Though I wasn't too hot on the hairdo, it would keep them together for several hours. That would be more than either of them could take. Right now though we had a funeral to perform at, and that was strange in itself.

Her answer broke my heart. "I'm leaving."

Brian gave me a knowing glance. There was so much disappointment in the look. I'd never seen Joyce in him before, but it was undeniable now.

"When will you go?" he asked. There was a little catch in his voice.

"Today," she said softly, surprising even me. I knew everything was still boxed up, but I didn't know she'd decided for sure to leave today.

He turned to me and smiled. "I guess we've just been having a reunion instead of getting ready for what we need to do. I sort of forgot that you were here for a while, Zeely. Sorry for being so rude."

"It's okay."

"Are we all set?"

"I think so. My husband has officially disappeared."

"That means we're all set."

I laughed. "Pretty much."

He slid a bracelet off his arm. My favorite of his, a sterling arm cuff and inscribed in swirls. He'd always told me no when I begged for it, said I'd never grow into it. He slid it over my wrist and up my arm. With one squeeze, it closed around my bicep. A perfect fit.

"Thank you."

He nodded. "Just take good care of him." He looked back at Grace. "He's all the family I've got."

Daddy was talking to the crowd, and the scent of baked chicken—a first for a Mount Olive repast—wound up the stairs.

Grace got a crazy look. "Where's the program?"

Brian shuffled through papers stacked beside the door. He held out a page with a picture of Joyce that we'd seen many times before. It was cropped from the photo of the first Imani class. Her smile was wide and there were arms all around her. I focused on one of the arms, knowing it was the same as the one that now held the photo. Grace, Ron, and Jerry were somewhere in the shot too.

"Here," he said, after looking at the picture for a few seconds himself.

It was all I could do to keep from snatching it from him. My heart sank as I read the first line aloud. "Remembrance, an African dance of celebration: Grace Okoye, dancer; Zeely Wilkins, narrator; Brian Mayfield, drummer."

My pulse quickened. Remembrance. Grace's solo from our first dance recital. The dance she'd been headed to do when Mal had dragged her from the bus stop and stolen her soul . . .

And now, it seemed, God had used Joyce once again to give us another chance. There was just one problem—there wasn't a vocal part to that dance. I'd have to make it up myself. I read it again just to be sure, but I knew I'd read it right the first time.

"She didn't," I said.

Brian shook his head. "She did."

The church was full, but we were empty. Especially Brian. He'd been putting up a good front all morning, but he was coming undone.

"What are we going to do?" he said.

I fanned myself with a hymnal. "I don't know what y'all are going to do, but I'm going to sing."

"What are you going to sing?" Grace said, half smiling. "The narrator is a griot, a storyteller. He never sings the same song twice. Admit it. She got you this time."

Ron popped out of nowhere. "At least you don't have to preach! How do you think I'm feeling? I'd prepared something but the program says that I'll be preaching on restoration, from Nehemiah. I preached that when I was sixteen, people. Give it up, you guys. There's nothing we can do but pray."

Brian nodded. "Yes, let's pray. I think that was the goal."

We formed a circle, a chain of prayer. Ron's voice was steady as he began to pray.

"Lord, we come to you asking for clean hands and pure hearts to do what you're asking. What Joyce is asking. Give us hearts to remember and minds to obey. Stir us with the spirit of Nehemiah, a spirit to rebuild all that has been broken."

"Give me the song, God. I don't know the words, but I know you. I knew her. I know the story. It's a good story too. Help me to tell it in a way that brings you glory."

It was Grace's turn, but it took her a minute to get herself together. She hadn't cried for Joyce at the hospital. She hadn't had room, hadn't had time. I cried when it was time, and I didn't feel sad now, but here, holding the hands of these people I loved, who I knew loved me, I felt Joyce among us. I felt the presence of God.

Grace looked like she wanted to scream.

Brian smiled. "Take your time, baby."

She took a breath. "Lord, we've had some good times in this church. Some bad times too. All our lives you've met us here. And now you've called us back again. I never forgot that dance, Lord. And I'll never forget the woman who gave it to me. Let us pour ourselves out this morning, God. For her. And for you."

Well, that about did it. I'd been feeling fine, but Grace's prayer made me want to step away and come apart, breathing fast and sob-bing deep. Ron pulled me back, tightening the circle once more.

"In Jesus' name, amen," Brian said, dropping Grace's hand and heading for the stage.

I got the feeling that he planned to do his praying on the drums.

48

Grace

I wasn't proud of myself for leaving the funeral, but I wasn't too upset about it either. I'd done what was asked of me. I'd gone farther, danced harder than I'd ever intended. God knew my heart. That should have been enough.

But it wasn't.

I'd run home to my empty house, thinking I'd make a getaway while everyone else was at the funeral. If only it had been that easy. From my futon, I scanned the bare walls and clean counter, remembering how Brian drummed his heart to me, how I'd flung myself to heaven, how the Spirit had poured down. I'd looked over at him in the middle of that and thought about the possibility of us being related and I just had to go. It was almost to the point where I wanted to get a DNA test or something.

Sometimes I convinced myself that it would be impossible for him to be my father's son. Then, I remembered the way my mother had looked at Joyce the few times we'd visited Mount Olive. Only then had I seen such a desperate fear in her. It was that same fear that had driven me from the church. If there was going to be some big announcement or new revelation that Brian was my brother, I hadn't been up for it. Not today. I'd rather leave without knowing.

I nudged my purse with my shoe. Everything I needed right now was inside: the keys to my new place, a Bible. There were a few other things I'd take with me, but most of it I'd have picked up by movers. It seemed silly with Columbus so close, but I felt like I needed to save my strength. For what I wasn't sure, probably for when school started up again in the New Year.

Everything would be the same, but so different. Brian was officially the principal now. I tried not to think of him in that office with all those books, sitting behind Joyce's desk. He fit there. He belonged there, just like Joyce had. It was me who didn't have a place. Except for at that funeral today. I'd belonged there. We all had.

Zeely went down first, right in the middle of a note. Brian went next. Smiling right at me. I don't think he meant to do it, but it fractured me somehow, watching him drown in the Spirit like that. It fractured me but healed me too. It was a closeness beyond any kiss we'd shared, deeper than any conversations we'd had. So deep that though I'd ended up on the floor too, eyes closed and heart open, I couldn't let myself stay there.

I'd run out into the snow, dragging myself from Brian. From God. It hadn't worked then. It wasn't working now. I got up, put on my coat, and walked to my car, dragging to the trunk what I could carry.

There was a sprinkle of snow, coming and going like an undecided woman.

Like me.

It hit my hair and melted, which made me laugh in spite of myself. I'd picked out all the matted pieces and washed my hair with liquid castile soap and conditioned it with coconut oil. I could smell the faint scent of the vanilla beans I'd infused in the oil months ago. It

277

was a welcome sweetness on a day like today. I'd put a little jojoba at my temples too.

As I closed the trunk, woman winter made up her mind and blasted me with a firm but thoughtful wind. My hair got away from me again, flying into my eyes. There wouldn't be much more of that. One thing I had decided in the short time I spent on the floor during Joyce's funeral was that it was time to lock my hair—to risk something permanent. I'd always been drawn to locks, always thought that one day I might have a set of my own.

I'd planned to just get someone in Columbus to do my hair, but when I got in the car and started it up, my hands dropped into my lap. I couldn't leave yet, not without saying goodbye to him. I had to take something with me besides pain. At the funeral, Brian had offered me one last gift—to do my hair. If he was still willing, I'd take him up on the offer and pray that we wouldn't both regret it.

As I backed out of the driveway, I ran my fingers through my hair—gently, but not as gently as Brian would have. For someone so smart, he had huge, weathered hands, like my father's. Working-man's hands. And yet, he touched me like I was blown glass. Pure silk. I closed my eyes, thinking of what it would be like to be alone with him one last time.

Impossible, that's how it would be, but I knew that I had to do it anyway.

I made a pact with myself to remain silent, to sit motionless as he twisted himself into my scalp, twined his love into my memory. It would be torture, but I didn't care. For the rest of my life, my hair would remind me of what love was.

Or what it could have been.

49

Brian

The old folks went first.

And I was glad of it. Reverend Wilkins' "few words" had everyone rocking in the pews and hugging themselves as he talked about who Joyce had been, what she had done in Testimony. He mentioned things that I'd never known about, but none of it surprised me. Joyce had mastered something I still struggled with—the art of giving oneself away. So far, the only time I'd truly been able to do that was when I was drumming. I hoped that today wouldn't be an exception.

"And now we're going to have a performance from some of the teachers at Imani Academy, some of Joyce's first students. Welcome them as they perform Remembrance, an African dance of celebration!"

"We're on." I whispered to Grace and Zeely as if they hadn't heard. As we got up, Zeely spiked her hair one last time and checked the spray of sequins on her dress. Why she'd needed that for a funeral I wasn't sure, but my mother had probably requested that too. They both had a flair for the dramatic, those two.

"It's all in place," I mumbled as Grace fumbled with her dress too. Grace narrowed her eyes at me, but didn't say anything. Zeely just shrugged and headed for the microphone in the dress she'd probably intended to be married in.

And perhaps that's just what she was doing, singing a song to God, the lover of her soul.

I took my seat at my drums while Zeely adjusted the microphone down to her height.

"You all just hold on a second, you know I'm short," she said into the microphone.

Laughter rippled through the crowd.

Grace took her place at the center front of the sanctuary. She was a blush of gold and brown, of hair and tears. Zeely was still messing with the microphone, but I couldn't hold it any longer. I clapped my hands to Grace as I had so many years ago.

The signal.

The heels of my hands rapped against the skins of the drums, speaking out all the things I couldn't say.

Be-de-re-bup-be-bum. Be-bum.

The notes were sharp at first—angry and confused—but then they slowed to a familiar rhythm, one that none of us had ever forgotten.

From the corner of my eye, I saw Grace take the first leap. Someone in the front row gasped.

It had begun.

Zeely's voice came in then, breaking over all of us like a warm rain. "There is a time to live, a time to die, a time to hurt, and a time to mend. Selah . . ."

I played on, drilling my palms against my loss. High-low-high-low.

Grace was near me now, head back and arms reaching high, again and again.

"They brought us on a big boat across many waters . . . but the Spirit was on the face of the deep. Selah . . ."

Boom-pu-cha, my hands said over and over before releasing a string of something that sounded to my soul like the waves of an ocean.

"One has made a voyage, but we all are in the boat. Cross over. Selah . . ."

Cross over. Cross over. Cross over.

The words were drumming into me like my hands were hitting the instruments. I took my favorite drum, the one Joyce had brought me back from the Congo, and strapped it onto my chest. I started for the middle aisle. Zeely snatched the microphone from the stand, not missing a beat behind me.

"Cross over, cross over, cross over. Selah . . ."

Grace circled down the side aisle, meeting us in the center. She was facing me, but not looking at me at all. Without turning around, I knew Ron was behind me, felt him calling the people to the altar for prayer. We moved to the back of the sanctuary. Somebody opened the doors. There were people out there too. They paused for a minute as we went on, me drumming, Zeely singing, and Grace dancing like I'd never seen her or anyone else dance before.

I could hear Ron now at the microphone. "Yes, yes. A healing season, a time to rebuild, says the Lord. This town, this church, our lives are broken. Our hearts are broken today. Well, rise up, church. It's a time to mend. A time to heal. Come down here, one and all. We're going to celebrate a life that was about love by doing some loving. Find the person you're not speaking to, the one you're mad at, and bring 'em down here. Right now."

"Cross over, cross over, cross over. Se-lah . . ."

As he passed us on the way up the aisle, a tall man almost fell as he ran to the altar. A woman climbed the pew to get to someone who looked like her sister. They danced down the aisle. Grace followed them, turning again and again, until all we'd been holding back, all we'd been hiding behind, shattered over our heads.

I wobbled, trying to keep standing, keep playing. I tried to keep upright, but I couldn't hold on. No one could.

Jesus walked among us.

I didn't know how long I'd been on the floor. Someone must have lifted the drums off my chest. Zeely was curled into a shiny ball a few feet away. I didn't see Grace. I couldn't remember how long it had been since I'd seen her last. I didn't see her anywhere. Ron walked toward us, almost stepping on my fingers. I blinked at the light overhead. We were still here. Still at the funeral.

"I'm not going to preach all day. The Lord has had his say in here."

I blinked again.

I know that's right.

"I'm not going to talk about death either." Ron moved down the aisle. "Or Joyce."

An old lady snorted.

"She asked me not to." He pulled a letter out of his pocket. "'Don't talk about me,' she said. 'I'm fine. Talk about living. Loving. Talk about restoration.'"

He stepped over me and walked to the back door, motioning for those in the foyer to squeeze inside the sanctuary. I couldn't do a thing but watch Ron's shoes slide across the carpet as he walked by.

"Sounds crazy, huh? Restoration . . . resurrection at a funeral." Ron slapped his Bible. "I thought so until I thought about it. It makes perfect sense—Joyce doesn't have a casket to climb out of, but we can climb out of ours."

I pushed myself up against the nearest pew, still sitting, but upright with my hands around my knees.

"Right. Right." A man nodded in agreement in the pew across from me.

"No matter what we've done. No matter where we've been . . . resurrection and restoration is available!"

I hugged my knees, taking in the people sitting near me. I could see Jerry, a few pews up with his crutches—and Carmel beside him. Monique was there with the baby.

Quinn was there too, looking like he'd aged ten years since I saw him last. His suit was a little short on him but familiar. Sean's suit.

Ron moved up the aisle like this was a revival instead of a funeral. "We all have something dead. A dream. A hope. A relationship. And not just the ladies. Men, do you think you're not good enough to be a husband?" He stopped and turned to me. "A father?"

My throat tightened. He was my brother, but Ron was going places I didn't want to visit.

He rounded the front of the aisle and stopped in front of Zeely. He pulled her to her feet. "I thought I wasn't good enough to preach. Too white for all of you. Too black for the people I'm supposed to be a part of. No place to fit. You ever felt like that?"

"Yes, Lord," someone called out. Many people nodded.

"But you know what?" He kissed Zeely's cheek and led her back to her seat. "It's time to stop being ashamed. It's time to get free."

Reverend Wilkins stood. He leaned forward and clapped his hands one time. "My God," he said softly.

That made me smile. I took a deep breath and thought about

my other mother, Eva, the woman who'd raised me. The last time I'd heard Rev say that was the one time I'd heard Eva sing.

Ron smiled and flipped open his Bible. "You don't have to turn with me. Just listen." He leaned on the front pew. "One day God told Hezekiah to set his house in order because he was going to die."

I closed my eyes, remembering the story . . . and the sermon. Ron and I had both preached that one. In matching suits. It was our first one with a title: "Fifteen More Years."

"Well, Hezzy wouldn't accept dying like that. He wanted more time. How many of you know you have to watch out what you pray for?"

Hands waved throughout the church.

"In the third year of the extra fifteen years God gave him, Hezekiah had a son. A bad seed. Went by the name of Manasseh. Spent his whole life undoing everything his daddy ever did. Some of you know what kind of child I'm talking about. They might even be here with you today."

A heavy woman next to Thelma, my elementary school lunch lady, howled so loud she forced the others to scoot down the pew. "I know the kind, Preacher." She narrowed her eyes at a boy on the next row.

I tensed as the lady called her son out. I hadn't had the chance to be disappointed in Quinn, or to be proud of him.

Yes, you have. You were there for all the good parts.

Not as a father, I wasn't. I'd missed his whole life.

"God waited fifty-five years for Manasseh to stop acting a fool, and finally he sent an enemy to drag him away as prisoner, with a hook through his nose."

"Nose wide open!" Reverend Wilkins clapped his hands.

Ron nodded. "Exactly. But you know what? With his face dragging against that dirt, Manasseh got ahold of something no prophet could explain to him—repentance."

"God just forgave him? After all that?" The sound of my own voice surprised me.

Somebody in the end seat reached out and squeezed my hand.

Ron walked toward me, his eyes cutting right through me. "Better than that, bruh. God didn't just forgive Manasseh. He restored him."

The man who'd taken my hand leaned over the edge of the pew. There was liquor on his breath.

"Ain't that something? Sounds too easy though. It don't happen like that for me." The man's voice rumbled in my ear.

Ron had heard it too, I could tell by the big smile on his face. "Manasseh repented, but his people didn't. They wouldn't turn away from the ways he taught them."

The man sighed and nodded as if he understood. "It's hard to change bad ways. I love God, I do, but sometimes I don't know if I can make it . . ."

This had to be the craziest funeral—no, craziest church service—I'd ever been to. It was also one of the best. It was forcing me to face things that I'd shoved aside since learning that Quinn was my son. Since knowing that Joyce was my mother. We'd all wasted so much time. Time when I'd needed a mother. Time when Quinn had needed a father . . .

"Don't waste any more time trying to do things your own way! Start loving where you are. Let God make up the rest. Manasseh had fifty-five years on you." Ron scratched his chin.

The man sitting near me leaned over and collected his change from off the floor. He wanted to hear the message, I knew, but it was hard to hear. Hard to think that you'd wasted that time for nothing and now you could start over just like that.

It must have been too hard, because the man gave me a small nod and stepped across me and then walked out of the church.

"God's peace to you, brother." Ron walked back to the front. "Listen now, everybody. Whatever we think we don't deserve—we're right. You don't deserve to be restored. I don't deserve to be resurrected." He stopped and cleared his throat. "But we have to reach out and take it anyway. We have to let God surprise us. It's His gift and it's His grace. To get it though, we're going to have to repent, to confess, to bring all our stuff out of hiding and place it at the cross."

The fabric on the pew pricked my skin as I pulled myself up to take the seat the man had left. I wanted God's grace. And my Grace too.

As the music started, people didn't move toward the altar this time. We just sat and let God deal with us where we were. I saw a sprinkle of sequins on the floor and knew that Zeely had gotten up too. My eyes met briefly with the organ player. He quickly looked away. Mindy's baby's daddy, no doubt. A fine mess we all were.

I dropped my head. Stared at the floor.

Ron went quiet now and I was glad. I needed to get home, take a bath, and sleep . . .

I looked up in time to see a dark finger approach my face. Reverend Wilkins' finger.

"You folks see this boy here? This big, fine man who played those drums so beautifully for you this morning?" Reverend Wilkins' voice shook with emotion as he lifted his hand above. "Stand up."

I pushed off the bench and found my feet.

The old preacher pointed to the picture of Joyce on the projector. "That woman up there? She is this boy's mother."

The buzzing crowd fell silent. My head started to hurt.

"Don't go quiet on me, church. You dressed up and drove over here to see her off, didn't you? Well, this here's her family."

My breakfast started to rise in my throat.

The Reverend went on. "He wanted to tell you all that in his own time, I suppose. Well, like Rodney—Ronald here said, time done run out. This is Joyce's son . . ."

We locked gazes.

"And mine."

"Welcome to the family, Brian."

"Thanks." I shook hands with Isaiah, my new brother. Ron and the other Wilkins men, all nine of them including the Reverend, circled me in a ring of acceptance. It should have been liberating. Empowering even. Instead, it felt a little . . . cramped.

"Let me through, he's my brother too." Zeely squeezed through the wall of giants and into my waiting arms. No wonder we'd never quite gotten along. She was my sister.

"Are you okay with this? I didn't know. Really I didn't—" I whispered to her.

She smiled. "None of us knew. I guess I should have. You always have worked my nerves." She pointed behind me at her other brothers. "Just like the rest of them."

Another of the brothers, whose name I'd forgotten, picked Zeely up and flipped her over his shoulder. What was his name? *Ezra.* His voice, deep like his father's, filled the room. "We work your nerves, do we, little girl?" He tickled Zeely's stomach while she struggled to hold down her skirt. Ron stepped out of the circle and watched, smiling.

She giggled until she could take no more. "Lazarus! Izzy! Noah! Stop it! Ron, help me, baby . . ."

The brothers kept talking as if they hadn't heard a thing. Ron watched in amazement as I attempted to rescue the tortured Zeely and arms grabbed me from everywhere.

"Ah, ah, ah. First rule of Wilkins brotherhood. Never rescue the sister until she says the magic words."

I raised an eyebrow in question, unsure if I really wanted to know.

The shortest of the brothers answered. "'Please kind sirs' is the ticket to freedom. Don't worry, she'll say it soon."

"I will not!" Zeely shouted, while Ron attempted to get her feet on the ground.

Ezra looked down at Ron and laughed. "Looks like we've got ourselves a knight in shining armor, fellas. What should we do with him?"

Ron laughed too, but his brow was knit together in a line. "C'mon, guys, quit playing."

Isaiah walked over and grabbed Zeely by the waist. "Yes, let's all quit playing. I know we're all glad to see each other and get to know Brian better, but I'd like to hear what Dad has to say about all this. I don't know about the rest of you, but I'm a little put out with how Dad handled this whole thing. No offense to you, Brian."

"None taken."

Reverend Wilkins gripped the chair at the head of a long wooden table in the choir room, where we were sequestered away from the mourners still hanging around after the dinner. The Reverend—my father, I had to get used to thinking of him that way—nodded at his son, then sat in his chair.

"Sit down, all of you. Your brother's right. I owe you all an explanation." He crossed his legs and laced his fingers around one knee.

I slipped into a chair next to Ron. Zeely sat almost in his lap. The rest of the brothers filed around the table, sliding into place from oldest to youngest. They were pastors themselves now, all eight of them. I imagined them seated around the dining table in the same order, growing up like plants around the table with my father, the one I'd always known, but never known, at the head.

He began the tale. "A long time ago, my daddy's church stood on this ground."

The youngest brother, Noah, frowned. "How? You built this place from scratch. I saw the pictures."

Isaiah snorted. "Boy, please. You saw the pictures? I did the work. Daddy like to killed us building this place—"

The Reverend raised his hand. "Hear me out, boys. I know we've got a lot of big-mouthed preachers in here, but now isn't the time. I'm an old man and these words don't come easy."

"Yes sir. We'll hear you out." Isaiah eyed the others. They nodded in agreement.

My father got up from his chair. He stared out the window. "It began for me and Marie like it did for Zeely and Jeremiah. Which is why I was always against that. My mother and your mother's mother were great friends. They picked Marie for me when I was born—"

Ezra shook his head. "I thought the fathers did the choosing. That's what Mama told me—"

Lazarus jabbed his brother with an elbow. "Go on, Dad."

I took a deep breath, trying to absorb both the family dynamics and the story I'd waited so long to hear. Both overwhelmed me. I looked from each of my brothers' faces and then to my father at the window.

My father. What would I have been like if I had grown up with them? I turned to Ron, who gripped my hand under the table. I squeezed back, wanting to reach out and tousle those red-brown curls tangled around his head from all that preaching. I chuckled instead.

Lord, I'm happy with the brother I've got.

The pastor cleared his throat. "Don't be confused, children. I loved your mother. I always will." He turned and stared at Zeely and Ron. "She did some things against my wishes, some wrong things, but she was a good woman. A good mother."

He stared outside again. "And I grew to love her more than I'd ever loved anyone. But that's not how it started. No, my loving started with Joyce."

I held my breath. He'd loved her? This preacher, so calm, so serious? Yet at the mention of my mother's name, the old man's voice cracked with tenderness. "I met her at a sit-in. I was the blackest thing there and she was the lightest, the whitest. She sat down beside me and introduced herself. We talked into the night . . ."

I turned to Ron and narrowed my eyes. Ron shrugged his shoulders. The whitest? Joyce was light-skinned all right, very light. Probably mixed for sure, just like a lot of people in Testimony, but white? What did my father mean? It didn't make sense.

The Reverend turned to face us. "Yes, white. Mixed up with a lot of things—Irish, Indian, and you guessed it, a whole lot of slaves. But according to the state of Ohio, she was white."

When would the surprises end? I cracked my neck, trying to process this information. Isaiah did the same thing. At the same time. I'd have to trip on that later. This Joyce being white, mostly white, or whatever Rev was saying, had my immediate attention. How could I, a scholar of African studies and African-American life, have missed that? I recalled Joyce's face in my mind, a face so similar to those fair women who'd come and comforted me at the hospital. I turned to my father. "What about those women, the ones at the hospital?"

The Reverend nodded. "The cousins? Oh yes, well, Joyce is white in the same way we are black, I suppose. The cousins are from Sadie's other side."

Ron shot up and almost dumped Zeely onto the floor. "Sadie? My Sadie? My great-grandmother?"

The Reverend smiled. "The same."

Ron was up now. Pacing. I almost joined him, but my mind was racing too fast for me to move. He'd told me the story enough for me to put the pieces together. Sadie, a mulatto raised as a slave owner's daughter, had come north and married two men: a black one and a white one. For the white ones to pass, the black ones had to stay away. Joyce had come from the "white" side. Eva and those women at the hospital had come from the "black" side. Joyce would have been Ron's father's sister. The aunt that we could never find.

Ron stared at me when he got it. Eva had taken both of us because, in a way, we were brothers. Family. Her real blood family. He walked across the room to me and slapped hands. We held tight before sliding palms, looking deep into each other, before he took his seat and pulled Zeely close to him.

Watching them, I realized what all of this meant for me, for Grace. She was my sister in Christ, but that was it. My father hadn't just given me a public acknowledgment or the key to my past. He'd given me the key to my future too: Grace and all the love I'd been waiting to give her, all the love I'd been waiting to get. She'd run off somewhere like always, but I could only pray that she hadn't gotten far. Either way, I'd find her.

I forced myself to pay attention.

"We didn't mean to do it, but we fell in love. Our parents wouldn't hear of it. I even left the church for a time." He walked toward my chair and lifted that same finger at me. "You were conceived then."

Okay, he had me going now. Left the church for a time? This man of God? This man who'd stood in this community longer than most of the buildings? I shook my head, trying to loosen the dizziness gripping me. Reverend Wilkins was human. He'd failed. And I'd been the result.

You were the result of his love.

Isaiah, the only single guy among the brothers, pounded the table with his fist. "So what about all that holiness talk? Chastity. We all waited. I'm still waiting. But you didn't."

The Reverend nodded. "And I've regretted my sin all my life." He walked to me and touched my face. "Not the result, but the act. I caused a lot of people a lot of pain: Marie, Joyce, Brian. I didn't want that for any of you. The Lord's ways are best. Always."

Though everyone kept trying not to offend me or hurt my feelings, I really just wanted to leave, to find Grace and make my own story, for once. I scratched my beard. The Reverend's hands touched my shoulders. "Trust me, son. I have no regrets about your life. You're the blessing out of all of it. I just wish I had known . . ."

I froze. "You didn't know?"

Reverend Wilkins shook his head. "Not until I opened my letter from Joyce." He squeezed my shoulders. "Your birth certificate, the original, was inside."

I pressed my lips together. The birth certificate no one could find. The Reverend slipped it from his pocket and laid it on the table in front of me. I tucked it into my pocket.

Ezra waved his hand like a schoolboy. "So what happened? How'd you end up with Mama? With us?"

The old man took a deep breath. "Joyce's family gave us a choice—break up or be broken."

Ron turned around. "What do you mean?"

"The church burned to the ground after our last night together. A cross burned in my yard at the same time."

I pushed back from the table. I didn't want to cry in front of these guys. Brothers or not, I didn't know them like that. They beat me to it. Isaiah hung his head first, and sobbed like a baby. "The fire that killed Grandpa?"

The Reverend nodded. "The same. Your grandfather had preached that night, and although I'd begged him to let me do it, he was down here cleaning up the instruments of the altar. Another man died that night too. The man who set the fire." He turned to Ron. "Your father, Joyce's brother."

Ron shook his head from side to side; slow at first, then faster and faster.

The old man patted Ron's arm. "Joyce was your aunt. Your mother must have known who Brian was, and when she saw the two of you getting so close—"

A gasp escaped Ron's lips. Zeely pulled him to her chest. He pulled away. "Is that why she beat me . . . She didn't want me to know?"

"I suspect so. Maybe she blamed us for your father's death. I don't know. Even now, Marie comes around, but she won't talk about that, not with me anyway." He sucked his teeth. "After the fire, I didn't see Joyce for a long time. She went to Africa and joined the Peace Corps. Then one day I looked down from the pulpit and there she was."

Ron stared off into space.

I grabbed my brother, my best friend. "Don't look like that. Remember what you preached today. Restoration. Resurrection. Let it out, man. We're all family here."

Chairs scraped against the floor. Everyone crowded around the two of us, hugging and crying.

Isaiah's voice rose above us in a timbre I knew he probably used with his congregation back in Detroit. "That's right. We're all family here. God's family."

50

Brian

"Please pick up." I gripped the phone as I raced to Grace's house. It'd been hours since she disappeared from the church, and she said that she was leaving today. All I could do was hope and pray that she was running late . . . as usual.

"The cellular customer you have called is unavailable." The automated message crashed against my ears.

I pulled into her empty driveway and got out of the car. The snow was coming hard, but I moved slowly, letting it fall on me. After the revelations of the day, I didn't want to live a life full of secret regrets, burdened with lost love. I wanted to come here and find Grace waiting so that I could tell her everything and offer her everything. The best of me.

But I was too late. Just as she'd promised, Grace had left Testimony. She'd left me. My hands refused to close my jacket, to protect me from the cold. I welcomed the biting wind. One step after another carried me to her door, though I knew she wasn't inside. As I approached, I could see through the open windows the piles of boxes. She'd left something behind. That gave me some hope.

Hope enough to notice the wet note fluttering in the door. I dusted the film of snow from it and tugged the note out from where it'd been shut inside the door. It wasn't addressed to anyone, but I knew that it was for me.

> *I changed my mind. I'm going to stop by around three*
> *to let you start my locks. If you still want to, that is.*
>
> *Yours,*
> *Grace*

Did I still want to? More than anything.

I ran to my car and jumped inside, racing to the church. I had to stop them before they took down those decorations.

51

Zeely

I wobbled on the ladder, placing the mistletoe in the correct position on the ceiling in the church basement. Ron's hands shot up and grabbed my waist.

He pulled me down. "Watch it, Zee. It still hasn't been that long since . . ." He squeezed my hand. "Let me do it."

I smiled at him, amazed that after all we'd gone through, he could worry about me climbing a ladder. "I hope Grace comes tonight. Do you think she will?"

"Don't ask me. She's your best friend."

"True, but Brian is yours."

"I'd have a better chance trying to figure out Grace." We laughed as we admired our decorations and went to see who else needed help. Across the room, Grace's mother was lining a table with a purple tablecloth.

Ron waved to her while whispering to me. "It was brilliant how you put this all together so quickly. I'm glad Grace's mom could make it. I really hope that Brian can get her here. It'll be a wonderful surprise."

I shrugged, trying not to melt as he kissed me. It was so wonderful to be married and not have to worry who was looking before kissing him back. Mother Riley did suggest we tone it down a bit. We were in church, after all. We were trying. "I hope she'll come. I can't believe it's Christmas Eve and we just had Joyce's funeral. It seems weird decorating for Christmas. I was so sick at Thanksgiving . . . I didn't even cook—"

"Tell me about it!" Ron rubbed his stomach. "I tried to make something and bring it to you, but—"

"Burned the turkey?"

He smiled. "Let's just say I'll need your help next time. We can have a do-over if you want. This weekend."

"I'd really like that. I have a lot to be thankful for." I touched his cheek and sighed. "I still can't believe you got Daniel and Mindy together. How'd you pull it off? And did you give them the check, from her father?"

He shook his head. "Bent gave it to them himself. I told him the whole story. Everything, including the baby. The old man cracked and apologized to Daniel. It won't be smooth, but they're going to face the future together. As a family."

I stared at the floor. "Have you talked with Jerry at all? Are he and Carmel going to work things out? I hope so. I feel so bad for coming between them for so long. I saw them together this morning, and it seemed so right."

Ron looked relieved to hear me say that. I wondered if we'd ever get over the things we'd done to each other. I hoped so. I prayed so.

"They're going to try. No fast moves. Pastor Rodriguez will counsel all of them this next year with the goal of moving into a house together next Christmas."

I squinted. "All of them? What if they let Sean out of jail? How—"

Ron patted my hand. "I don't know. I'm working on it, but I don't know."

"Does he have a chance?" I took a deep breath with the words, wondering if I was asking for Grace or for me. Since I'd probably never have any children now, if Sean did get out, I planned to make it up to him for how I'd treated him. Even if he didn't get out, I would do it. Somehow.

"There's always a chance. I firmly believe that."

I swallowed hard and laid my head on Ron's shoulder, thankful that we'd finally taken our chance. "Yes, always a chance. Even for us."

He stroked my face. "Especially for us. You were worth every minute that I waited." He pointed across the church basement at my brothers and my father, the tight fist of men bustling in the kitchen. "Though I hope I can survive those brothers of yours."

"Don't worry. They always did like you." I shook my head. "You're just what the family needs—another preacher. They'll be fighting over who'll have you come to preach first." I laughed to cover up my tears. They surprised me, those tears. Before Grace moved back here, I don't know when I'd cried last. Lately, I was turning into a faucet.

Ron buried his face in my shoulder. "There are still some things we need to talk about. Children—"

"Not now, okay? Not now. I'm just full."

He nodded, knowing just what I meant. "I feel the same way too, only opposite. I'm so full of love for you, so full of happiness, but the rest of it . . . It's like I'm empty at the same time."

That, I could understand. For so long, all I'd been able to feel was the hollow of my womb, the empty space in my bed. And yet, in giving Ron my empty, broken heart, God had filled it somehow. Still, I knew from the way he was talking, that it wouldn't all be easy. There would be hard parts too. Like when I would have to tell him that there wouldn't be any children.

"What is it, Birdie? Why are you looking like that?" He held me tighter.

"That time, when I came to UC and that guy said that you couldn't marry me. When you paused, what were you thinking?"

Ron stared at me with hurt in his eyes. "Does it matter?"

I thought about it. "Yes, I think it does. It doesn't change anything, but I would like to know. If you don't want to talk about it, I respect that and accept it. To be honest, I've just wondered all this time."

"Our mothers, yours and mine. I wondered how Marie would treat you, whether she would come to our wedding. And your mother, well, she came to visit me a few days before you did. She said I'd leave you alone if I really loved you. She told me how hard it would be for our children. When that guy said the same things, it just startled me for a minute. It wasn't because I didn't love you. I did then and I do now. I followed you, but I got there too late . . ." He hung his head.

I clung to him, laid next to his heart as it beat like a racehorse. Mama. If only she'd given us a chance, given me a chance. I knew now that it wasn't just Ron's race but the blaze of our love that had worried my mother. She'd been burnt by that kind of love, she'd built her life on the ashes of it. But our blaze was different than that one. A forever flame. My head dropped to his shoulder, into the cranny of his neck. My voice sounded miles away. "I'm so happy and so scared. Even now."

Ron took my face in both hands and stared into my eyes. "Good. I'm terrified too. And thrilled." He lifted my chin and kissed me—barely. Just a whisper of skin across my lips, my cheek. "Let's just accept the love, not try to analyze it. We've spent enough time being afraid."

I pinched his side. "It's not you I was afraid of. It was me. Fifteen years is a long, long time."

Ron exploded in laughter, pulling me into his arms. He shook his head. "And so I've learned. I'm going to have to start taking stretching class or something. You're limber, girl."

"You do all right yourself." I gave him a mischievous look.

"All right? Okay, we'll see what you say when we get home. What time is he supposed to get here again?"

I shook my head. "Focus, okay? You know I'm just playing with you. Don't start anything. I'd hate to have it be said that I ran out on my best friend to go home and be with my husband—"

"It would be trifling to be sure, but we are newlyweds after all."

"Boy . . . You make my day, do you know that? Every day."

He kissed me again, this time for real.

I kissed him back, ignoring Mother Riley's wagging tongue across the room.

"It's my pleasure, Mrs. Jenkins," he said.

I closed my eyes. "And mine, Mr. Jenkins. And mine."

52

Grace

The code to Brian's house was still the same: John316. He should have changed it but I was glad he hadn't. I didn't stop to look at the beautiful houses as I sped through his neighborhood. I didn't want to wonder what it might be like to live here, under these trees, with a man like him. I had a new goal now—get my hair done and run away.

Again.

I parked on the street, avoiding Brian's steep driveway. Despite the wind, he sat on the porch, waiting. As I stepped onto the landing, he pulled off his hat revealing . . . a head shaved bald! I almost tumbled back down the stairs, but he caught me.

My hand flew to my mouth. "Your hair!"

He smoothed his scalp with a gloved hand. "What hair?" He smiled.

"But why? It was so beautiful . . . Not that this doesn't look good too—"

"Look good, do I?"

I sank into the wicker couch beside him on his porch. A

wraparound porch, the kind for lemonade and long talks with neighbors. My favorite kind. But all I was supposed to do was get my hair done. None of this was supposed to happen.

My eyes wandered over him anyway: his bald head, his beautiful eyes. It took some getting used to, but crazy as it was, he looked good like this too. Maybe even better.

Nah. Don't get carried away.

I swallowed hard "You—your hair looks great. You shocked me though."

"Good," he said, taking me by the hand and leading me inside. "It's just the first in my bag of tricks."

The house smelled of lemongrass and violin rosin, a combination I never would have thought of, but wished I hadn't smelled. It was intoxicating, so much so that I almost reconsidered getting my hair done.

He led me to the deacon bench that had once been on the front row at Mount Olive and sat me down on a big satin pillow on the floor. There was a wooden box of combs and things on the seat. The box smelled like honey. When he sat down and put his knees around my shoulders, I almost screamed.

"Karyn put those locks in my hair. I planned to cut them after five years and start a new set, but after she died, I kept them. Today, I decided it was time for a fresh start."

I turned to face him and cringed at the look in his eyes. Passion. Determination. What was he trying to do? Rub it in? "And here I am starting my first set. A new beginning for both of us, I guess."

He raked the comb down the center of my head. "I hope so."

My whole body shivered. "Before we start, I'd like to lay some ground rules—"

"Be quiet." He reached into the box and took out a bottle of sweet-smelling something. It smelled like his beard. I strained to peek at it so I could get some wherever I was going. Where was that again? Columbus, yeah, that's right. Columbus.

"I have something to tell you." He sectioned my hair faster than any woman ever had.

"Okay." I crossed my arms against myself to hold things together, just in case.

"You are not my sister. Zeely is."

Suddenly Brian's haircut was old news. I tried to pull my head from his hands, but he didn't let go. "What?"

I felt a metal clip slide into my hair, near to my scalp. He'd planned the big sections and was diving in with the first twist. "You heard me right." He paused. "And about Quinn . . . I know I said I'd tell you later."

I sank back into the cushions, feeling suddenly hungry. Thirsty. "You don't owe me an explanation. You don't owe me anything."

"Of course I do. I got drunk at Mal's once. She was young. We were both—"

I shook my head, taking all the joy of knowing that my father hadn't been Brian's father with it. He'd had a baby with Lottie and not recognized her all these years later when she stepped up to him? No wonder that girl was so crazy. "Oh please. No more. If I didn't know better, I'd think we're all nuts."

"He was all right this morning at the funeral. I don't know how he'll handle all his uncles though." He rubbed his chin. "Did you know Joyce was white?"

Huh? "I mean I guess she was as white as anybody around here."

"That's what I thought too. You know how it is in this part of Ohio. Everybody's got white folks. Everybody's got secrets. I'll start to work on the detailed genealogy over the holiday, but it turns out that Ron and I aren't brothers, but we are related. Joyce was Ron's aunt. His father died burning down the old Mount Olive."

I remembered that story. My mother had always been agitated when Daddy brought it up. Ku Klux Klan did it, people said. Mama said those times were over. Daddy never said anything except once when he admitted that he worked with a lot of men who still belonged to it. And here we were all these years later, still dealing with it.

"Somehow none of this surprises me."

Brian laughed a little. "I guess it would take a lot to shock you now." He leaned across me for a tortoise shell comb. I closed my eyes, for a moment forgetting his new bare head and waiting for the tips of his blond locks to tickle my skin. Many times during the months we'd taught together, they had done just that and I'd had to excuse myself from the room to pull it together. There was no hair to run from now, but there was still the man behind the hair. And there was nowhere to run.

"Thanks for telling me." I didn't know what else to say. To do. What did this mean now? Were we supposed to date or something? I was too old for this.

His only response was the slip of his fingers through my hair. He was almost through the back now.

"Sean got a record contract," I said, still trying to convince myself to leave when my hair was done.

Brian made a sound deep in his throat. A laugh. Joy. "I'm so glad. I know he'd never believe it, but I've always loved him. He just hurt me by getting in trouble like that. I'm sorry for what I took him through. You too."

He should have been apologizing for what he was taking me through right now, touching my neck, my ears . . .

"What'd you wash your hair with? It turned out so nice. And it smells good."

You smell good.

I turned to face him while he reached for another clip. "Some liquid castile. Coconut and olive oil. I'll give you some."

He froze for a second and stared at me. I thought about how that probably sounded to a man.

I'll give you some.

I had to get out of here. For real.

Whatever he thought about the comment, Brian never said it out loud. He spoke instead with his hands, pleading with my scalp, my hair, my neck—dipping into different containers, each one containing a new scent, another slice of heaven. He touched me so sweetly that it almost hurt, like a child's belly after she's been tickled too long.

I forced myself to say something just to get him to stop. And to slow him down. He was already in the middle of my head.

"What's that one? It smells divine." I hoped for a lengthy answer. I needed a break from his touch or I was going to jump all over him. And not in a violent way.

Brian leaned across my shoulder, turning my chin gently. "Rose water, sage oil, and rosemary. To fight the itchies that'll kick in after a few days." He lifted a spray bottle from the table. "I packed you some for the road. If you're still leaving, that is. Since you know things can be different between us now, I'm praying that you'll stay."

What do you say when the finest man on earth says that he is praying that you'll stay? Idiot that I am, I said nothing.

"Or am I wrong? Are you staying?" His fingers flew over my head, parting, twisting.

And I thought Zeely did hair fast.

Brian propped a mirror on the table so I could see his progress.

Though we'd never discussed how big I wanted my locks to be, the sections were just the right size—not too big, not too small. Perfect. As I put down the mirror, I caught a glimpse of his face. His eyes looked red.

"I hoped you'll stay, but I know hope doesn't go as far as it used to." He leaned in again, this time his beard brushed against my cheek. Without thinking, I reached out and touched his face.

Make up your mind, girl.

He made a purring noise before snatching himself backward. My hair was still in his hands. He jerked that too.

"Ouch!"

He cleared his throat. "That's the last one. Do you want to see the back?"

I didn't. Everything I wanted to see, all I wanted to know, lay behind Brian's eyes. "Sure."

He produced another mirror, held it behind me, while I held the other one in front. I marveled at what I saw. Pencil-sized twists formed perfect lines like soldiers. He'd made a center part and two side parts for different styles—everything I wanted but forgot to ask for. "They're beautiful!"

Brian stood. "I'm glad you like it. Before you go, I have something for you." He reached into his pocket for a small cuff, an ornament I'd seen in people's hair before. "It doesn't mean anything really, just something to remind you that I'm joined to you, that I'm here. That I'll always be here."

I accepted his gift with a smile, hoping that my disappointment didn't show on my face. Despite all my wishy-washy-I'm-moving-away mess, I thought that the man was about to give me a ring. And if he had, I would have taken it. Gladly. That too would have been wrong. He deserved better than a grown woman who was too scared to accept the best thing that had ever happened to her.

He smiled back. A knowing smile. "You look disappointed."

I *was* disappointed.

In myself.

As Brian slipped the copper cuff onto a lock of my hair, I realized that I'd been the biggest fool of all.

Brian took my hand and kissed my knuckles, then turned it over and kissed the center of my palm. "Did you expect something else?"

His tone stung. I pulled away. It served me right. I'd asked God for the opportunity to love and then I'd been too afraid to take it.

Brian spoke again, but he didn't touch me this time. "I know what I want—a wife, a family, all of it." A look right into my heart. "All of you."

I closed my eyes, trying to find the right words. "I want all of you, all of your life. Do you know that even though Mal had hurt me, one of my biggest regrets about leaving here was that I wouldn't grow up and be your wife?"

He pulled me close. "It doesn't have to be a regret."

"But it will be one, don't you see? I don't know how to love anybody, not really. And one day you'll figure that out. How long will it take for you to decide you wanted the wrong thing? That you made a mistake?"

"Grace, we know the worst about each other already."

I didn't know what to say to that. "Maybe."

Brian didn't answer. He let me go and walked away.

Just like that.

My sadness switched to anger for a second. Where had he gone?

Then I heard the music.

"Here's my story, you can lean on me . . ." The song drifted toward me from the next room, where Brian was sitting on the couch.

He patted the seat beside him. "Talk to me."

"Don't say anything until I'm finished, promise?"

He nodded. "Promise."

"That night in the hospital when you said you loved me, I didn't know what to say. I was afraid if I loved you, something horrible would happen." I wiped my face. "Well, horrible things have already happened. That's life. I made it through the past few months because of God and because of you—because of your love."

He tried to say something, but I shook my head. "But in all my pain, I never stopped to consider what you needed, that maybe you didn't really understand the extent of what I feel for you. I do love you. I love you so much that it scares me."

He crushed me against him. "And now? Are you still afraid?"

I punched his arm. "You're supposed to be quiet, remember?"

Brian laughed. "I thought you were done. You've never said this much to me at once."

I shook my head. "Just taking a breath."

"Answer the question. Are you still afraid?"

Perfect love casts out fear.

"No. I'm only afraid of missing out on love with you." I adjusted the cuff in my hair. "A life with you." I slipped down onto one knee.

Brian jumped up like something had bit him. "Oh, no you don't. Hold that thought." He pressed a finger to my mouth and then took off down the hall. "Be right back."

"What are you doing?"

"What I should have done a long time ago," he said, already returning with a small box in his hand. A jewelry box. I got up to greet him, but he was already on his knees in front of me. He looped an arm around my waist. I relaxed against his arm, so strong, so familiar.

"Did I mention that I love you?" I was fighting back tears.

"Keep saying it. I'll never get tired of hearing it." He smiled, lifting the box in front of me. "Here's the gift I really wanted to give you tonight. Will you marry me?"

I grabbed the box and started to open it before I realized that I hadn't answered him.

Brian laughed again. "Is that a yes?"

A million times yes. "Absolutely."

He got up and hugged me. I hugged him too, even the part of his shirt in the middle of his back, where he sweat when he got nervous. I opened my fingers and touched him there, gripped the shoulders of the man who was soon to be my husband. Suddenly I was curious about a lot more than the ring . . .

Brian shook his head at me and opened the box. I gasped. Inside was a slim ring made of stone, a sliver of blackness. Onyx.

"Read the inscription."

I kissed his wrist as he tilted the ring so that I could see what he'd had inscribed on the inside of the ring.

For my Grace, my glory. Yours, Brian

On the outside of the ring, like a wise eye, a pearl stood watch over the words engraved inside.

I completely lost it.

"I didn't mean to make you cry."

I laughed through my tears, my new locks brushing my eyelids. "These are happy tears."

"Now that's what I'm talking about," Brian said, kissing me like I'd wanted him to all day long.

I laughed to myself, devouring his mouth, melting into his arms.

Brian pulled back and took a much needed breath. "I know you probably wanted a long engagement, but—"

"I don't, actually. If that kiss was any indication, we need to head for the justice of the peace right now. Too bad it's a holiday."

"I'm glad you feel that way." He kissed me again. This time more cautiously, but as sweet.

Maybe I should move to Columbus. Just until we pick a date. There's no way I can be in the same town with him and—

"Will an hour from now work for you?"

I dropped the ring box. "Today?"

Brian salvaged the ring, while I stared at him in disbelief.

"You're serious, aren't you?"

"I am."

"But—but my hair!"

"Just got done."

"A dress. I don't have a dress . . ."

Brian took my hand and started down the hall. For the first time, I noticed something under the sprinkle of hair on his head. A tattoo on his scalp. A cross. Under all that hair, all that time, had been a cross. Talk about the mind of Christ . . .

"Come on," Brian said. "You need a dress, don't you?"

We stopped at his room.

I held my breath as he pushed the door open and walked inside. I paused against the doorway, taking in the scene, every bit as glorious as it was in my dreams. The king-sized bed caught my eye first—cherry wood climbed into an open frame overhead, draped with linen. Circles of cranberry, crème, and forest green interlocked across a handmade blanket. I swallowed, recognizing the pattern. A wedding quilt.

"Don't be shy. It's going to be your room too. Come in." Brian disappeared into the closet.

I touched the pillowcase, black satin. Probably to keep lint out of his locks. I lifted the pillow to my face and sniffed it. My stomach growled like when I was starving. Patchouli and pineapple. The fruit of the earth. All man was made of.

Hangers rattled in the closet. "Are you in here? Come on."

"I'd better stay out here."

He laughed. "Suit yourself."

Next to the bed there were shelves of alphabetized books. I stared at the Cs, trying not to think about what was happening. Calvin. Chaucer. *The Chitlin Sourcebook*, still in the wrapper. Knowing Brian's infamous aversion to chitterlings, that had to have been a gag gift. I couldn't help but smile. There was music too, enough CDs to cover almost an entire wall. Classical music, jazz, and a surprisingly vast gospel section. A violin case in the corner. An easel by the window. A Bible on the nightstand.

Brian was everything I'd thought he was, everything I'd prayed for. And more.

"Put this on."

I hadn't heard him leave the closet, but he had my full attention now. He was holding a full-length African dress and matching head wrap across his arm—cornflower blue with gold piping, just like the suit he'd worn this morning. Like the one he was wearing now. He laid the hanger across the bed.

I fought the heat rising in my middle as I took the clothes.

"Are you trying to do this now? Today?"

"Not if you don't hurry up. Mother Riley's cousin can't hold the license office open much longer." He rested against the bedpost, smiling.

On the way to the bathroom to change, I ran a hand across the bed and stared back at him.

He shook his head. "I don't even want to know what you're thinking about."

"You sure don't." I called from the bathroom as I tugged the dress over my head. It fit perfectly. "How did you know my size?" I asked, stepping back into the room to wrap my hair in the head wrap.

Brian reached under his pillow and held up a slip of fabric. The tag that had been ripped from my dress the night we'd been reunited and Sean and the Golden Boys gang had almost shot up the school.

I knew what it said without looking.

Virtuous woman. Size 16.

Brian reached out and tucked in the last bit of fabric into my wrap and handed me my shoes. He put on his coat and grabbed his keys. "I knew you'd dropped a good bit of weight since then, so I got a twelve."

He kissed my forehead. "I'm going to work on that though. A baby will put some meat back on you."

My nostrils flared. Not long ago, a husband seemed an impossible thing to pray for, but a baby?

He gives us exceedingly abundantly more than we could ask or think.

Brian's eyes danced with amusement. "Come on. You can do more prettying up at the church if you want, but we have to rush and fill out the marriage certificate. I already paid for it. The notary said she'd wait until six. Six thirty at the latest."

I didn't know what to say. "Anything else I should know?"

He checked his wall clock before grabbing my hand and leading me to the front of the house. He handed me my purse. "There's our family at the church, of course . . ."

"Who? How?"

He held my coat for me. "Ron. Zeely. Quinn. The church. My brothers. My dad . . . and your mom."

"My mother? Is she really here?"

He glanced at the wall again. "She should be by now. Come on. Let's not keep them waiting."

I punched his shoulder. "I can't believe you did all this. Pretty sure of yourself, huh?"

Another kiss. The tingle ran to my toes.

"Every bit of it was faith. I wasn't even sure that you'd show up. But if you did, you weren't getting away."

I nodded, crying again. Giggling too.

He held the car door open for me. "What's so funny?"

"Zeely. I always wished that she was my sister . . . We'll be sisters now for real."

"You always were."

I took a deep breath and laughed again.

Lord, you are too much.

The notary had kept her word. Brian had to run back to my apartment for Peter's death certificate, but in the end, we got it all taken care of. And now I was trying not to cry.

Again.

"You probably think I'm a wimp crying like this."

He shook his head. "Never. I've seen you in action. I know what's up. You know how to do a lot more than cry. Besides, these are happy tears, right? Those don't count. And I used to share an office with somebody who told me that there's strength in weakness."

"I must be the strongest person in the world right now," I said, as we got out of the car at the church. My "prettying" had consisted of a few pats of mineral makeup and some lipstick, which already needed to be reapplied.

A gust of icy wind beat over the both of us as we got out of the car, flinging the door out of Brian's hands before he could close it.

It made a peaceful sound, like a woman's voice, as the wind slipped between us. Brian tried to block it, but I could still feel the needling breeze cutting my skin.

As quickly as it had come, the cold rush died away. Something in my heart blew away with it.

Peter's itch, the part of my late husband that had felt like he was there even though he was gone, no longer existed.

Brian pulled back his cap and stroked his head. "Did you feel that? Was it . . . them?"

"I think so. Maybe it was their blessing."

Some piece of Karyn, the part of her that had protected his love and kept him sane, had blown away too. The memory remained, but the pain cleared from his eyes. "What did they call that in the Bible. A mighty rushing wind?"

I nodded, whispering a prayer. "Thank you, Lord, for never stopping the music on us. I know that no matter how hard things get, we just have to keep moving toward you. We just have to keep dancing."

He raised his head and looked into my eyes. "That shouldn't be hard. He's given me a great partner."

The parking lot overflowed with the same cars from the funeral, plus a few more. I recognized a silver Lexus with a sorority plate. My mother's car. I swallowed the lump in my throat, glad we were already dressed.

Brian smiled. "Are you ready?"

I nodded. "I just wish I could stop crying. It's getting on *my* nerves."

Brian laughed, walking with me up the steps. "Cry all you want. As long as I know they're tears of joy, it doesn't bother me a bit."

As we reached the front doors, I pulled myself together.

For a minute anyway.

"It's them!" someone screamed from the other side. Even Brian looked like he didn't know what to make of that. He opened the doors wide anyway.

Any hope of making it through the service dry-eyed died when I stepped inside. Dried flower petals—red, purple, and gold—crunched under my feet. My shoe brushed a daffodil. My daffodils. The ones I'd tended all winter and forced to bloom indoors. I'd given them to Zeely weeks ago because I couldn't stand to look at them anymore. I turned to Brian. Those flowers had made me think of hope.

They'd made me think of Brian.

The rest of my daffodils wreathed the arch in front of me, mixed in with other flowers, like the ones beneath my feet. There were bows too, joined by a garland of ribbon. I stood there, amazed and unable to move.

Then the organ piped up with "Here Comes the Bride," beckoning us into the sanctuary. Brian nudged me. I guess we'd both been married before and had some idea of what to do, but this was crazy. My mother appeared in the hall with a tiara and bouquet of white roses.

You are altogether beautiful, my darling. There is no blemish in you.

"Buds of promise," my mother said with a smile and pointed down the aisle. Both she and I had sung in the choir here, the Buds of Promise choir. I crossed into the church, smiling at the crowd.

My eyes tried to focus as I took in the sight at the altar. Ron, Jerry, and Quinn held up the wedding canopy. I'm not sure how Jerry was doing it since one of his arms was in a sling. One of Zeely's brothers, Isaiah, I think, held the fourth pole. Each pole was attached to a canopy at the top. Jerry shifted and the fabric, striped at the sides and fringed at the ends, rippled in a wave above me. I closed my eyes, remembering the linen draping Brian's bed . . .

His banner over me is love.

As I approached, Quinn smiled wide and blew me a kiss. He moved his lips. "Keep going."

Thelma smiled at me from her seat at the organ. I joined her there, making it past the tulle and satin—purple, gold, and . . . blue. Exactly the right shade. My breath caught in my throat on the next step. The decorations from Joyce's funeral. She had picked out these decorations herself.

She's here too. Even now.

I wiped my face, thinking of what she'd written to me in my letter—*Stop crying. You'll get wrinkles.* With every step I took toward the wedding huppah, the one that Zeely had been the bride of Christ under back in Vacation Bible School, I smiled at Ron, remembering when they'd stood beneath it.

The crowd gasped behind me, many of them seeing Brian's shaved head for the first time since . . . this morning, when his hair had been down to his waist. I turned, watching him cruise the aisle, smoothing his bald head and winking at the crowd. My belly fluttered.

The music changed. Zeely rose from the front pew in the sequined sheath from this morning. It was perfect for a wedding too.

My friend took a step forward and lifted the mike to her lips. "He gives beauty for ashes . . ."

"Strength for fear . . ." Quinn's voice joined the harmony. His pole shook beside me.

The two voices combined, high and low, penetrating my soul. "Gladness for mourning. Peace for despair."

Brian ended his walk, joining me under the canopy. I covered my face with my bouquet as the song rolled on. He pulled me close. This was too good to be real. At the last note, Reverend Wilkins rose and stood in front of us. He looked out over the congregation. "Well, it's been a busy day, hasn't it, church?"

"I'll say," someone said behind us.

The pastor laughed. "That's all right. The Bible says weeping may endure for a night, but—"

"Joy cometh in the morning." The church answered loud, their response peppered with laughter.

Reverend Wilkins rubbed his hands together. "We're getting our Christmas joy a little early. How about that?"

I wiped my eyes. Christmas. I'd been so wrapped up in taking, in getting away, that the holiday had blurred against everything else. I'd sort of forgotten about it. My eyes rested on the man beside me, my friends and family around me.

God didn't forget.

Brian took my hand.

"This ceremony won't be long, but it will be a little different. Especially the vows." The Reverend pulled an envelope from his pocket.

I glared at Brian, who had assured me that his father would just do the traditional vows since this was all last-minute. Had he managed to write vows without telling me? I could improvise if I had to, but I'd really rather not. Brian looked just as confused as I did, so that made me feel better, until I realized that we were both in trouble.

"Joyce put this in the envelope with my son's birth certificate." The preacher held up two pieces of stationery covered with flowing script. "The vows for this wedding." The old man laughed. "I didn't think we'd be using them so soon or I would have asked if you two minded."

Brian stared down at me with questions in his eyes. I nodded. He turned back to his father. "It's fine."

The pastor nodded and handed a page to both of us. He positioned a microphone stand between us. I smiled as Brian looked at me and licked his lips. He nodded slightly, never looking down at his page. "Go ahead, princess."

The paper shook in my hand. "Brian, my beloved." My voice cracked. "How I have waited, my darling, for you to come for me. To bring me to your banquet hall. Your banner over me is love—" I paused, staring up at the canopy above our heads.

Brian stepped closer, so that all I could see was his face.

"I was a wall. A princess . . . trapped in my tower. Your love has made me a door. A door of hope."

The canopy wobbled as Jerry wiped his eyes.

"Do you, Brian Gabriel Mayfield, knowing my love for you and returning it, promise to draw on my strengths and learn from them, to recognize my weaknesses and help me overcome them, to—"

Gabriel? An angel.

I lost it again. I held up one hand. "I'm sorry, everybody."

Reverend Wilkins shook his head. "You're fine. Take your time, baby."

Brian kissed my hand.

"Do you promise to make music for me, to dance with me before the Lord, to wash me in the water of God's Word? Do you take me, Diana Grace Okoye, to be your lawfully wedded wife as long as we both shall live?"

He didn't even blink. "I do."

I tensed, reading the next line.

Place the ring on his finger.

His ring. In the fuss, I hadn't even thought of it . . .

My mother's voice filled the awkward silence. "Here. It was your father's." She rose from her seat on the front pew to hand me a gold ring with a cross at the center. My father's wedding band.

"Thank you." I took it and slipped it on Brian's finger. It fit.

"Man. This is deep," Quinn whispered.

I smiled over at Brian's son, my son too, now. If only he knew how deep this really was, he'd drop that pole. I sighed as Brian lifted his page and began to read.

I hope he does better than I did.

"Grace, my beloved, I welcome you into my garden, my bride, and my sister in Christ. Open to me, my dove, my perfect one. Let the myrrh drip from my fingers . . ." He choked up. I stared up at him and smiled. He cleared his throat. "Let me drench your life with love until your locks are damp."

Quinn looked at us with wide eyes.

I wanted to assure him that it was all in the Bible and that the Bible was passionate in places, but I was too busy closing my eyes and letting Brian's voice wash over me.

"You struck me—" He chuckled, probably remembering me hitting his car. "And wounded me. I was lovesick and thirsty. You led me to the stream of living water and bid me drink."

"Thank you, Jesus." Reverend Wilkins lifted his hand high.

"Do you, Diana Grace Okoye, knowing my love for you and returning it, promise to identify my strengths and share in them, to recognize my weaknesses and help me overcome them . . ."

He sniffed. "To respect me when I'm disrespectable, to pray for me when I do the unthinkable, to keep me dancing until the music stops?" Brian let the paper fall to the floor. He stared into me. "Do you take me, Brian Gabriel Mayfield, to be your lawfully wedded husband?"

"I do."

Ron handed Brian the ring. Brian slipped it on my fingertip and paused, a silly grin on his face.

He's killing me.

I shoved it down the rest of the way and threw my arms around his neck. My roses crackled against the microphone, which Reverend Wilkins grabbed.

"These two are ready, aren't they? In the sight of our Lord Jesus Christ and the witnesses gathered here, I now pronounce you man and wife."

Cheers rose from the crowd.

"You may kiss—"

A smacking sound echoed through the room. As I closed my eyes and accepted Brian's kiss, my husband's kiss, I could have sworn I saw the Reverend laughing.

The old man sighed into the microphone. "A little quick on the draw, but at least they follow directions."

The basement overflowed with people. And food. I watched Quinn holding Justice, both face deep in a piece of chocolate cake.

I sighed. Brian's son. My granddaughter. I wished that Sean could have been here too. Just seeing these two gave me hope.

Brian walked up behind me and hugged me around my waist. "You got away from me after the kids finished dancing."

I turned to face him. "They got me with that one. I didn't plan for Rhythms of Grace to do that piece until next year. They were awesome."

"Just like their teacher." He licked his lips. "You ready to jump de broom, missy?"

I hooked my arm in his. "Lead the way."

Brian's brother Isaiah waited for us at the front table. Zeely shuffled past us with a regular broom tied with ribbons, missing many of its straws. "It's the best I could do. Sorry," she whispered on her way by.

"It's good enough for me," I said.

Isaiah raised his hands and called to the crowd. "Form a circle around them, everyone." He handed the broom to Brian. Quinn played Brian's drums in the background. "Jumping the broom is an African tradition that denotes a new life. Many slaves kept the practice, even though their divided lives kept them from being married. Today we are free in mind, body, and spirit. Grace and Brian jump into a new union, an unbroken circle of fellowship between them and God." He bowed to Brian. "You may lower the broom."

The groom knelt and put the broom on the floor. He grasped my hand.

"One, two, three . . . Jump!" the crowd screamed.

I closed my eyes and felt Brian jump beside me. I jumped too. And tripped.

Zeely sucked her teeth. The Reverend laughed. My mother shook her head and checked my hem for tears.

My husband smiled and lifted me into his arms. "She's a dancer, not a broom hopper." He had someone get our coats, then he carried me to the door and pushed it open with his foot. It closed quickly, shutting out our family's laughter.

Freezing despite the coat that covered me, I fought to get down, but Brian held me tight, his lips brushing my ear. "You ready to go make Sean and Quinn a little sister?"

"Will you hush? We're still on the church grounds."

"Don't be embarrassed, princess. The marriage bed is sacred, remember?"

He stepped into the street, gently put me down, and kissed me completely, tangling his fingers in my new hair. I laced my arms around his neck and returned the kiss with equal enthusiasm.

I stared back at the church. "Are we really leaving? Just like that?" My mother would have a fit. Such things were the height of being "ill-mannered." "Where are we going?"

Brian kissed my ear. "We are going to our car, then to our house, and then to the church."

I managed to get to my feet when he reached into his pocket for the keys.

I stared back at the building behind us. "Church? Back here or Tender Mercies?"

Brian shook his head. "Neither. The church I'm talking about meets in my—our—bedroom." He opened the car door and slid me across the seat.

I rested my head against the window, trying not to blush. Despite being married before, I'd never known much about love.

But I was ready to learn.

Acknowledgments

Books are born through the hope and hard work of many people. This one, especially so.

Special thanks to Jennifer Leep for believing in me and giving me a chance. Your insight is a blessing.

To Barb Barnes, Cheryl Van Andel, Nathan Henrion, Michele Misiak, Carmen Sechrist, Claudia Marsh, and all the wonderful folks at Revell, thank you, thank you, thank you!!! You all make an amazing team.

To my agent Wendy Lawton, thanks for everything.

To Claudia Mair Burney, your love is such a comfort. Always.

To Sharon Ewell Foster, thanks for coming and for giving me back my name, sistah. I needed it.

To Stanice Anderson, you inspire me. Selah.

To Barbara Joe Williams, Katina Amoah, Linda Dwinell, Annette Ponder, Shantae Charles, Carmita McCall, Rosalyn Webb, Mary Ardis, Leeshun Fryson Jackson, Coleen Hagood, and Lisa Brown, thank you for your friendship. I appreciate you.

To the young ladies of Young Lives Tallahassee: You are amazing. K.I.S.S. the King!

To Calvary Chapel Tallahassee and Kent and Debbie Nottingham, thank you for your kindness and love.

For Doc (Dr. Joseph D. Lewis, professor emeritus, Central State University): In a summer when all was lost, you saw me. Thank you—Bantu Onyedika.

To my family, thank you for enduring the frozen dinners and pizza at the end. It was worth it.

Mom, thanks for the support, love, and well-timed deliveries. You rock.

For my cousin, Mike Swain, thanks for all the books you've talked your friends into, all the bookstores and malls we've walked, the events you set up, and the thousands of e-mails you've sent. It all means so much. Really.

For Ashlie, I going to miss you, babe. Never stop dancing.

For Jewell, wherever you are, I pray you hear this song.

For Fill, my love and thanks. Without you, there is no story.

For Jesus, Alleluia.

Reader's Note

Dear Reader,

I pray you have enjoyed *Songs of Deliverance*. I certainly enjoyed writing it.

Thanks to each of you who emailed asking when the book was coming out or what would happen next. Opening your messages always makes my day.

Visit my website at www.MarilynnGriffith.com or drop me an email at marilynngriffith@gmail.com.

May each day bring you a new song of deliverance.

Blessings,
Marilynn

Marilynn Griffith is a freelance writer who lives in Florida with her husband and seven children. When she's not helping with homework or tackling Mount Fold-Me, her ongoing laundry pile, she writes novels and speaks to youth, women, and writers.

If you enjoyed this book, please drop her an email at marilynn griffith@gmail.com.

She Finally Found
the Love of Her Life . . .

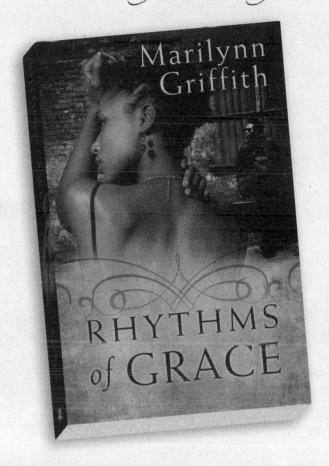

But can she choose between him and God?

"Griffith's dialogue is engaging and her characters deeply memorable;
she deserves a wide audience."—**Publishers Weekly**

 Revell
a division of Baker Publishing Group
www.RevellBooks.com

Available wherever books are sold.

NOVELS WITH *Spirit* AND *Soul*

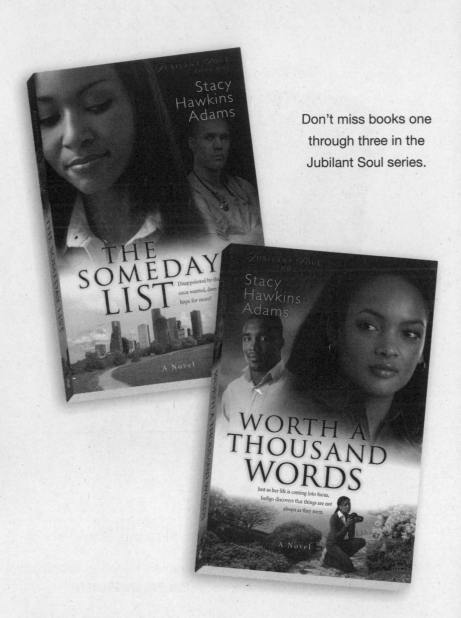

Don't miss books one through three in the Jubilant Soul series.

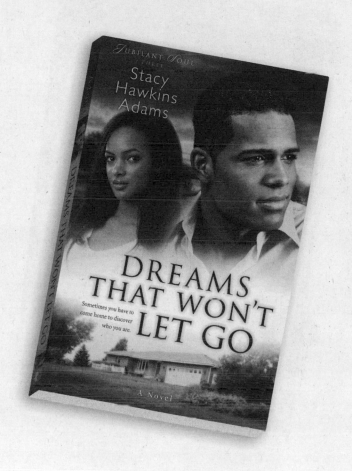

Man, I Just Want to Make It . . .

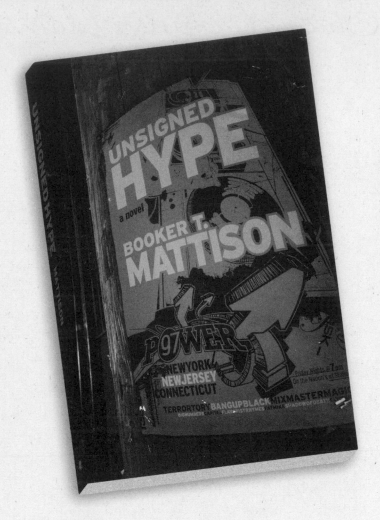

"A great story. . . . [Tory's] life, music, and personal situations were stepping-stones to becoming someone great in hip-hop music. That's a beautiful thing."

—**Pete Rock,** legendary hip-hop producer and DJ